"The Ancients were taught that their Gods would return every hundred years, and they would expect a sacrifice."

Sebastian showed Lex a large-scale mural depicting the Great Serpent and the Gods clashing in mortal combat. "Like gladiators in a coliseum those two alien races would battle," he explained. "Only the strongest survived. And the survivors would be the ones deemed worthy to return to the stars, to return *home*."

"What if they lost?"

Sebastian showed Lex three images in a sequence, a grim, doomsday triptych. The first was an image of a great pyramid, three stylized Predators standing on the pinnacle, a horde of Great Serpents slithering up the sides. The next image showed the Predators, arms raised, with wavy lines radiating from their wrists.

The third image was hauntingly familiar. It showed an explosion—a green-tinted blast with a mushroom cloud hanging over it, an explosion that destroyed everyone and everything in its path.

"If the Gods were defeated, then a terrible disaster would overtake the land, and their civilization would vanish overnight . . . Total genocide . . . An entire civilization wiped out at once."

Lex went numb. "Then these creatures have been here before," she said.

"Undeniably," Sebastian replied. "Thousands of years ago, and many times since—perhaps even recently."

ALIEN VS. PREDATOR

NOVELIZATION BY
MARC CERASINI

BASED ON THE MOTION PICTURE
SCREENPLAY BY
PAUL W. S. ANDERSON
AND SHANE SALERNO

STORY BY
PAUL W. S. ANDERSON

BASED ON THE "ALIEN" CHARACTERS CREATED BY
DAN O'BANNON AND RON SHUSETT
AND THE "PREDATOR" CHARACTERS CREATED BY
JOHN THOMAS
AND JAMES THOMAS

HarperEntertainment
An Imprint of HarperCollins*Publishers*

HARPERENTERTAINMENT
An Imprint of HarperCollins*Publishers*
10 East 53rd Street
New York, New York 10022-5299

ISBN: 0-06-073537-6

First HarperEntertainment paperback printing: July 2004

Printed in the United States of America

Visit HarperEntertainment on the World Wide Web at www.harpercollins.com.

10 9 8 7 6 5 4 3 2 1

*To Hope Innelli for being the perfect, patient editor.
To my agent, John Talbot, for being so cool.*

*Most especially to my wife, Alice,
who endured the rigors of Antarctica
and the terror of alien invasion with poise and class.*

PROLOGUE

The first columns of sunlight stabbed through the canopy of tangled branches. Birds took flight, cawing a greeting to the dawn, their scarlet wings staining the pale sky as they skimmed the hard gray angles of a massive stone pyramid. Nearby, the air quaked with the incessant rumble of the river as it pulsed over a serrated cliff then broke on the ragged rocks far below.

Along the jungle floor, where thick vegetation muted the waterfall's roar, a wet snout parted a knot of vines and branches. Leaves stirred, sending a rustling hiss down an overgrown trail. The wild pig sniffed, then listened. With a satisfied grunt, it penetrated the underbrush and burst into the clearing.

Short tail swishing, the pig trotted onto a carpet of moss near a grove of ancient trees. Aggressively it snuffled the damp, fetid ground. At the twisted base of a mammoth trunk, its body stilled. Then its spotted hide quivered with excitement, and its front paws dug into the soft, black soil, spilling chunks of fungus and a knot of squirming worms onto the green moss. Finally, with loud snorting gulps, the animal began consuming its prey.

Behind the gorging pig, leaves parted again, this time without a sound. A pair of mud-brown eyes peered through the opening in the tight branches, focusing on the wild pig's twitching hide. Funan the Hunter lifted his paint-streaked face to the sky. Like the pig had before him, he sniffed the air and listened.

Monkeys chattered on high and a single bird cried out, but not in alarm. In the lower branches tree apes leaped and chattered, sending twigs and foliage raining down on the jungle floor. Closer to the cool, moist earth, insects crawled, squirmed, cackled and buzzed through the curling fingers of mist.

Funan smiled. He and his hunt mates had patiently stalked their prey. The time for the kill was almost upon them. But not yet. Only when Funan was satisfied that all conditions were right would he signal his men with his sun-bronzed hand.

Slipping like shadows out of the underbrush, twin brothers Fan Shih and Pol Shih moved to either side of Funan. Like their chief, they clutched wooden spears tipped with chipped obsidian. Camouflaged for the hunt, their faces, torsos and chests were darkened by ash and slashed with brown and green mud. Leafy vines encircled their arms and legs and crowned their heads.

Adorning their hips, untreated leather thongs displayed trophies of previous hunts—skulls, bones, rows of sharp teeth and curved fangs belonging to a dozen species. Dangling from cords around their necks were bits of fur, feather and quartz, magical charms meant to ensure a successful hunt.

As a breeze moved over him, Funan stroked a dried monkey's tail hanging at his throat and sniffed the air once more. He could smell the pig, the vegetation, and the river in the distance—but nothing else. Yet tension preyed upon his nerves, and his men seemed on edge, too.

Never before had they hunted this close to the sacred temple. Although the jungle around the stone pyramid teemed with wildlife, hunters always shunned this forbidden place. Only during the time of sacrifice, when the local tribes offered up their young men and women to the gods, would the people enter these grounds.

Funan knew he was reckless to hunt near a site deemed so sacred. The hunt should really end now, but he decided otherwise, signaling the last member of their group.

A giant of a man called Jawa moved forward in a crouch, then ducked behind a lump of ropy vines. He clutched a long spear that seemed tiny in his immense hand, and a stout club hung from the leather thong at his hip. Like the others, Jawa was camouflaged with mud and vegetation, and from his belt hung bear's teeth and a piece of bone from a large jungle cat. His powerful chest still bore the angry scars from the cat's savage combat.

Unseen at Jawa's feet, another hunt had reached its lethal climax. A ruddy, gray-green lizard and a horned, black beetle were locked in a death struggle on the jungle floor, oblivious to the giant in whose shadow they warred. When Funan made a chopping motion with his left hand, Jawa stepped out of his hiding place, crushing both lizard and beetle under his brown, callous foot.

Slipping through the brush, Jawa moved to his position, flanking the pig. He cackled once, imitating the call of the red-and-green bird that inhabited this region. From their own hiding places, Funan and the two Shih brothers rose, spidery mist hugging their legs as they moved.

Funan took the lead. Soon he would be near enough to strike a fatal blow with the first throw—or be gouged by the creature's tusks should he miss. In a flashing spasm, his muscles quivered, his heart raced. Then, as suddenly as it came, the tension evaporated and a cold calm washed over him.

Lifting his spear, Funan was about to take aim when something went wrong. The pig's snout, black with dirt, jerked high to sniff the air. Ears twitching, the pig snorted nervously.

Funan did not dare breathe. Behind him, Fan and Pol Shih paused in mid-stride. As a fly buzzed around his head, Funan drew back his weapon. But before he could strike, the startled pig ducked under a log, then vanished in the bush. The echo of the pig's crashing retreat lingered for a moment, then faded.

Funan looked at Jawa in bewilderment. They had done everything right—yet somehow they had spooked their prey. Behind their chief, Fan and Pol lowered their weapons, perplexed.

Then, abruptly, all sound in the jungle ceased. Every bird, every insect seemed to fall silent. Only the distant pounding of the falling river water penetrated the thick vegetation. In the quiet echo of the thundering pulse, Funan warily scanned the clearing but saw nothing. Fan and Pol Shih also raised their spears, poised to attack. But attack what?

With a loud crack, a black, whiplike appendage shot out from the underbrush and encircled Fan Shih's legs. Without even a cry of alarm, the hunter was dragged into the bushes, quivering leaves the only sign of his violent passage.

Pol Shih raised his spear, ready to avenge his brother. But suddenly the spear was torn from the man's hand. Kicking helplessly, he, too, was hauled across the clearing and into the bush. Only after Pol vanished from sight did he scream—once, twice, three times, the last a sustained howl of agony.

Pol's terror-filled shriek broke the courage of the others. Jawa bolted into the undergrowth, followed a moment later by Funan.

Like the pig before him, Jawa fled blindly through the trees, ignoring the trail to trample through the jungle. Vines caught his arms, and he dropped his spear to move faster, fright driving him on.

Finally out of breath, Jawa stumbled into a clearing domed by interlocking vines. He braced his heaving form against a tree trunk. Panting, legs wide, Jawa listened in the heavy shade for the sound of pursuit. Behind him, he heard Funan's whipping movements through the jungle, but nothing else.

The black, formless shadow dropped out of the tree with no warning. Landing in a crouch, the large, insectlike beast unfolded itself and faced Jawa. A doglike whimper escaped the warrior as he took a step backwards. He fumbled for the stout wood-and-stone club that dangled from his rawhide belt. But there was no time to fight, only to die. The final imprinting on Jawa's senses were sharp teeth and gnashing jaws, hot drool and red blood.

Seconds later, Funan stumbled into the same shaded clearing—in time to see Jawa hauled helplessly into the vines above. A scarlet rain sprinkled the ground, and warm drops splashed Funan. The chief hunter, his fist still choking the neck of his spear, searched the branches above for any sign of Jawa.

But the man was gone.

Spear raised, Funan scanned his surroundings. He stood in a cove of ancient, thick-boled trees, the largest covered with shiny black bark. Struggling for calm, Funan halted his anxious wheezing to listen for his enemy's approach. Only then did Funan hear a wet, ripping sound from behind. He spun, his spear thrusting forward.

With mounting horror, Funan watched the dark, oily bark begin to move, peeling itself away from the trunk. With a fleshy, popping sound the shapeless mass sprouted limbs. Then an oblong head emerged, the appendage covered with glistening, near-translucent skin. A bony, segmented tail unwound itself from a heavy branch, and with a wet thump, the writhing obscenity dropped to the ground.

The creature, chattering like some terrible giant insect, rose to its full, immense height and shambled toward the cowering hunter. Gnashing jaws parted to extend a long, veined mandible tipped with yet another snapping, drooling orifice.

Weapon forgotten, Funan attempted to flee. In his panic, he stumbled over the entangling vines. Twisting his ankle, Funan struck the ground hard, spear flying from his numbed fist. Then the mightiest hunter of his tribe curled up into a cowering ball and waited for death to claim him. This, he knew, was his punishment for encroaching on the sacred ground around the Temple of the Gods.

Hot spittle splashed his cheek and burned his skin. Chattering jaws snapped at his throat, and a deadly shadow, black as death itself, loomed over him, ready to strike, when an astounding thing happened.

Another abomination emerged from the jungle.

Funan first saw the creature as a blur—for the world seemed to shimmer with its passing. Wherever the apparition stalked, the jungle melted and reformed itself. In a blinding flash of movement, the translucent figure shot across the clearing and struck the black monster at Funan's throat, penetrating its segmented armored shell with a bone-crushing stab and tossing it away.

The black monster's exoskeleton clattered as it hit the ground, and Funan saw that the armored plates at the creature's throat had indeed been pierced and shattered. Fountains of green, acidic blood spurted from the black monster's wound, spraying leaves and branches and vines. Every place the venomous fluid touched began to smoke and burn. The molten hot drops struck Funan, too, and he rolled on the ground and cried out with raw agony.

The phantom paused to hover over the fallen hunter, and as Funan pulled his hands away from his face and looked up, the ghostly blur formed into a solid thing—

a nightmare that appeared part man, part reptile, part demonic beast. The phantom stood on two legs as thick as logs. Its torso was scaled, its wide face covered by a metal mask. Barbarous eyes burned from behind that mask—eyes Funan desperately tried to avoid.

Then the phantom stepped past the human, moving with giant strides toward the black monster still writhing on the ground. Funan watched as the phantom raised its enormous arms. Then, with a sharp and sudden click, a trio of silver blades burst out of the band around the creature's wrist. Sunlight glinted off razor-sharp tips. The phantom grunted in satisfaction and looked down at Funan once again.

Funan covered his eyes and prayed to all the ancestors of his people. He begged for mercy from a dozen tribal deities, great and small. And to Funan's eternal surprise, one of those gods answered his pleas.

Shaking its head in pity, as if the fallen human was not worth the time or effort to kill, the Predator turned once again to face its real prey.

The chattering black monster, its ragged neck wound still spewing poisonous green bile, put its back against a tree. Tail whipping, claws extended, the monster prepared for its final battle.

Legs braced, the Predator tossed its head and let loose with a savage howl that shook the jungle. Then it charged.

Funan heard flesh rip and chitinous armor crack. Then came the wet sound of green phosphorescent blood and acidic poisonous venom as both splattered the clearing.

Branches shook and trees quaked in the wake of the terrible life-and-death struggle. While the jungle smoked and burned around him, Funan watched in helpless fascination as two primeval creatures, whose unearthly origins were beyond his comprehension, fought savagely to the death.

CHAPTER 1

Bouvetoya Whaling Station,
Antarctica, 1904

The *Emma* sailed for the shores of Bouvetoya Island at the start of the 1904 whaling season with a full complement of sailors, harpooners, boats and oil processing equipment—enough to slaughter whales and extract their oil for a full year on the Antarctic ice before returning to Norway the following year.

Emma's newest skipper and part-owner Sven Nyberg intended to make his first and last voyage as a whaler a profitable one. Sven's brother, Bjorn, had been the *Emma*'s captain for nineteen seasons, but Bjorn had died of a fever during last year's return voyage, which had compelled his brother to assume command on this, the final commercial venture of the Nyberg Brothers Oil Company of Oslo. Upon his return to Norway, Sven fully intended to sell his family's business to the highest bidder.

The dawn of this new century was bringing an end to traditional whaling. Magnate Christian Christensen had opened a modern processing facility in Grytviken that would eventually edge out smaller Antarctic whaling concerns like the Nyberg brothers—men who'd followed methods practiced by Norwegians since the days of the Vikings. Like seal hunting, an activity that had made many a family fortune back in the 1870s, whaling was becoming an unprofitable enterprise. Declining herds and rising competition from British and Scottish whalers—and recently even the Japanese—along with giant conglomerates like the Christensen corporation were gradually ending the era of the self-sufficient, independent whaler.

Still, Sven Nyberg would try to make the Nyberg Brothers a viable oil company for a little while longer. It was the only way to ensure a profitable sale of his family's interests. To that end Sven had offered Oslo's most experienced whale hunter, Karl Johanssen, a position as first mate, with a five-percent share of the expedition's profits. If successful, the *Emma*'s journey to the South Pole would make Karl a very wealthy man.

The offer could not have come at a better time for Karl Johanssen. A whaler since he'd been twelve years old, Johanssen had weathered twenty-seven seasons on the ice and survived them with all of his limbs, fingers and toes intact—no mean feat where temperatures could reach 50 degrees below zero. From past voyages with brother Bjorn, Johanssen was also familiar with the Nyberg Brothers' oil processing facility on Bouvetoya Island, one of the world's most remote locations.

A few years before, in 1897, Karl Johanssen thought he'd given up the sea for good. Lured to northern California by his brother's promises of wealth, Karl had squandered his meager savings trying to strike it rich in the Alaska gold rush. Forced to return to whaling out of financial desperation, he'd been ready to sign onto one of Christensen's ships for a paltry one-half of one percent share when Sven Nyberg had made his offer. A berth as first mate with a full five-percent share was Karl's lucky second chance at a comfortable retirement.

Of course, Karl would work hard for the money. Sven Nyberg was an indifferent seaman, and he'd never spent even a single season on the Antarctic ice. Fortunately, during their long twelve months of backbreaking labor, Sven had been wise enough to defer to Karl's judgment in nearly every situation. Under the harpooner's tutelage, the younger Nyberg brother had learned secrets of the whale hunting trade that it would have taken him years to discover on his own. The result, after a year, was an incredibly successful hunt, with *Emma* towing over three hundred carcasses into the cove at Bouvetoya Island. There the remains of blues, minkes and sperms would be cut up and the blubber rendered for its oil.

It was during the grimy rendering process, when the men were outside for lengths of time attending the huge iron vat dominating the harbor, that the whalers began to see strange lights in the sky, and *not* the southern lights they were used to seeing.

Over Lykke Peak and the taller, three-thousand-foot Olav Peak that overshadowed the oil processing facility, bursts like distant cannon fire lit the sky, and explosions on the ice could be heard in the distance. Then a strange reddish glow appeared on the horizon, illuminating the ceaseless twilight with the brilliance of a thousand cook fires. The light danced crimson off the ice and tinged the millions of whalebones that littered the beach a sickly hue. Often—but not always—the eerie lights were accompanied by tremors deep beneath the ground under their feet.

While volcanic activity on the island was not unusual—sometime in 1896 part of the island had even been destroyed by a volcanic eruption—the phenomena unsettled the whalers, who were trapped on Bouvetoya until the spring thaw no matter what happened. So after a few days of these strange events, in an effort to calm the whalers' fears and discover the cause of the eerie pyrotechnics, Karl led a group of sailors away from the harbor's ramshackle wooden buildings and onto the glacial ice that covered the fifty-square-mile island.

On a vast frozen plain, they recovered a large, metallic object shaped like a coffin built for a giant. The object was embedded in the ice in the middle of a huge crater. Its silvery surface was smooth and bullet-shaped, with no visible joints or openings. There were markings etched into the metal—a strange, alien scrimshaw no whaler in the party could read or even recognize. Though the metal coffin appeared to be hollow, no one could figure out how to open it, or what was inside.

Karl Johanssen thought it best to leave the thing where it lay, but in this one instance the skipper overruled him. Captain Nyberg was eager to find another way to make the voyage profitable, so he ordered the sailors to load the object onto a sledge and use a dog team to drag it back to camp. It took five men and fifteen dogs a full day to fulfill the captain's wishes, but when they were finished, the shining metal coffin was stored in the warehouse, among the barrels of whale oil waiting to be loaded into the ship's hold. In just a few weeks, moderate temperatures would slowly free the *Emma* from the icy prison of the frozen bay. Then the crew could return to Norway and claim the reward for twelve long months of labor.

But hours after the object was brought into their camp, Karl was jolted out of his narrow sleeping bunk by the sound of screams. Yanking on boots but leaving his coat, Karl dashed across the icy street to the warehouse. The doors were ajar, and one of them had been torn off its hinges. In the center of the room Karl found four dead men—more than dead, they were ripped apart, and their heads and spinal columns had been severed and removed. More ominous, the strange coffinlike object was now wide open and empty, and inside the drafty warehouse, mingled with the smell of freshly spilled blood, was a dank, reptilian stench.

Back outside, and shivering on the street, Karl discovered mammoth, bloody footprints leading out of the warehouse and across the street. The crimson spoor formed a path right up to the rough wooden building where the sailors bunked. There, at the door, he saw a ghostly shape shimmering in the frigid air. Before he could shout a warning, Karl watched some invisible force smash down the door and surge into the sailors' quarters. He heard cries of surprise and panic—then fear and agony—from inside the building. There was a single shot, then a severed human hand flew through the door, still clutching a small pistol.

Finally, Karl watched as a sailor flew toward the

window, his nightshirt bloody, his face a mask of terror. The man's eyes met Karl's for a split second before a silver blur slashed across his naked throat. Then bright red arterial blood coated the glass, and Karl could see no more.

Choking down his panic, Karl ran back to the warehouse and searched for a weapon—anything to defend himself. Finding none, he sought escape instead. Karl knew it was certain death to go outside without protection from the elements, but when he tried to remove the coats from the dead men, he found them torn and soaked with blood—blood that would freeze in an instant. Finally, Karl wrapped himself in a dirty canvas tarpaulin and stumbled out the back door, slipping down an icy slope that led to the whalebone-littered beach. There, among the skeletons of sperm, minke and blues, he hoped to find shelter enough to protect him until whatever it was that had emerged from that silver coffin returned to the hell from which it had come.

A tremor under the ice woke Karl Johanssen from a dreamless sleep. With the perpetual twilight sky above, he could not know how long he'd been unconscious. But the canvas that covered him glistened with ice, and his limbs refused to respond to his brain's commands. More ominous, Karl could not even feel the cold that had seeped into him while he'd been unconscious. Instead, it almost seemed as if a languorous cocoon of warmth enveloped him—a sure sign that he was freezing to death.

It took all of his willpower, but Karl forced himself

to stand. Without a proper coat, even the heavy canvas was not enough covering to retain his body heat. A fire might save him, but he dared not risk attracting the invisible demon that had slaughtered the camp. And anyway, he had nothing to burn. Karl knew from experience that if he did not find warmth in less than an hour, he would be dead. He could never cross the frozen bay and make it to the ship in that time. Which meant he had to return to the camp and hope that the thing that had murdered his crew was gone.

With leaden footsteps Karl crossed the field of bones. Shards of shattered whale ivory clattered under his feet with each step. Finally, he reached the icy slope that led to the camp. With raw, blue-veined arms and black fingers swollen to the size of sausages, Karl hauled himself out of the boneyard. He crawled across the snow, rising only when he reached the cover of the buildings.

Cautiously approaching the greenhouse, where he hoped to find food and warmth, Karl discovered a scene of carnage. First he noticed that most of the windows were broken, the paltry array of herbs and vegetables frozen solid. Then he spied a bloody handprint frozen on a pane of glass. Finally he saw the near-frozen body of a whaler. The man lay in the middle of the greenhouse floor, among shards of shattered glass. Like the corpses Karl had found in the warehouse, this man's head and spine were missing.

Turning, Karl moved down a narrow alley between two structures. At the end of the corridor, he tripped over a sledge and tumbled into a pile of dog harnesses.

Snarling jaws snapped at his face, and Karl jumped

backwards. The mad dog's tether went taut just before the creature's fangs closed on his throat. Eyes black and terrified, the dog howled and pulled at its leash.

Karl got to his feet and staggered to the mess hall. His shoulder hit the door, and it flew open with a slam. Inside a fire still burned in the hearth, oil lamps glowed, and simmering pots steamed and boiled over on the cast-iron stove. The long tables were set for a meal, but the mess was empty—hastily abandoned, by the look of things. Turning, Karl slammed the door and lurched into a table.

He was ready to slump into a rough wooden chair when he heard movement behind him. Whirling, Karl thought he saw a black shape moving across the mess hall. Cautiously, he squinted into the shadows.

With a snarling hiss, something emerged. Karl saw the slavering jaws and the eyeless head and reeled backwards, tripping over a bench. Whimpering, he watched the black nightmare stalk him, long tail swishing back and forth like that of an angry cat.

Karl crawled backwards, his eyes locked on the evil thing. Finally, his back struck a seemingly immovable object. Turning slowly, Karl looked up to find another demon towering over him. Humanlike but not human, the creature was clad in armor from head to toe, its face covered by a metal mask. With a quick backhand, the humanoid monster threw the human aside.

Crashing into the tables, Karl felt his rib cage and the bones in his frostbitten arm shatter. Moaning with agony and the certainty of death, he crawled into a corner, where he lay forgotten as the twin horrors began to tear one another apart, piece by bloody piece.

CHAPTER 2

Whistling tunelessly, Francis "Fin" Ullbeck tipped his Boston Red Sox cap to the bored guard, then whisked his access card through the magstripe reader, punched in his code, and waited for clearance. When the security doors hissed, then yawned, Fin squeezed his considerable bulk through the opening and sauntered along the climate-controlled tunnel.

On the other side of the wide, tinted windows that lined this concrete tube, the high desert of New Mexico shimmered under the ruthless assault of the afternoon sun. A forest of radar dishes stretched for miles across the sandy plains and red-brown hills, their faces tilted toward the heavens. Out there on the desert floor, temperatures topped out at 106 degrees with near zero-percent humidity. But on this side of the glass and concrete, the temperature was a cool and constant 72 degrees.

Fin grinned when he spied a gangly, long-limbed man approaching from the opposite direction.

"Headley, my man. Leaving so soon? Do that and you'll miss the maestro in action."

"Shift's over," Ronald Headley replied dully.

Unlike Fin, whose skull appeared rather small on his short, rotund body, Headley's defining feature on his flagpole form was his oversized cranium—an ironic trait, considering his name. Consequently, Headley was the only technician working in the Telemetry and Data Monitoring Center who didn't have a nickname. In everyone's opinion, "Headley" was just too perfect.

"So, Headley . . . did you manage to move that Air and Space Museum reject out of my bad old baby's orbit?"

Headley nodded wearily.

Fin blinked in feigned surprise. "You mean that relic actually responded to your command?"

"Come on, Fin, GO7 isn't *that* old."

"Headley my man, when GO7 was launched, *Miami Vice* was the hottest show on television and I did my homework on a Kaypro." He patted Headley's back. "Don't worry, you'll get your chance to drive a sports car—someday, when you're all *growed* up."

Headley ignored the slight. In his view, Fin Ullbeck mainly got through life by projecting an attitude of smug superiority peppered with "jovial" disdain. Headley had long ago resolved to treat such insufferable behavior as a genetic malfunction—along the lines of a cleft palate or stunted arm.

"Hey, Fin. Don't forget the big show at 1400 hours—"

"I know, I know! Just keep it to yourself, man," said Fin, shushing him. He eyed the overhead security camera anxiously.

"Well, got to go," Headley called over his shoulder. "Happy motoring."

Scratching the scraggly beard that covered his double chin, Fin continued through the tunnel until he reached a second set of climate-controlled automatic doors. Beyond that barrier, an elaborate air filtration, cooling and purification system double-scrubbed the air to protect the computers from sand, plant pollen and ordinary dust. The entire facility was built over a five-foot-thick concrete foundation as near to earthquake-proof as human engineering could achieve. Insulated, soundproofed walls muted the whisper of wind on sand and the occasional howl of coyotes baying at the moon.

Beyond those doors the computer-lined Telemetry and Data Monitoring Center was staffed by a dozen scientists and technicians. All of them looked up as Fin entered the room. He smiled and flexed his pudgy fingers.

"Daddy's here. Let's get this show on the road!"

Flickering on walls and on desk consoles, high-definition television screens digitally projected data gathered by dozens of surveillance satellites. Generated by radar or microwave transmissions, by ultraviolet light, thermal imaging or simple photographic equipment, this data was gathered, assessed and sorted by multimillion-dollar Kray computers.

Fin tipped his baseball cap to Dr. Langer. The day supervisor scowled and turned his back.

Tossing his cap on the console, Fin flopped into a groaning office chair and spun in a half circle to face the largest and most advanced workstations in the entire complex. Every bit of data collected by Big Bird's array of scanners could be accessed from this single station. More importantly, the ergonomic keyboard and joystick in the center console controlled PS12's propulsion system.

Cracking his knuckles, Fin emptied his pockets to create a mound of Snickers, Milky Ways, PayDays and Baby Ruths on the desk. With a keystroke, he activated the console and began to type. Minutes, then an hour, passed as Fin fed information into Big Bird's telemetry computer. Finally, he activated the large HDTV screen above his workstation and slipped a hands-free communications unit over his head.

"This is Waystation One, Waystation One, commencing scheduled telemetry alteration for satellite P as in Peter, S as in Santa, One-Two. That's PS12 moving in five minutes from right. . . . Now. Stand by to receive data stream."

Fin flipped a switch and sent Big Bird's coordinate changes to computers at dozens of space agencies, observatories and satellite tracking facilities all over the world.

"Data confirmed, Waystation One. Good luck," a voice announced into Fin's ear.

Ready now, Fin grasped the joystick and pickled the activation switch. Thousands of miles above the earth's surface, the propulsion system aboard satellite PS12 came to life. Back on Earth, Weyland Industries technicians strained at their workstations to watch the self-styled "Master of Telemetry" in action.

Legend had it that both Microsoft Game Studios and LucasArts had courted Fin to design game systems for them, but the "Game Shark," Fin's nickname before he'd come to Weyland Industries, had found a new passion during his years at M.I.T.—satellite technology. In the end, the National Video Gaming League's highest scorer ever had chosen a lower-paying position at Weyland's TDMC because management had let him achieve an entirely new level of kicks with his joystick by driving the big satellites.

And Fin had never lost the skills he'd honed as a dedicated game player. Now, through barely perceptible movements of his hand, he skillfully inched two-and-a-half tons' worth of orbital mass out of its current orbit and into a new one—an orbit that would take the Big Bird satellite cruising over the bottom of the world. Each subtle move of Fin's hand was followed by minutes of gazing at the figures dancing across the tracking computer to see if the satellite needed any adjustment. Sweat beaded his forehead as Fin hunched over his console, eyes focused on the telemetry data that continually poured in. Occasionally his white-knuckled fingers twitched, gently moving the joystick to one side or another. Throughout the intense ordeal, Fin's eyes never left the screen.

Finally, after two hours of toggling the joystick, Fin sighed and sat up, blinking his eyes as if he had just awakened from a long sleep. He stretched his arms and tilted back his chair.

"Mission accomplished," Fin announced into the communicator. "PS12 is in its new orbit. Systems are running normally. Nothing to do now but sit around and wait."

Fin tossed the hands-free on the desk and checked his watch. It was almost time. Fingers flying across the keyboard, he activated Big Bird's onboard sensors. As the satellite began its assigned task of deep-mapping the Antarctic continent from orbit, Fin propped his feet up on the console, snatched a candy bar from the pile, and tore at the wrapper with his teeth. Munching chewy nougat and crunchy peanuts, Fin touched another button. A television screen near his foot came to life.

"Right on time," said Fin with a sigh of satisfaction. On the monitor, the black-and-white credits for Universal's 1943 classic *Frankenstein Meets the Wolf Man* began to roll.

Sixty-two minutes later—just as Bela Lugosi's Frankenstein monster was about to square off against Lon Chaney, Jr.'s, Wolf Man in the ruins of Frankenstein's castle—a blinking red light interrupted Fin's much anticipated downtime. He bolted upright in his chair and switched off the television, to activate the main HDTV monitor above his console. A real-time digital image shot by Big Bird filled the big screen. Fin studied the flickering picture for nearly a minute, trying to comprehend what he was seeing.

"Oh my God," Fin gasped at last, his legendary cool shattered. Then he whipped his head around and called over his shoulder, "Dr. Langer! Over here, quick. Take a look at this."

"What is it?" the day supervisor demanded.

Fin's gaze never left the screen as he replied, "It's the data stream coming in from PS12."

"Where is she now?"

Fin triple-checked the satellite's navigational data before answering. "She's right above Sector 14."

Dr. Langer blinked. "But there isn't anything in Sector 14."

Fin pointed at the image on his monitor. "Well there is now."

Over Fin Ullbeck's shoulder, Dr. Langer saw a series of interlocking square shapes—perfectly symmetrical and, if PS12's sensors were correct, very large. Too large to have formed naturally.

"What are we looking at?" Langer asked.

"Thermal imaging," Fin replied immediately. "Some kind of geologic activity tripped the heat-sensitive sensors, which activated the cameras. Then Big Bird's computers alerted me."

Dr. Langer studied the image. The shapes mimicked precisely the look of man-made structures as seen from high earth orbit. But that, of course, was impossible. Nothing existed in Sector 14, unless you counted polar bears and penguins. So if those interlocking shapes really were structures, then they were built a long, long time ago—which made this the most important archaeological discovery of the twenty-first century, perhaps of all time.

"Wake them up," said Dr. Langer.

Fin reached for the phone, then paused. "Who?"

"Everybody . . ."

As he spoke, Dr. Langer's eyes never left the screen.

CHAPTER 3

Mount Everest, Nepal

Climbers had two ways to ascend the Khumbu Icefall. The sensible route up the four-thousand-foot frozen waterfall was with Sherpa "icefall doctors." These expert mountaineers would scout ahead, lay aluminum ladders across deep crevasses, plant anchors, and string rope so that climbers could proceed with some amount of caution—accompanied, of course, by their experienced Sherpa guides.

The reckless way to conquer the single most hazardous site on Everest was to go onto the ice alone, stake out a point at the base of the waterfall and start your ascent, placing your own anchors and stringing your own ropes as you went, hoping there weren't any deep crevasses that needed bridging. In this type of climb, anyone who became trapped by an ice slide, buried by an avalanche, or swallowed by a crevass that opened then closed without warning (all pretty much daily occurrences on Khumbu) would likely remain frozen in place until global warming thawed the entire planet.

This was how Alexa Woods chose to make her ascent.

After hours of hard climbing, the young woman's lone slender form appeared as a mere speck on the vast, shimmering wall of ice. Buffeted by fifty-mile-an-hour winds, she now dangled less than a hundred feet from the icefall's summit.

With a controlled swing of her leanly muscled arm, Lex buried the head of a Grivel Rambos ice axe into the frozen waterfall. As the blade bit into the ice, water trickled around its head, reminding Lex that underneath this icy shell, tons of fresh water poured off the mountain. Nearly half the fatalities on Everest occurred right here on the Khumbu's shifting wall, but she did not let this thought linger or break the rhythm of her climb. For Lex, the universe and all its stressful potentialities had condensed themselves into a few economical motions—swing the axe, kick the crampon, pull on the rope and move up. Every move was calm, deliberate and careful.

Wrapped from head to toe in extreme-cold-weather gear, Lex sank the spiked crampons strapped to her boots into the icy wall. As a gush of fresh, cold water continued to bubble out of the hole her axe had gouged, Lex anchored her safety line with an ice screw and paused to rest. Risking frostbite, she pulled off the face mask that covered her delicate features and put her lips near the ice.

The bracing, near-frozen water refreshed and restored her. After drinking her fill, Lex stuffed her long, dark curls under her thermal mask and pulled it down over her face. Hanging on the rope with the safety harness pressing against her breasts, Lex listened to the constant wind and the steady sound of her own heartbeat.

Below her icy perch, the magnificent and brutal topography of this rugged ecosystem appeared uninhabitable—a trackless expanse of snow and ice broken only by black granite mountains so high their summits towered over the clouds themselves. Yet Lex knew this seemingly unlivable landscape was inhabited. In fact, it was the ancestral homeland of the Sherpas, the "People of the East" whose society and culture were as old as Tibet. Thousands of Sherpas dwelled in the forbidding Khumbu Valley, planting potatoes and herding yak in the shadow of the mountain they revered.

Before the coming of Westerners, the Sherpas had guided yak trains across the mountains along dangerous, shifting routes to trade wool and leather with the people of Tibet. Today their descendants routinely risked their lives leading groups of international tourists who flocked to Everest up the mountain—and rescuing those who ran into trouble.

A short, stocky people with Mongolian features, the Sherpas were the backbone of any mountaineering expedition attempted in the Himalayas. Called "the Gods of the Mountain," their skill and stamina were legendary. And though they had constant contact with the modern world, the Sherpas retained their traditional religion and customs; Lex admired them for that.

Tibetan Buddhists of the Nyingmapa sect, Sherpas still grew or raised most of their food. Herds of yaks provided wool for clothing, leather for shoes, bone for toolmaking, dung for fuel and fertilizer, and milk, butter and cheese for consumption.

Most Sherpas who worked on the mountains spoke English, and Lex had shared many a meal of *daal bhaat*—rice and lentils—and a savory yak-and-potato stew called *shyakpa* with the bold icefall doctors and pathfinders, the bearers and guides, and the emergency rescuers who lived at the base of Everest. Open and giving people, the Sherpas were as generous with their trade secrets as they were with their heavily sugared tea, which they drank from Western thermos bottles, or the rice beer, called *chang*, that each Sherpa household brewed.

Much of the kinship Lex felt with the Sherpas was a result of their shared profession. Her work—providing survival training and guidance to scientific expeditions into the Antarctic wilderness—was the modern equivalent of the Sherpas' age-old livelihood. And like the Sherpas, what Lex did for a living was risky. If she made a mistake, and even if she didn't, in the extreme climate of the Himalayas, death was always hovering near, always a possibility.

Mount Everest, though tamer now than at any time in her grim history, was still an unpredictable killer and always would be. Hundreds of corpses were scattered across the rocky pinnacles of the higher elevations, or buried under tons of ice and snow, where they would never be found. Most of those corpses belonged to Sherpas.

For Lex, her own death now held little terror. She had watched others perish, including those she'd loved, and on several occasions she'd almost died herself. Facing death so often had somehow blunted its power and diminished its dread. Personal extinction was something Lex could face and accept. What she could *not* abide, however, and what she would *never* accept was the death of another human being in her charge.

A blast of unexpected wind and a rain of dusty snow set Lex's adrenaline flowing. She cocked her head and listened for the telltale rumbling that would herald an avalanche. When it didn't come, she took a deep breath and prepared to resume her climb.

That was the moment the GSM phone rang on her belt, bursting into the epic landscape of this natural world like some kind of mechanized explosion.

Silently, Lex cursed a string of obscenities. Then she hung her axe over her wrist and reached down to check the device's digital screen. Lex didn't recognize the number blinking there and was tempted to ignore the call. But the phone continued to ring, so she tore off her mask and placed the hands-free receiver over her head and into her ear.

"Who is this?" she demanded.

The voice on the other end was liquid velvet, cut with a precise English accent.

"Miss Woods? A pleasure to make your acquaintance."

Lex tucked her mask into a pocket and resumed her climb without a reply.

"My name is Maxwell Stafford," the man purred. "I represent Weyland Industries."

"Let me guess," spat Lex as her axe bit into the ice. "You're suing us again?"

"You misunderstand. I speak for Mr. Weyland himself."

"What's one of the world's biggest polluters want with us?"

"Mr. Weyland is interested in you personally, Ms. Woods."

Lex kicked her crampon into the ice and grabbed the safety line with both hands.

"He's offering to fund the *foundation* with which you are associated for a full year," said Maxwell Stafford. "If you'll meet with him."

Lex hesitated a moment. As a professional guide and explorer, she had long ago committed herself to the Foundation of Environmental Scientists, an international group that actively advocated the preservation of all life on Earth—human and nonhuman. Species were disappearing from this world at an alarming rate. Lex agreed with the foundation's members who strongly believed that the loss of even one species put those that remained at greater risk.

Like the rope from which Lex dangled, the foundation was a lifeline for many—the deciding factor between the certainty of life and the finality of death. And though this offer sounded like a deal with the devil, she couldn't help but ponder what a deal it was. With Weyland's money, the foundation she loved, in danger of extinction itself, would be in a position to do some truly remarkable work.

"When?"

"Tomorrow."

"I presume you know how bad we need the money," Lex replied. "But tomorrow is going to be a problem. It will take me a week to get back to the world."

As she spoke, Lex continued to climb. Just a few feet

above her was the Khumbu summit, the icefall's highest point—a frozen river that formed a flat, icy shelf the size of a tennis court.

"I told Mr. Weyland that," said Stafford.

Lex swung the axe, kicked in the crampon, and hauled herself up on the rope.

"What did he say?" she said between pulls.

"He said we didn't have a week."

Throwing her arm over the edge of the icefall, Lex pulled herself up to the summit—and found herself staring at a perfect pair of brown Oxford Brouges. Still dangling, Lex looked up into the face of a handsome black man wearing light-cold-weather gear. Behind him, a Bell 212 helicopter sat waiting, its door open.

Lex unhooked her safety line and took the man's proffered hand. With surprisingly little effort he lifted her off the ledge and placed her onto the ice.

"Right this way, Ms. Woods," Maxwell Stafford said, gesturing toward the chopper, which immediately began revving up.

Speaking loud enough to be heard over the engine roar, Stafford took Lex's arm and led her to the aircraft.

"Mr. Weyland is quite eager to get started."

CHAPTER 4

Thirty miles from Mexico City, at the base of the towering Temple of the Sun, under the chiseled stone gaze of the Aztec sun god Uitzilopochtli, hundreds of men and women toiled in the sweltering heat.

Perspiring day laborers gouged the ground with picks and shovels, tossing clots of earth into sifters—large barrels with wire mesh bottoms used to separate out rocks and pebbles, bits of metal or pottery, and anything else larger than a Mexican peso. Archaeologists and graduate assistants scrabbled on their hands and knees, picking at the ground with garden shovels to unearth shards of broken pottery and blobs of lead fired from the guns of conquistadors 400 years before.

The founder of this excavation project, Professor Sebastian De Rosa, observed the controlled chaos from the fringes of the site. De Rosa was an athletically built man with a face that reflected both the olive-skinned warmth of his Sicilian mother and the chiseled, patrician angles of his Florentine father. It

was to his father, a steely pilot who'd flown for Mus-
solini in World War II before becoming a successful
businessman, that Sebastian owed his tenacity and
nerve. From his mother came his remarkable compo-
sure, patience and charm—attributes admired by most
of his students and many of his peers.

As the professor walked the perimeter of the site,
however, an approaching limousine with a Republic of
Mexico seal set Sebastian's characteristic cool on
edge. Waving off a bandana-clad site manager, the professor changed the direction of his stroll to coincide
with the arrival of the vehicle.

The black limousine, grimy from the road, was
heading for an area beside the main site that had been
established as a staff camp. Tents were pitched, and a
bank of portable plastic outhouses had been erected
downwind. There was a mess hall with a kitchen and a
makeshift shower made from a barrel suspended over a
square of water-stained plywood planks.

Beyond the camp, a dusty clearing was overrun with
battered pickup trucks, grimy Land Rovers, dented
Jeeps, and three faded yellow school buses used to
transport the day workers to and from the surrounding
Mexican towns. Those laborers—carpenters, electri-
cians, diggers—ranged in age from energetic teenagers
to weather-beaten old men. All spoke Spanish, smoked
American cigarettes, wore dusty jeans, and drank
cervezas from the early afternoon until late at night.

As Sebastian passed the tents to meet the limo, he
waved to a group of graduate students taking a *cerveza*
break themselves. All were young, enthusiastic and
American. They wore fashionable, name-brand gear—

Banana Republic shorts, L.L. Bean boots, J. Crew vests and jackets—and as "associates" and "archaeological assistants," they were handed the worst jobs on the site, which was, of course, the academic order of things. As one grad student had put it on a sign over his tent, in that typically blunt American fashion: "Grunt Work Is Our Fate."

It wasn't easy being a neophyte, and Sebastian well remembered the arduous, eternal centuries of paying his dues. But before basking in the glories of published papers, private grants, and *Good Morning America* appearances, this uber-educated breed had to earn its chops through painstaking study and tedious labor at archaeological digs.

Higher on the excavation's pecking order were the specialists: computer experts, technicians, archaeologists, anthropologists and site managers, all under Sebastian's direct supervision. As he continued moving to approach the limousine, they continually approached *him* with questions, demands or proposals. He slipped past them all with the serene calm and soothing apologetic words that usually salved the bruised egos of Type A professionals whose demands were either denied or ignored.

Unfortunately, Sebastian's brand of cool charm registered zero on the efficacy scale of the slightly wrinkled government suit who climbed out of her limousine strangling a sheaf of papers in one manicured hand.

"Ms. Arenas, how delightful to see you," Sebastian began, relieved to see that it was not her boss, Minister Juan Ramirez, who was paying a visit. He smiled with sincerity as he strained to find a few pleasant aspects of the woman's demeanor on which to concentrate.

One of the more valuable things he'd learned growing up in the long shadow of his father, the gregarious, highly driven, and deceptively easygoing head of his own import-export business, was to concentrate on the positives during human interactions. In Ms. Arenas's case, Sebastian settled on her lovely, somewhat intelligent eyes and admirable hygiene.

"I see you've received my report," he pleasantly told the woman, glancing curiously at the choking fist she'd made around his perfectly innocent papers. "Have you had the time to read it yet?"

"This is very troubling, Dr. De Rosa. Very troubling indeed," said Olga Arenas, the assistant minister of the interior for the Republic of Mexico. "You have been promising results for three months now, but so far we have seen nothing. This report only confirms your failure. When the minister reads this, he will be furious."

"We're close," Sebastian lied smoothly. "Very close."

The woman frowned. "You've been 'close' for a year and a half."

Perspiring, Ms. Arenas tugged at the lapels of her slightly wrinkled business suit and squinted up at the hot afternoon sun. Sensing her anger, Sebastian thought it best to put the woman's negative energy to better use. Hoping his "motion spends emotion" lecture to his students worked equally well in application, he began a brisk walk right through the debris-strewn center of the busy site. Ms. Arenas trailed him, stumbling unsteadily on high heels as she crossed the broken ground.

"Archaeology is not an exact science," Sebastian told her.

Ms. Arenas opened her mouth to speak, but her reply was drowned out by the sudden roar of a gasoline-powered motor, followed by loud cheers.

Dr. De Rosa waved his encouragement to the men who'd managed to get the generator started—two electrical engineers and a retired electronics expert from the United States Navy. They had set up an experimental sonar device that was—theoretically—capable of detecting underground buildings, tombs, ruins or other solid structures buried by the passing of centuries. But testing their device had been impossible because the gasoline-powered electric generator had been broken for days.

As the generator's juice now flowed to the sonar device, the navy man threw a switch, and the sonar screen sprang to life. The triumph was short-lived, however. In a shower of sparks and a blast of black smoke, the generator exploded. Tongues of fire leaped into the sky until a quick-thinking bystander doused the machine with an extinguisher.

At this sight, Sebastian frowned. And Ms. Arenas scowled.

"I don't see any science here at all, Professor," said the woman, her lovely eyes hard, her hot tone apparently unwilling to be put on ice.

Most unfortunate, thought Sebastian.

Concluding that the woman would not be charmed, he resorted to one last trick. Turning quickly, the professor attempted to flee from the bureaucratic barracuda. But his escape route was blocked by a bank of sifting barrels, and Ms. Arenas pounced.

"You're holding up the development of this land for tourism at great cost to the Mexican government," she barked. "The Ministry of the Interior gave you a permit to dig for eighteen months. Your time is up, Professor."

"Now wait a minute—"

But it was Olga Arenas who stalked away this time. "Results by the end of the week or we pull the plug!" she called over her shoulder.

Sebastian De Rosa squinted in the burning sun as the woman climbed back into her limousine and sped off. Cursing, he kicked a rock into the bush, then sagged against a tree. He and his team had been working like tireless mules for eighteen months and had found nothing. How was he going to make a significant discovery in only five days, let alone prove his theory about the origin of Mesoamerican culture and civilization? Impossible.

He cursed himself for not working harder on the politics. Only recently, Sebastian had learned that a rival archaeologist had been working behind his back to gain the ear of Mexico's minister of cultural affairs, the influential and no doubt corrupt Juan Ramirez. The unknown rival had undermined Sebastian, speaking out against his project, his theories, and against him.

Such predatory behavior was nothing new in the academic world, and nothing new to Sebastian. After all, he'd grown up admiring his father's ability to best men who would smile in his face while thrusting a self-serving dagger in his gut. But what Sebastian hadn't expected was the campaign of personal and professional destruction that had been waged against him ever since he'd broken with the herd to question a few of the cherished "facts" of modern archaeology—a scientific discipline he had naively assumed was in pursuit of the truth.

The controversy had begun when Sebastian had published his doctoral dissertation challenging the notion that the Egyptian pharaoh Cheops had built the Great Pyramid. When irate Egyptologists had demanded that he prove his "absurd" theory, Sebastian had published a second paper—his own translation of the inscriptions found on the mysterious "Inventory Stela" discovered in the ruins of the Temple of Isis in the 1850s. A record of the pharaoh Cheops's reign carved in limestone, the inscriptions clearly indicate that both the Great Pyramid and the Sphinx were already on the Giza plateau long before Cheops was even born.

This second paper was the academic equivalent of setting a hornet's nest on fire. The implications of Sebastian's theory, if proven, were staggering and would change recorded human history. And Sebastian had gone even further. He'd declared that the Great Pyramid and Sphinx were both far older than the Egyptian civilization that had sprung up in their shadows, and both were likely the remnants of an older and *still unknown* civilization.

Dr. Sebastian's reputation had suffered after the mainstream press had misrepresented this theory. Upon obtaining a copy of his dissertation, a Boston tabloid reporter had twisted his ideas. Hence the unfortunate headline: "Archaeologist Claims People from Atlantis Built the Pyramid."

Other tabloids had picked up on this misrepresentation, and the resulting wave of speculation among the Roswell, UFO, *X-Files* crowd had done little to uplift Dr. De Rosa's reputation among his peers.

Of course, Dr. De Rosa had never uttered the word "Atlantis," and he publicly objected to the simplistic characterization of his research. But the damage had already been done, and all his protestations only threw more fuel on the fire.

Since the publication of those first erroneous reports, Dr. Sebastian De Rosa's work had been both praised and condemned in the archaeological community—but mostly the latter. Sebastian generally ignored his critics and doggedly pressed on with his quest to find the connection between the pyramid-building civilizations of the Nile Valley and those in Central and South America. Two years ago, that quest had landed him in Mexico, where he'd been granted a rare opportunity to examine a unique and inexplicable artifact.

In the 1960s, a peasant farmer was digging around at the base of the Temple of the Sun when he unearthed a burial chamber filled with priceless Mesoamerican artifacts. The farmer later claimed to have discovered vessels, implements of gold, and other finds his untrained mind could not recognize. Most of the stuff was sold on the black market and vanished, but one object fell into the hands of a Mexican archaeologist curious enough about its origins to pursue the matter back to the farmer himself.

It was a metal object roughly the size and shape of a U.S. mint silver dollar. The artifact was inscribed with characters that resembled the earliest form of hieroglyphics used by the Egyptians. Potassium-argon dating techniques that accurately measure when a metallic ore was last heated to a temperature above 227 degrees Fahrenheit subsequently revealed that the artifact was made around 3000 B.C.—about the time the Egyptians first developed their pictographic writing system.

But how, Dr. De Rosa asked himself, could such an object appear in Mesoamerica, thousands of miles across the Atlantic Ocean from the cradle of Egyptian civilization in the Nile Valley—long before any known human culture existed in the rain forests of Central America? The tenets of traditional archaeology could not answer that question, so the object was declared a forgery by the prevailing experts and locked away in a vault at the Universidad de Mexico until Dr. De Rosa received permission to study it three decades later.

After a careful examination, Sebastian concluded that the artifact was genuine and that it represented the first physical link between Egyptian and Mesoamerican civilizations ever unearthed. But he also knew that the only way he could convince other archaeologists that the object was real was to somehow "repeat the experiment." In other words, unearth a *similar object* buried at around the same time at the same site—probably over a burial chamber similar to the one the farmer discovered forty years before. So when Sebastian De Rosa learned that the Mexican government was preparing to build on the land around the Temple of the

Sun, he appealed to the president of Mexico for the time and the funds to search for just such an artifact.

For a year and a half Sebastian De Rosa and his team had been hunting and had come up empty-handed. Now their time had run out.

"Professor! Professor!"

Sebastian looked up, glad for the distraction. Marco, a worker hired locally, was waving a long sheet of computer paper over his head. Marco's job was to scan the ground with a metal detector mounted on a long pole. The data collected by that device was fed to a lap-top computer manned by Thomas, an archaeologist Sebastian had trained himself and a digital imaging specialist whose job it was to interpret the vague, shifting forms that appeared on his monitor.

"Over here!" Sebastian called to Marco.

Breathless, Marco crossed the excavation site, and, with a Cheshire cat grin, he thrust the computer printout into the archaeologist's hand.

"We found it!" Marco declared as Sebastian examined the image on the printout.

"Where?"

Around the Temple of the Sun a series of deep, long trenches had been excavated by Sebastian's team. The main trench was close to six feet deep. Marco pointed in the direction of that main trench, and Sebastian took off in a run, legs and arms pumping.

By the time Sebastian arrived, the diggers had already abandoned the pit and stood on the edge watching, curious to see what all the excitement was about. Only Thomas remained at the bottom of the deep trench, waiting for Dr. De Rosa to arrive. Sebastian leaped into the middle of the pit and paused to study the digital image on the computer sheet once again. The printout indicated that a solid object—round and possibly metal—was buried just beneath the earth under his feet.

Dropping to his knees, Sebastian fingered the rich, black soil. Marco leaped into the trench to kneel next to the archaeologist. Around them, work ceased as rumors of a major find raced through the site.

"It's right here," Marco said, patting the ground with the flat of his hand. "Thomas says it could be metal of some kind."

Sebastian looked up at Thomas. The computer expert leaned against the wall of the trench, arms folded, his open laptop perched on a wooden crate.

"What do you think?"

Thomas pondered the question. "It's too small to be the chamber."

Sebastian waved the comment away. "Of course it's not the chamber," he cried. "It's a burial offering. The Teotihuacans would bury a hundred or so gifts around the burial chamber. Obsidian blades, pyrite mirrors, shells . . . we must be right on top of it."

As Sebastian crouched over the spot where the object was buried, Thomas placed a small brush and an archaeological probe into his hands.

"You do the honors," Thomas said, stepping back.

As a crowd gathered around the pit, chattering in Spanish, English and French, a tall, mustached man in a dark suit moved unnoticed to the front of the group, where he watched Dr. De Rosa.

Sebastian began by carefully pushing the dirt aside

with his bare hands. Then he positioned the archaeological probe and gently thrust its sharp tip into the soil, slowly piercing the crust until the long metal spike was nearly buried. Dr. De Rosa felt nothing on the first attempt, so he drew the probe out and tried again.

It wasn't until his fourth attempt that Sebastian struck pay dirt. Almost as soon as the tip disappeared in the soil, it touched something hard. The artifact was buried less than an inch below the surface. Dr. De Rosa immediately withdrew the probe and set it aside.

"He's found something," someone in the crowd whispered.

Sebastian cautiously pushed the dirt away with the brush until he could just make out the rough outline of the object. It was small, about the size of a coin. And round like a coin, too.

"What is it?" Marco asked.

Dr. De Rosa did not reply. Instead, he dug his fingers deep into the soil around the object until his fingers closed on the thing. Sebastian held his breath as he lifted the artifact out of the ground.

"Professor?" Thomas whispered breathlessly.

Finally, soil fell away and the object was revealed. Sebastian let out the breath no one knew he was holding. Eyes strained, but Dr. De Rosa still crouched over the artifact, shielding the thing he had unearthed. When he looked up, Dr. De Rosa found a host of eager, expectant faces surrounding him. He stood, still concealing the mystery in his hand.

Finally, without fanfare, Dr. De Rosa presented the artifact to his audience.

They saw a glint of blue, and a familiar white swirl,

and some characters etched onto a circular, rusted surface. There were murmurs. Then gasps of surprise. Finally, Sebastian held the object high enough so that everyone could get a look at the only significant discovery his expedition had made during eighteen months of grueling, backbreaking work—

A rusty metal cap from a cola bottle.

"Vintage nineteen-fifties, I'd say," a slightly accented voice announced.

Sebastian looked up to see Mexico's minister of the interior, Juan Ramirez, staring down at him.

"Minister, I—"

But the bureaucrat cut Sebastian off. "According to you, the Teotihuacans' final gift to their dead king was a Pepsi?"

"Give me one more month," Sebastian said, still clutching the bottle cap.

Frowning, Minister Ramirez shook his head.

"Can't do it, Sebastian. Department of the Interior needed results six months ago. We're putting in another team."

As the sun set, the Mexican afternoon grew slightly cooler, down from 107 degrees to a pleasant 99. Sebastian De Rosa was in his tent, packing, when Thomas arrived.

"How bad?"

"We lost half the crew," Thomas said, frowning.

"Bobby leave?"

"Yeah. And Joe. And Caroline. Nick. Jerry and all of Jerry's crew."

Sebastian took the news hard. He slumped down on his cot, his shoulders sagging. "Thomas, the burial chamber is here. I know it." His fingers made a fist. "We're going to find it—and a link to the Egyptian culture."

"I know it, too," the younger man replied, pushing the blond hair from his face. "But without a crew and a new permit to dig, we're out of business."

Sebastian stared at Thomas a moment, then got back on his feet. With renewed determination, he threw more things into his pack.

"Hold the rest of the team together for two days. I'll go to Mexico City . . . talk to the suits. I'll get our dig back."

"I might be able to help you accomplish that, Professor."

The voice was a stranger's, deep and with a precise British accent. Sebastian and Thomas turned to find a tall black man standing at the door to the tent. De Rosa estimated the man to be well over six and a half feet tall, and the perfectly tailored London business suit did little to hide his broad chest and thick-muscled arms. Despite his size the man moved with polished grace.

"Do I know you?" Sebastian asked.

"My name is Maxwell Stafford," the man replied. Then he stepped forward and handed Sebastian a bone-white stationery envelope that bore the embossed monogram of Weyland Industries.

Sebastian tore it open and stared at the piece of paper inside—a personal check from Charles Weyland made out to Dr. Sebastian De Rosa. The number on that check was followed by more zeroes than a carbon-dating estimate. Sebastian looked up at the stranger.

"In exchange for a little of your time," Maxwell Stafford explained.

CHAPTER 5

Near the Antarctic Circle,
325 Miles Off the Cape of Good Hope

The massive, British-built Westland Sea King helicopter designated *Weyland 14* flew through a brewing storm. Outside, leaden clouds roiled and wind gusts intensified, making for a bumpy ride, but the Sea King's shudders and sudden dips went unnoticed by one passenger.

Alexa Woods slept soundly, sprawled inside the chopper's main cabin. She was still clad in the cold-weather gear she'd been wearing when she'd been plucked from the Himalayas. A copy of *Scientific American* lay open across her chest. On the cover there was a recent photograph of the founder and CEO of Weyland Industries, and the headline read "Charles Bishop Weyland, Pioneer of Modern Robotics."

Standing at the window near Lex was a tall, skinny man with gangly limbs and a prominent Adam's apple. On his nose was perched a pair of bottle-thick glasses; he gripped a digital camera in his hand. He placed the camera on a seat in an attempt to take his own photograph. On his first try, all he succeeded in doing was blinding himself. On his second, the chopper lurched and he bumped into Lex.

"Sorry," the man said when Lex woke. She nodded and was about to close her eyes again when he said, "But since you're awake, would you mind?"

He held up the camera and tried to flash Lex a seductive smile. It only made him look geeky.

Lex took the camera and snapped the photo.

"I'm documenting the trip for my boys so they know that their father wasn't always boring," the man explained. He reached into his parka and pulled out a thick wallet of photographs. He presented a picture to Lex.

"That's Jacob, and that's Scotty," the man said proudly.

"They're cute," Lex said out of politeness. "Is this your wife?"

"Ex-wife," he replied. Then the man thrust out his hand. "Graham Miller, chemical engineering."

They shook.

"Alexa Woods, environmental technician and guide."

"Do you work for Weyland?"

Lex shook her head.

"I split my time between working for a small environmental foundation and taking scientists on expeditions on the ice. One pays for the other and neither pays very well."

"The ice?"

"Arctic and subarctic environments, the Himalayas, Antarctica—"

Just then the copilot stuck his head into the cabin. "Lex, you and your friend buckle up. We're close to the ship now, but we're going to hit some major turbulence."

Lex buckled her seat belt. Miller sat down across from her and did the same.

"Friend of yours?" he asked.

"Of my dad's. He trained most of the pilots down here. During the summer my sister and I tagged along."

"Does your sister work with you?"

Lex nearly laughed at the notion. "No way. She hates the cold, moved to Florida. If you see her skiing, she's being pulled by a boat."

The copilot, back in his seat, turned and yelled from the cockpit.

"Just passed the PSR!"

"Damn," said Miller, clutching his camera. "I wanted a picture."

"Of what?"

"The PSR. They should really call it out *before* they pass it."

Lex shook her head. *Where'd this guy come from?* "The PSR is the point of safe return," she gently explained to him. "It means we've used more than half our fuel so we can't turn back."

Miller visibly paled.

"We could ditch," Lex added to the engineer's relief, ". . . but the temperature of the water would kill us in three minutes."

Miller grew a bit paler as the helicopter continued to shake and rattle.

"Antarctica," Miller said softly as he gazed out of the window.

The 278,000-ton Icebreaker *Piper Maru*, 270 Miles Off the Cape of Good Hope

Captain Leighton stood, legs braced, on the ship's heaving bridge and squinted through rain-soaked windows. Gray, foam-flecked waves crashed over the bow of the pitching vessel while stinging wind lashed the superstructure. At this time of year, there were long nights and short days this close to Antarctica, with a continuously twilight sky that seemed forever dominated by roiling purple clouds. The storm that battered the ship showed no sign of abating, and powerful gusts sent salt washes across the deck.

Leighton, who'd spent close to forty years at sea, had navigated the Cape of Good Hope many times before, and he didn't need to check the barometer to know that weather conditions were only going to get worse. The first European to circumnavigate this region in 1488, Bartholomeu Dias had christened these waters *Cabo Tormentoso*—"The Cape of Storms" in Portuguese. On days like this, Leighton wondered why the cape's original name hadn't stuck.

"*Weyland 14* to *Piper Maru*. We are on approach," announced a voice through the crackling of the ship's radio.

Captain Leighton slipped on a hands-free communicator and spoke into the microphone. "This is *Piper Maru*. You're cleared for landing, but watch yourself,

Weyland 14. We have severe wind sheer. It's going to be rough."

He broke communications with the aircraft and faced his executive officer. "Gordon, I want you to send out a crash team, just in case. Put them on deck, but out of sight. We don't want to spook the fly boys."

The bridge crew chuckled.

A few moments later, they watched from the relative comfort of the command deck as the huge helicopter touched down on the storm-tossed icebreaker. Sailors hurried into the rain to lash down the aircraft with hooks and cables.

After the engines powered down, the side hatch slid open, and the passengers disembarked, crossing the steel deck in the pelting rain.

From his command position, Captain Leighton counted the bodies through water-streaked windows. "Two new arrivals. I hope we have enough room."

Silently Max Stafford appeared at the captain's shoulder. "This should be the last of them."

Down on the tossing deck, the final passenger to disembark was Lex Woods. Itchy, stiff, and tired, she'd paused at the chopper's hatch before finally stepping onto the slick metal deck. After being plucked from her mountain perch, she'd shuffled from helicopter to private jet to helicopter again, crossing entire continents and vast oceans without benefit of clean clothes, a long bath, or adequate REM sleep. Now that she'd reached what she hoped was her final destination, Lex had little patience left. Whatever billionaire industrialist Charles Weyland had in mind for her, she certainly expected to find out sooner rather than later.

A hot meal wouldn't hurt either, thought Lex. The last thing she'd ingested, other than the caviar canapés and smokehouse almonds on Weyland's private jet, had been a Ziploc bag of cold yak jerky back on Khumbu.

After disembarking, Lex quickly caught up with her fellow traveler. Miller, the photo-happy Chem. E., was having trouble finding his sea legs.

"Careful!" Lex cried as she deftly caught the lanky, bespectacled man before he fell. Scrambling to retrieve his suitcase, Miller accidentally kicked it. The case hydroplaned like a hockey puck across the deck's slick surface, and Lex snatched it up before it tumbled over the side.

"My savior! Thank you," Miller gushed in unembarrassed gratitude. He gazed at Lex through dewy glasses thicker than the windows on a bathysphere. When Lex handed the young man his suitcase, she noticed his sneakers were already sopping wet.

"You need to find some better shoes."

Miller shrugged. "I came straight from the office."

So did I, Lex thought.

Fighting wind and rain, they made their way across the ship, Lex striding and Miller stumbling. Ahead, a sailor waved them forward with a red flashlight, toward metal stairs that led below deck, down into the ship's hold.

From his position on the bridge, Max Stafford watched, amused, as the stunning Lex walked side by side with the awkward Miller.

"Alexa Woods . . . unusual first name," he remarked to Captain Leighton.

It was another man who responded. "She's named after her father, Colonel Alexander Woods, United States Air Force."

Captain Leighton turned toward the deep voice to find a muscular man swaggering onto the bridge. Max continued to stare out the window.

The newcomer grinned, an unlit Cuban cigar clenched between his white teeth. Quinn radiated a raw, animal power and usually spoke with testosterone-fueled vulgarity, though his brutishness was blunted by quick wit and an innate intelligence. His sinewy frame and leathery skin reflected his life lived at war with the elements. Prickly stubble lined his square chin, and unruly, sandy-blond hair protruded from the sweat-stained rim of a battered cowboy hat.

Quinn touched the brim in a casual salute to the captain, then sauntered over to join Max Stafford at the window.

The two men stood side by side watching the lovely, athletic African-American woman stride across the pitching deck with perfect balance, oblivious to the storm swirling around her.

"Her old man was a tough bastard with a big reputation on the ice. Probably wanted a son," said Quinn. After a pause, his jaw muscles clenched. "He got one."

"Nice toys," murmured Lex in a stunned breath as she moved farther into the cavernous main hold of the *Piper Maru.*

Tracked vehicles, heavy lifting and earth-moving machinery, prefabricated shelters, electric generators, hydraulic apparatus, harsh-weather gear, oxygen tanks, saws and handheld digging tools crammed the vast area. Thanks to her father, Lex had already experienced more Antarctic expeditions in her twenty-eight years than most scientists saw in their lifetimes, but she'd never before seen this amount of expensive equipment in one place.

Vehicles—including *ten* Hagglunds—dominated the deck, while mountains of packing crates were secured to the four walls. Most of the crates were branded with Weyland Industries' ubiquitous *W*—the same *W* that Lex had seen on every damned vehicle, jumpsuit and flight attendant uniform during her trip to this icebreaker.

In one corner of the mammoth hold, Lex noticed a makeshift briefing area. Dozens of folding chairs had been arranged in an unbalanced circle around packing crates piled high enough to create an elevated stage.

Lex estimated there were thirty to forty other passengers milling around the hold, ogling the expedition toys. She divided them into two groups—*scientists*, of which she was one; and *roughnecks*, the folks who would be operating the heavy machinery. The latter were a different breed, common in Antarctica and one that Lex was, unfortunately, all too familiar with.

Lashed down in the center of the hold was a pair of enormous vehicles, each roughly the size of an eighteen-wheeler. Lex recognized them from her stint as an environmental specialist at the Natural and Accelerated Bioremediation Research Center at the Oak Ridge National Laboratories. They were self-contained mobile drilling rigs equipped with multi-spectrum sampling labs, though the prototypes at ORNL were nowhere near as advanced as these models. She approached the machines to get a better look. A moment later, Miller appeared at her side, sans luggage and wearing dry clothes.

"That's some pretty fancy gear over there," she noted, nodding toward the drilling rigs.

Miller nodded. "Wonder what it does?"

Before Lex had a chance to tell him, someone else did.

"Well," said Sebastian De Rosa, stepping up to them. "That right there"—he pointed to a collection of pipes on the side of the machine—"is a sophisticated thermal exchanger. So my guess would be some kind of drilling device based around heat."

Miller raised a finger. "Don't tell me . . . physicist?"

"Archaeologist, actually," said Sebastian. "My colleague Thomas and I have an interest in anything that digs or tunnels."

"The mystery grows," Miller said, obviously enjoying every minute of this adventure. "We have a chemical engineer, an archaeologist, and an environmentalist. I even met an Egyptologist over there. So what are we all doing on the same boat?"

Sebastian arched an eyebrow. "I presume one of us is the murderer. That *is* the tradition, isn't it?"

Lex smiled, her first since her forced departure from Nepal. She could not help being charmed. When Lex noticed an unusual object dangling from a leather thong around his neck, she asked him, point blank, "What's with the bottle cap?"

"It's a valuable archaeological find," he replied without a trace of irony.

Miller, meanwhile, had become so insatiably curious about the drilling rigs that he climbed a metal ladder to investigate without permission. He stood on top of one machine, then climbed down the opposite side. The cab was unlocked, so Miller hopped behind the wheel and began bouncing around like a kid on a hobby horse.

Suddenly, Miller was surrounded by four large, muscular men wearing battle fatigues. They wore tags that read Verheiden, Boris, Mikkel, and Sven. None of the men was smiling. Instead, they were looming. Sitting between them Miller looked like a thread of dental floss. The biggest man—Verheiden—had a long scar running down his cheek. He thrust his head into the cab and leaned into Miller's face.

"Having fun?"

Miller nodded. "My first real adventure. I can't wait to tell my kids about all this."

Verheiden sneered. "This might be an adventure for you, *Dad,* but for the rest of us it's a job. Get off the equipment and go back to the suburbs before you walk us all off a cliff."

When Miller didn't respond instantly, Verheiden yelled, "Keep your hands off the hardware or you'll be wearing your ass for a hat!"

Miller quickly scrambled out of the cab as Lex approached.

"Nice team spirit," she said.

Verheiden looked at Lex, then at Maxwell Stafford.

"Keep the Beakers away from the gear," he barked.

Max Stafford sighed. A meticulous organizer, he had worked long and hard to put this very expensive expedition together. The last thing he needed was a personality clash, which led to bruised egos and wasted energy. The endeavor they were about to embark upon was too important for either. He stepped between Miller and Verheiden's team.

Verheiden turned his back on Lex and Miller and contemptuously surveyed the collection of overeducated, underdeveloped brainiacs milling around the hold, examining everything as if they were peering through electron microscopes.

"Just keep the goddamn Beakers away from my gear," he snarled again.

This time Verheiden's remark evoked applause, catcalls and derisive laughter from his own men and some of the roughnecks.

"What's a Beaker?" Miller asked.

Lex crossed her arms. "It's what they call scientists out here. You know . . . Beaker? Like in *The Muppet Show*?"

Miller's face lit up. "Beaker . . . I kinda like that."

"The briefing is to start in five minutes," said Max Stafford. "Please take your seats."

Sebastian De Rosa found a place in the front row, close to the makeshift podium. As he sat down and crossed his legs, Thomas hurried across the hold to his side.

"Weyland's check cleared."

"Good," said Sebastian. "We're going to listen to whatever he has to say. We nod, we smile, and then we politely decline whatever offer he makes, take the money and head back to Mexico."

Five minutes later, everyone in the mammoth hold was seated in folding chairs, grouped together by profession. The muscle—Verheiden, Sven, Mikkel, Boris, and Adele Rousseau—sat together in one clique; Quinn, Connors and the roughnecks in another. The third group was more casual and was comprised of the scientists and researchers from diverse disciplines that Charles Weyland had assembled from the four corners of the world.

Stafford noticed that Lex had aligned herself with them.

As an experienced leader of men, Max Stafford felt the tension rippling through the ship's hold like charged particles before a lightning strike. Some of the heightened emotion was due to the team's uncertainty about why they'd been brought here and what was expected of them. But once these people were made aware of the reasons for this voyage, uncertainty would be replaced by other emotions—scientific curiosity and the joy of discovery, perhaps, along with baser instincts like greed and ambition.

Forging such a diverse group into a functional and efficient team would be a challenge, Stafford decided as he stepped onto the makeshift platform. Then again, his job usually was.

"Everybody, please, your attention!" Stafford announced into the microphone. His amplified voice reverberated hollowly in the cavernous space.

"Most of you already know me, and I know all of you, by reputation if not yet personally. My name is

Maxwell Stafford and I've been authorized by Mr. Weyland to assemble this team—"

Suddenly a pale hand fell on his shoulder. Max turned.

"Mr. Weyland," he said, surprised.

"Thank you, Max. I'll take it from here," Charles Weyland replied. Stafford stepped back, and the billionaire leader of the mysterious expedition took center stage.

Though well into his fourth decade, not a trace of gray could be seen in his thick shock of black hair. With his broad, commanding forehead, wide mouth, piercing, ice-blue eyes, and sinewy frame, Charles Weyland looked more like a sports enthusiast than an industrialist—an illusion he fostered by appearing in public with a golf club slung over his shoulder. Waiting patiently for the murmurs of surprise and recognition to fade, Weyland twirled his nine iron once, then leaned on it with both hands.

"I hope you've all had a chance to freshen up, perhaps catch a little sleep," he began. "I know some of you have just arrived, and all of you traveled a long way to be here, and at very short notice. Let me assure you, however, that your journey has not been in vain."

The lights in the hold dimmed, and a digital projector illuminated a large square of the peeling metal bulkhead behind the platform. Weyland stood silhouetted in the light.

"Seven days ago one of my satellites over Antarctica was hunting for mineral deposits when a sudden heat bloom beneath the earth outlined this—"

The square of white light was replaced by a hazy, red-and-yellow-hued satellite image. Outlined in blood red on a background of pale yellow and burnt orange, a pattern of interlocking square shapes was clearly visible.

"This is a thermal image," Weyland continued, gesturing with his nine iron. "The red lines indicate solid walls. The orange, solid rock. My experts tell me it's a pyramid. What they can't agree on is who built it and when. . . ."

Sebastian De Rosa found his interest piqued for the first time since he'd arrived on the ship.

"What caused the heat bloom?" Thomas asked.

"We don't know. But one expert tells me that this feature is reminiscent of the Aztecs. . . ."

The image behind Weyland shifted angles.

"Another tells me that this is probably Cambodian. . . ."

Yet another satellite image of the pyramid silhouette appeared on the wall over Weyland's shoulder.

"But everyone agrees that the smooth side is definitively Egyptian."

Thomas, an acclaimed Egyptologist, nodded in agreement.

"Why would anyone build a pyramid out here?" Miller asked.

"Ancient maps show Antarctica free of ice," said Thomas, echoing his mentor Sebastian's theories. "It's likely that the continent was once habitable."

Sebastian De Rosa rose and stepped closer to the image on the wall. Weyland's penetrating blue eyes searched him out.

"Mr. De Rosa?"

"I think your experts are right."

"Which one?"

Sebastian smiled. "All of them. The Egyptians, the Cambodians and the Aztecs all built pyramids. Three separate cultures that lived thousands of miles apart—"

"With no communication between them," Thomas added.

"Yet what they built was almost identical." Sebastian stepped right up to the wall and stared at the projection. "This is clearly a temple complex. A series of pyramids, probably, and there is the ceremonial road connecting them."

Sebastian De Rosa's words caused a ripple of excitement on the Beaker side of the room. Pausing for effect, Weyland swung his nine iron with one hand, then rested it on his shoulder.

Oblivious to the growing clamor, Sebastian remained focused on the projected image. "Almost identical," he said again.

"Meaning what, exactly?" Lex asked.

"This might be the first pyramid ever built," Sebastian replied.

Miller scratched his head. "Built by whom?"

It was Sebastian De Rosa who replied, in a voice that barely contained his growing excitement. "The master culture from which all others are derived," he announced.

"If it could be the first pyramid, it could also be the last," Weyland said. "An amalgam of the ones that came before it. There's no proof of any connection between the cultures you cited."

Sebastian shook his finger at the image. "This photo is the proof."

Weyland smiled at Dr. De Rosa, somewhat condescendingly, Lex felt.

"I can't tell you who built it," said Miller, speaking up. "But if I could take a sample from it, I could tell you how old it is."

"Within how many years, Professor?" Max Stafford asked.

"Actually, it's Doctor," Miller replied. "And I'll give you the exact year . . . I'm that good."

"Well, *Doctor* Miller," said Weyland, "I'm offering to put you right next to the thing."

Lex stared at the image, clearly puzzled. "Where exactly on the ice is this thing?"

"Bouvetoya Island," Weyland answered, sending a sickening jolt through Lex. "But it's not on the ice. It's two thousand feet under it."

The thermal image of the pyramid disappeared from the wall, to be replaced with a satellite image of what looked like a Montana ghost town in the winter.

"The pyramid is directly below this abandoned whaling station, which will serve as our base camp."

A babel of voices erupted from all sides.

Weyland pointed his nine iron at the tall roughneck wearing a cowboy hat. "Mr. Quinn."

The man rose. When Lex spied him she frowned.

"Mr. Stafford, Mr. Weyland," Quinn began. "You're looking at the best drilling team in the world. We'll chew to that depth in seven days."

"Add three weeks on top of that to train everyone here," Lex Woods said.

On the podium, Weyland shook his head.

"We don't have that kind of time. I'm not the only one with a satellite over Antarctica. Others will be here soon, if they're not here already."

"Maybe I wasn't clear," said Lex. "No one in this hold is ready for this trip."

Weyland offered Lex a smile meant to be charming. It reminded her of a hungry shark.

"That's why I invited you here, Ms. Woods. You're our expert on snow and ice."

Lex didn't like being put on the spot, as was obvious from her expression. But she refused to back down.

"Bouvetoya is one of the most isolated places in the world," she said. "The nearest land is a thousand miles away. There's no help for us if we run into trouble."

Weyland nodded. "You're right. It's a no-man's-land. But the train has left the station. I think I speak for everyone aboard this ship—"

The image behind the billionaire shifted again to show another angle of the mysterious buried pyramid. Weyland pointed to it with his nine iron.

"—This is worth the risk."

Lex looked around the room. She saw curiosity, interest, and greed etched on the faces all around her. But no fear. Not even the slightest apprehension. And that's what concerned Lex the most.

The projected image vanished and the lights returned.

"That concludes our briefing, gentlemen—and ladies. Mess call is in ninety minutes. I hope you enjoy it. I had the chef flown in from my hotel in Paris . . . the filet mignon will be excellent."

Charles Weyland looked directly at Lex Woods. "Will you be joining us?"

Lex turned her back on the billionaire and strode across the hold.

"Find another guide," she called over her shoulder.

CHAPTER 6

Charles Weyland began to wheeze in the corridor before he even reached his stateroom. Eyes tearing, he tucked his head into his chest and choked back a cough. If he started now, Weyland doubted he could stop. So he suppressed the urge, but at a cost. He stumbled and nearly fell, the nine iron clattering onto the steel deck.

Then a powerful arm circled his waist, a deep voice rumbled in his ear. "Lean on me."

"I'm okay, Max," Weyland rasped.

Steadier now, he pushed Max aside and rose to his full height. "Hand me my club and open the door before anyone sees me like this."

Using the club for a cane, Weyland hobbled to his cabin. Max quickly closed and locked the door behind them, then helped Charles Weyland slump into a padded leather chair. Max leaned the nine iron against the wall and offered his boss a clear plastic oxygen mask. Weyland took several long, deep breaths, and some color returned to his gaunt face.

"Thank you," he said between gulps.

When his strength returned, Weyland discarded the mask and scanned the stateroom, which more resembled a hospital ward. His nose curled from the medicinal stench of the sickroom.

"The mirror, please."

Max rolled a portable vanity table and mirror in front of Weyland's chair and stepped away. Weyland gazed at his wan reflection for a moment, then sank into his chair and even deeper into his memories.

At twenty-one, Charles Weyland possessed a Harvard M.B.A. and a small satellite mapping company inherited from his father. Two years later he'd purchased a cable franchise in the Midwest, then a telecommunications grid in Nevada. Within a decade marked by shrewd and calculated expansion, Weyland Industries had become the largest satellite systems operation in the world, the company worth in excess of three hundred billion dollars. His financial empire secure, Charles Weyland had set out to change the world.

"Expanding the range of human endeavor" was more than the Weyland Industries catch phrase—it was the sum of Charles Weyland's personal philosophy. His mother dead before he was two, raised by a succession of nannies under the cold eye of a harsh, agnostic father, Weyland had lacked parental love or even the comforting faith in a higher power. So he'd made progress his creed, vowing to use his wealth to advance the frontiers of human civilization.

To that end, he'd begun to lead a double life. The

public Charles Weyland threw lavish parties, attended openings and charity events, bought luxury hotels in San Francisco, Paris and London. Billionaire Charles Weyland built a casino in Las Vegas and was very much a fixture of the society page, a shallow playboy who always had a beautiful woman on his arm and his signature nine iron draped over his shoulder. But like the hotels, the casino and the golf club, the women were mere props—part of an elaborate and calculated deception that enabled Charles Weyland to accomplish his real goals behind the scenes and under the radar.

While hosting the opening of the Weyland West Hotel in San Francisco, Weyland's representatives had been secretly purchasing a nanotechnology firm in Silicon Valley. As he'd attended London's theater season, Weyland's lawyers had been closing the deal for a robotics plant in Pittsburgh. While he'd attended fashion week festivities in Paris, Weyland's shell company had engineered a hostile takeover of a pharmaceutical company in Seattle and bought a genetics research firm in Kiyodo. By the time he was forty, Weyland had become the foremost financial supporter of cutting-edge scientific research on the globe.

Four years earlier, Weyland had told Max Stafford that, given forty more years on earth, the scientific research his company funded would enable Weyland Industries to open a branch in a moon base on the Sea of Tranquility. But that was before he'd been diagnosed with advanced bronchogenic carcinoma. Now, because of the cancer that was eating away his lungs, Charles Weyland no longer had forty more years. If he was lucky, he might have forty more days.

That was why the remarkable find in Antarctica and this expedition were so important. It was Charles Weyland's last chance to make a mark on humanity. And that was why Weyland was so grateful to the one man in his organization who made this last chance possible.

"Fifteen minutes rest, and then I get back into my . . . costume . . . and go across the hall to my office."

"Are you sure? Perhaps it would be best to retire for the night."

"Why? I won't sleep." Weyland took a deep breath and forced a smile. "Over the last three months you really have become invaluable, Max. Finding the right personnel, putting this whole expedition together in days—"

"Just doing my job."

Disgusted by his reflection, Weyland pushed the mirror aside. "I didn't think it would happen this fast. . . ."

Max crossed the room and rested his massive hand on Weyland's shoulder. The man's touch was surprisingly gentle. "You exerting yourself like this only accelerates the cancer. . . ." He hesitated, reluctant to bring up the same arguments, though he felt he must. "Perhaps you should reconsider accompanying us. You could stay here. Monitor our progress on the radio—"

With the wariness of a trapped animal, Weyland eyed the hospital bed, the oxygen tanks, the medicines, and he shook his head.

"I'm dying, Max. And I'll be damned if I do it here."

Sebastian De Rosa followed the executive officer's directions and located his cabin. He unlocked the door and stepped inside, delighted to discover that his quarters more resembled a stateroom on a luxury liner than a cabin on an icebreaker. For a moment Sebastian wondered if he'd been handed the wrong key, until he noticed that his luggage—what there was of it—had been deposited in the center of the room.

Sebastian opened his battered suitcase and removed an armful of clothes. When he opened the closet door, he was surprised to find clothing already hanging there—casual wear that fit his rather unexacting taste, along with cold-weather gear and even some equipment. He found waterproof pants and jackets, woolen sweaters and socks, thermal underwear, ski-style gloves, boots, woolen hats, and several bright-yellow Polartec pullovers stamped with the ubiquitous Weyland logo. A quick inspection revealed that everything was sized to fit.

"Mr. Charles Weyland, where have you been all my life?" he chuckled.

Sebastian was still feeling the high he'd gotten from Charles Weyland's briefing. At last he had a chance to prove to the archaeological community that the history of the world as currently written by scholars and academics was nothing more than a string of assumptions, conjectures, half-truths and outright lies. The discovery of a temple complex in Antarctica shattered every preconception of modern archaeology, which was why so-called objective scientists resisted the truth—even when confronted by evidence. This was a phenomenon Sebastian had experienced firsthand, early in his career.

While still a graduate student, Sebastian had gained access to the Library of Congress collection of portolans—maps used by fourteenth- and fifteenth-century seamen to travel from port to port. One of the maps he'd examined had been created in 1531 by Oronteus Finaeus. It displayed an accurate depiction of the entire continent of Antarctica as modern science now allowed it to be seen from outer space. Every bay, every inlet, every river, every mountain—all of the land hidden under tons of ice had been accurately reproduced on the Finaeus Portolan almost five hundred years before.

But how? Sebastian had wondered.

He'd learned from cartographers that most portolans used in the Age of Exploration had actually been copies of far older maps created by the ancient Romans and Egyptians. But even when the Egyptians had flourished, as far back as four thousand years, the South Pole had been completely covered by pack ice up to three thousand feet thick. Even if the Egyptians had sailed to Antarctica—which was absurd, because they hadn't had a navy until Cheops's father created one in 2000 B.C.—the ancient sailors would have found nothing but ice. It wasn't until the latter half of the twentieth century that modern scientists discovered the actual topography of the hidden continent under the ice, and they had used deep-sounding sonar techniques to do it.

So who had mapped the territorial features of Antarctica in ancient times, and how?

Sebastian had concluded that only two theories were possible. The first was put forth in 1967 by Erich Von Däniken in his book *Chariots of the Gods?* Von

Däniken concluded that space aliens had visited earth thousands of years ago and had helped primitive man create maps, build the pyramids, formulate calendars and construct ritual sites, where humans and aliens had interacted.

Sebastian's theory was far less outrageous. He believed that the original map Finaeus copied had probably been made at a time when Antarctica had been warm and habitable, and home to a now-forgotten civilization. The existence of the Finaeus Portolan, along with the Piri Re's map discovered in Istanbul, were solid evidence that Sebastian's theory was correct.

Yet when he'd presented his findings to his fellow archaeologists, his work had been rejected out of hand, despite the fact that physical evidence to prove his conjectures existed at the Library of Congress for anyone to examine.

After this sobering incident, Sebastian had been forced to conclude that either his fellow archaeologists hadn't bothered to read his paper, or they'd refused to face the truth. Either way, the pyramid complex Weyland had discovered in Antarctica—if indeed it *was* a pyramid complex—would slam the door on rigid, conventional thinkers in the academic crowd.

Just let them try to dismiss this!

As he shaved and dressed for dinner, Sebastian whistled tunelessly. He could not help but think that now, after years of controversy, scorn and neglect, all of his work would soon be vindicated, all of his theories proved.

* * *

Lex closed her eyes and felt the hot water wash over her. After two weeks in the wilderness, followed by a day of travel, the shower felt almost like a religious experience.

Searching the stall for a bar of soap, she found a packet of Savon de Marseille, an expensive handmade olive oil soap from the south of France. She sniffed, then frowned. Probably the same soap Charles Weyland offered to the fancy set at his Parisian hotel. She wasn't surprised. Like the high-end clothes and expensive gear she'd found in her closet and these ridiculously opulent accommodations, everything Weyland had provided was top of the line. But Lex still didn't like to be bought—a gilded cage was still a cage. And she much preferred a pitched tent 15,000 feet up Everest's North Face.

On the other hand, she did need to get clean. Ripping open the packet and squeezing the soap into her hand, Lex considered her opinion of Weyland, now that she'd actually met him. All evidence so far pointed to one conclusion: another billionaire eccentric. And this expensive expedition: a singular waste of time, and a dangerous one that would probably get most—if not all—of them killed.

She'd seen Weyland's type before—too rich, too bored, too full of themselves. Dilettantes who become temporarily fascinated by a subject, only to flit like a magpie to the next bright, shiny idea that flashed across CNN. Lex resented their ilk, not because she was jealous but because men like Weyland possessed money and power, and wasted both. They drifted through life without accomplishing anything beyond building a Godzilla-sized stock portfolio, while scientists and researchers who dedicated their entire careers and reputations to a cause were forced to bow and scrape for the crumbs they'd toss as an afterthought or a tax deduction.

As Lex rubbed the pricey soap into a thick lather and applied it to her taut body, she could almost hear the voice of Gabe Kaplan, the foundation's fundraising director, ringing in her head with all the charm of a never-ending Nike commercial: "C'mon, Lex, get with the program. Bowing and scraping costs us nothing and gains the foundation everything. Just do it."

Lex accepted the money Weyland promised to help the Foundation of Environmental Scientists, but she refused to be a party to the expedition's collective suicide.

At best, Lex figured Weyland and company would sail to Bouvetoya Island; Quinn and his cronies—walking environmental disasters to the last man—would poke a hole in the ice; and all those archaeologists talking about a pyramid would find a huge pile of quartz, or shaped ice, or volcanic fissures or one of a dozen other natural formations that somehow mimicked the appearance of a temple complex.

The worst scenario was too horrible to contemplate.

Lex well recalled her climbs to the summit of Everest. Air so thin she felt like she was breathing through a half-collapsed straw. Temperatures at 40 below, winds at 100 miles per hour. The excruciating pain of moving her body up 3,000 feet in a day and trying to breathe, let alone eat or drink, at the 29,000-foot mark.

That was a picnic compared to what Weyland and his expedition would face if something went wrong.

Without Lex, they didn't stand a chance. As she rinsed the luxurious suds off her cocoa-hued skin, Lex tried to convince herself that their odds wouldn't be much better if she did go with them. She lingered a moment longer under the warm water. The shower may have washed her free of any hypocrisy she felt having contemplated Weyland's offer, but it didn't wash her free of the guilt she was feeling leaving this team behind.

Lex dressed in a pair of Levi's and a sweater from the stocked closet and left the rest of the clothes untouched. She didn't have any clean clothes of her own, or she wouldn't have taken anything.

As she was packing up her meager belongings, there was a knock at the stateroom door.

"I spoke with Mr. Weyland," Max Stafford told her. "The money has been wired to the foundation's account. The helicopter is refueling to fly you back home."

Max turned to leave.

"Who did you get?"

He paused in the doorway but did not turn.

"Gerald Murdoch," he said, closing the door.

Fifteen minutes later, Lex pounded on the door of Charles Weyland's shipboard office.

"Come—"

Lex burst through.

"—in."

Weyland was seated in a leather chair behind a large oak desk. Though not opulent, the office was large and well appointed. Before Lex arrived, the industrialist had been reviewing personnel records. Ironically, it was her file he was reading.

"Gerry Murdoch has two seasons of ice time. He's not ready."

Weyland looked away. "Don't worry about it."

Lex leaned across his desk. "What about Paul Woodman or Andrew Keeler?"

"Called them."

"And?"

"They gave the same bullshit answer that you did," said Max Stafford as he came through the door.

"Mr. Weyland. What I told you in there wasn't bullshit. If you rush this, people will get hurt, maybe die."

Weyland faced her again, his eyes angry. "Ms. Woods, I don't understand your objections. We're not going to Everest. We need you to take us from the ship to the pyramid and then back to the ship. That's all."

"What about inside the pyramid?"

"You don't have to worry about that. Once we're at the site we have the best equipment, technology and experts that money can buy."

Lex met his anger with her own. "You do not understand. When I lead a team I don't ever leave my team."

Weyland slapped his palm down on the desk. "I admire your passion as much as your skills. I wish you were coming with us."

But Lex just shook her head.

"You're making a mistake," she told him.

Weyland tapped the weather report on his desk. "The wind sheer is dangerous right now. Captain Leighton assures me that we're moving out of the worst of it, but he thinks you should postpone your helicopter ride for a couple of hours." He rose and stepped around his desk. He reached out and touched her arm.

"Think about my offer. Join the others for dinner, and if you don't change your mind, I'll have the helicopter fly you back in a couple of hours."

"He wasn't kidding about the food," a wide-eyed Miller exclaimed between bites of succulent crabmeat.

"More wine? Chateau Lafite '77, an excellent year."

Miller nodded and Sebastian poured. Then the archaeologist raised his glass. "A fine vintage, for a French. And, for the record, it tastes even better out of plastic."

Sebastian's first meal aboard the *Piper Maru* was a study in contrasts. Fine food and superb wine served up, cafeteria style, on battered standard-issue metal trays and plastic glasses. The noise level inside the mess hall reminded him of college.

It didn't look as if Mr. Weyland would be dining with them tonight, or that fellow Stafford. Fortunately, Sebastian's dinner companions more than made up for any disappointment.

"That fellow dishing up the chow. I think I saw him on The Food Channel," said Miller.

"Watch a lot of television?" Sebastian asked.

"Not much else to do in Cleveland. . . . Not since my divorce."

"So you're from Cleveland?" said Thomas.

"That's right. I was born in Cleveland. Bought my first chemical set in Cleveland. Blew up my parents' garage there, too. After I got my degree I found a job in Cleveland and got married there and I live there now."

"Don't get around much, do you, Miller?" Lex teased.

"No, no! Not true . . . I left Cleveland to go to college."

"You studied overseas?"

"Columbus."

Lex noticed Sebastian wince, then rub his knee.

"Are you okay?"

"Busted my knee a few years ago. I have a metal pin holding it together. Hurts like hell in this cold weather."

"You get that in some dashing archaeological adventure?"

Thomas snickered, then took a sip of wine.

"I got it in Sierre Madre."

Lex was surprised. "The mountain range?"

"The Tex-Mex bar in the United States. Denver. I was lecturing there. Drank one tequila too many and fell off the mechanical bull."

Lex leaned back in her seat and laughed. So did Sebastian.

Across the mess hall, sitting among the workers, Quinn spied Lex sitting at a table with a few Beakers.

Connors, his partner, paused, a forkful of dripping steak inches from his toothy mouth. "Do you think she's here to shut us down?"

Quinn sneered. "She can't shut us down. Weyland is our employer. Ms. Woods and her farm team of environmentalist Beakers don't have the clout to stop Weyland."

"Well she sure did shut us down in Alaska. Her and that foundation of hers. . . ."

Quinn ignored his partner and continued to stare across the room.

"I think I've run through all my damn unemployment insurance," Connors continued. "I'm on welfare if this job falls through."

"Blow it out your ass, Connors."

Connors chuckled and poured wine into Quinn's glass. "I think you need another drink, boss."

Quinn slammed the flat of his hands on the table.

"Damn right I do," he roared. "But no more of this fancy French grape juice. Get on down to the hold and grab us a case of Coronas. Hell, make it two. Let's all get whup-ass drunk."

"Who is that guy?" Sebastian asked, noticing the open glare being sent in their general direction.

Lex sipped her wine before answering.

"I ran into Quinn in Alaska. He and his boys were pushing for more oil exploration. Had a lot of Alaska natives on his side, too. But we shut him down—the environmental group I work for. Guess he carried a grudge."

"I would," said Miller. "If someone put me out of a job, I mean."

"This pyramid," said Lex, changing the subject. "You really think it could be under the ice?"

"I would like to think so," Sebastian replied. "It would be the discovery of the century. In fact, it would validate some of my own theories. I believe that four thousand years ago . . ."

Sebastian's voice trailed off. Lex was no longer paying attention to him. Instead, she was gazing at something over his shoulder.

"Am I boring you?"

Lex pushed her chair away from the table and touched Miller's and Sebastian's arms. "Come outside . . . all of you. You too, Thomas."

"What is it?"

But she was already up and out the door. Sebastian rose and followed, Thomas on his heels. Miller swallowed the last bit of his filet, washed it down with Chateau Lafite '77, and hurried to catch up to them.

Lex led the others through a thick waterproof bulkhead, then onto the deck. A stab of icy wind cut through them, stealing their warmth. But any discomfort was forgotten when they saw the spectacle in the firmament.

"My God!" Thomas exclaimed.

The entire night had become a waterfall of shimmering radiance. Vertical ribbons of light snaked across the southern sky, a colored profusion of visual chaos. Successive bands of brighter colors flamed while darker patches pulsated rhythmically. The vast curtain of reds, greens and blues seemed to move as though ruffled by an interstellar wind.

Lex threw her arms wide, as if embracing the panorama. "It's an X-class flare accompanied by a halo coronal mass ejection. Otherwise known as aurora australis . . . the southern lights."

Sebastian was transfixed. "I don't think I've ever seen anything so beautiful."

Miller adjusted his glasses, then pulled the digital camera out of his jacket pocket.

"It's in the upper atmosphere," he explained. "Streams of protons and electrons from the sun are being deflected by the earth's magnetic field, causing a solar radiation storm."

"Whatever. . . . It's beautiful," Sebastian replied, "even the way you describe it, Doctor."

"Thanks," Miller replied. Then he snapped a picture. "And I agree."

Lex leaned on the rail and gazed up at the sky. "Shackleton called Antarctica the 'last great journey left to man.' It's the one place left in the world that no one owns, that's completely free . . ." Then she grinned. "Me? I'm kind of partial to the penguins."

"I wish you'd reconsider coming with us," said Miller.

Lex looked at him and smiled. But she shook her head.

"Not for me. Obviously," said Miller. "But I think a lot of the other guys really need you." He poked her arm. "C'mon, don't make me pull out pictures of my kids again."

"Your kids aren't that cute."

Sebastian chimed in. "What if we got pictures of other people's kids? Would that do it?"

Lex looked at them both. "Want my advice? Stay on the boat."

It was Sebastian who bristled. "We're not staying on the boat."

"Guys, the first rule of this job is to not take people to places they're not ready to go."

"Listen," Sebastian replied. "I was on the next plane

to Mexico. My team's waiting. But if Weyland's even half right, this find could change history."

"Weyland is more concerned with making another billion than with anything else," Lex replied. "*Including* your safety."

Sebastian stepped up to her. "Let me ask you something. You're here. You know this place. Do we stand a better chance of surviving with you than with the number two choice?"

Lex did not reply, but her face gave the answer away.

"Because if we do and you don't go with us, and something goes wrong, are you going to be able to live with that?"

Lex opened her mouth to reply, but no answer came. Suddenly a tall, blond woman strode onto the deck.

"Ms. Woods? Your helicopter is refueled and ready. They're waiting for you."

CHAPTER 7

Two Thousand Miles Above the Sea of Tranquility

Just beyond the reach of the moon's gravitational pull, an enormous vessel dropped out of hyperspace. Gracefully following the curvature of the moon, the craft passed across the sun, casting an ominous shadow along the lunar surface.

Nearly a kilometer in length, the ship's sleek, organic form more resembled an oceangoing manta ray or predatory bird than an interstellar vessel. As the craft plunged silently through the void, the warp engines disengaged and a thin stream of charged ions began to spew from the engine nacelles, propelling the ship on the final leg of its journey to the cloud-wreathed, blue-green orb still over 238,000 miles away.

Inside the ship, energy and life-support systems self-activated. Mazelike corridors and domed chambers were flooded with the hot, muggy, oxygen-rich atmosphere of the tropics. One by one, decks were illuminated by a green reptilian glow. The architecture was primitive, and many sections of the craft could pass for the interior of a samurai warlord's fortress or the grim torture chamber of a medieval castle.

In the half-light, shadows danced along walls etched with sharp-edged hieroglyphics. High, vaulted ceilings resembled those in a Gothic cathedral, but here they gleamed with the blood-red hue of the abattoir.

Other sections of the ship were more organic in appearance. The armory mimicked the fleshy interior of some vast monster's belly. Curved terra-cotta rib bones festooned the space. Between those faux-ribs, the walls were frescoed with pictographs and were hung with an array of fierce, techno-medieval weaponry: spears with retractable shafts; curved blades carved from yellow bone and bundled together like the fasces of ancient Rome; double-bladed ceremonial knives with serrated edges and ornate handles; metal clubs studded with raked white teeth; hubcap-sized shuriken edged with needle-thin blades; sharp-finned throwing darts larger than rail spikes.

The bloodstained trophies of previous hunts were also mounted in this bleak chamber—skulls of varying shapes and sizes, some broken, with empty sockets and jaws lined with fangs. A panoply of weapons, ranging from a quartz-tipped spear to a meson-interrupting particle beam weapon powerful enough to cut a mountain in half, hung in stasis behind a translucent metal bulkhead.

Beyond the armory, deep within the heart of this otherworldly ship, a computer screen brightened to reveal a thermal image of the *Piper Maru* floating on the vast expanse of ocean. Foreign cryptographs scrolled across the screen as the spaceship's cybernetic brain calculated the distance between the icebreaker and the array of interconnected squares on Antarctica.

Process complete, the computer sent out an alarm—a sibilant hiss audible throughout the alien vessel. Around that central monitor, lights flickered to reveal a circular chamber heavy with moisture. A deep pool of dark liquid dominated the floor. A white mist curled over the ooze. Surrounding the pool like petals on a flower, massive shapes drifted inside of five translucent cryostasic cylinders.

Suddenly the cryo-tanks burst, spilling their contents into the central pool. The liquid roiled as colossal shapes began to stir in the muck. Broad, mottled faces surfaced in the rippling fluid, their features a nightmare amalgamation of insect, shellfish and reptile. Sentience burned behind eyes that seemed strangely human—intelligent eyes that focused on the image of the *Piper Maru* still flickering on the monitor. Around the mouth of each creature, fingerlike mandibles flexed.

CHAPTER 8

The sky was a canvas of lead, a low full moon occasionally visible through breaks in the clouds. After the unsettled weather of the past few hours, the sea was now surprisingly calm, its smooth surface broken only by chunks of ice, many the size of an SUV. This moment would seem almost temperate for the Antarctic Circle if a frigid wind weren't cutting across the steel deck, sending icy claws into the men huddled there. Despite their layers of wool, flannel, cotton and the Polartec coveralls that supposedly protected them from the elements, a few shivered.

Sebastian De Rosa and Thomas came onto the deck to find themselves among the busy workers. Avoiding stares from the roughnecks, who were hauling tracked vehicles out of the hold with a crane and lining them up on deck, Sebastian drifted over to the scientists and mercenaries gathered near the rail. Although he wore so many layers of clothing that he felt like a walking teddy bear, he was shivering and sporting a thin layer of frost on his chin by the time he reached Miller's side.

"You okay?" Miller asked.

"Too much time spent in the tropics."

"Yeah, that tan does make you look like the odd man out around here."

Sebastian turned his eyes skyward, hoping for a ray of warm sunshine. But only the moon was visible in a slate gray sky. "What time is it anyway?"

Miller glanced at his watch. "Midday."

"Then where's the sun?"

"This far south they have six months of darkness. The sun never rises. Perpetual night . . . or whatever this is."

Sebastian suppressed a shudder. He should have guessed that already, of course, but he'd been distracted, his mind on the ancient pyramids of Mexico, Egypt and Cambodia. "Charming."

"When is this survival lesson to begin?" Thomas asked. "I have way too much to do before we reach the excavation site."

Sebastian watched Alexa Woods approach from across the deck. "Recess is over. Here comes the teacher now."

Miller grinned when he saw her. "See," he said. "I told you she'd stay. It's my animal magnetism. It's irresistible."

"Everybody gather round," Lex began without preamble. "It is my job to keep all of you alive on this expedition and I need your help to do that. Antarctica is *the* most hostile environment on God's earth. It is difficult to thrive in this climate, and very easy to die."

As Lex spoke, Thomas took out a video camera and began to record her briefing. As she spoke, Adele Rousseau—a tall, striking woman with a shock of blond hair and an Amazonian physique—began to issue everyone communication devices. Meanwhile, a Weyland technician laid an array of cold-weather tools and equipment on the deck for demonstration purposes.

"Since I don't have the time to properly train you, I'm laying down three simple rules," Lex told them. "One. No one goes anywhere alone. *Ever.* Two. Everyone will maintain constant communication. Three. Unexpected things do happen. When they do—no one tries to be a hero."

"For some of us it comes naturally," said Miller, chuckling.

"Laugh it up, Beaker," barked the mercenary Verheiden. He pointed at his own cheek. "You get scars like this when some hero on your team screws up their assignment."

Lex stepped between them.

"If one of us goes down, we're all going after them. Understood?" she said, directing her question to Verheiden.

"Understood," said a consensus. Verheiden said nothing.

Next Lex directed their attention to the identical, bright yellow Polartec coats issued to all the scientists and technicians. She held one up, turned it inside out, walked in a circle so everyone could get a good look.

"What you are wearing now are state-of-the-art cold-weather suits. The outer material is fabricated from recycled plastic soda bottles and is practically airtight. The polypropylene inner lining will whisk perspiration away from your skin before the moisture freezes.

"Our gloves are also manufactured from Polartec, with Capilene lining that will absorb a moderate amount of perspiration—but your hands sweat a lot, so always carry an extra pair of gloves.

"This gear is the best there is, so if you feel cold now, get used to it, because it is only going to get worse—"

"Great," muttered Sebastian.

"Temperatures out here drop to below minus fifty Fahrenheit on a regular basis, with wind chill that can become minus *one hundred* and fifty." Lex paused in front of the workers and locked eyes with Verheiden.

"Stay still for too long, you *will* freeze, you *will* die. Exert yourself too much, you will sweat, the sweat will freeze, and you *will* die. . . ."

She looked at Sebastian and Thomas. "Breathe too heavily and moisture will enter your lungs, the moisture will freeze within you and you *will* die."

She paused to let her words sink in. "Okay, I want you to take a look at the equipment I have spread out here. In a few minutes we'll go over their uses. Any questions so far?"

Smirking, Sven, one of the mercenaries, raised his hand. "Is it true you were the youngest woman to climb Everest?"

"No, that is not true."

Miller nudged Sebastian. "She was the youngest to

climb Everest *without oxygen.* . . . I looked it up on the net."

The group broke up as individual members checked out the equipment they were expected to use—ice axes, tents, stoves, safety harnesses, ropes, thermarests, neoprene water bottles and several types of first-aid kits for various illnesses and trauma.

Lex noticed that the mercenaries—readily identifiable by the khaki parkas they wore—were pretty much ignoring the equipment. They were either experts at cold-weather survival or just arrogant. Lex wanted to know which.

She crossed the deck to Adele Rousseau, who was cleaning a handgun.

"Seven seasons on the ice and I've never seen a gun save someone's life," Lex began.

Rousseau looked up. When she spoke, there was a hint of amusement in her blue eyes.

"I don't plan on using it," the blond replied.

"Then why bring it?"

Rousseau shrugged. "Same principle as a condom. I'd rather have one and not need it then need it and not have one."

She tucked the weapon into her belt and thrust out her hand. "I'm Adele."

"Lex."

"I'm glad that you decided to stay."

Lex shrugged. "Couldn't let you have all the fun."

Adele was about to reply when there was a noise like an explosion. The ship shuddered and lurched violently to starboard, tossing men to the deck. Miller was thrown backwards, against the rail. He nearly tumbled over the side, but Lex, standing near Adele, caught him just in time. Miller looked up at her through thick glasses.

"This is getting to be a habit."

Lex tossed her wavy dark hair. "Doesn't mean I have a thing for you."

"Oh, you hide it well, Ms. Woods, but I know."

Another massive impact shook the *Piper Maru*. This time a ten-ton Hagglunds tracked vehicle dangling from the crane swung over their heads like the Sword of Damocles. There were cries of surprise and panic. Sailors scurried onto the deck to secure all watertight hatches, and Captain Leighton suddenly appeared among them.

"Everybody off the deck please!" he commanded. "We have hit the ice pack. Return to your cabins, secure everything that is not nailed down. Quick as you can, people. . . ."

The reinforced steel bow struck the ice pack again. The ship lurched before plowing through it with a sound like ripping metal. Miller and Thomas became anxious.

"Nothing to worry about," Captain Leighton declared. "This ship is an icebreaker by name and nature. She can take it, and she can dish it out."

When the deck was cleared of all but essential crewmen, Captain Leighton climbed the superstructure until he reached the bridge. He found his executive officer at the helm, as well as Max Stafford and Charles Weyland, who were studying the data spewing out of the navigational system.

"Holding steady at five knots, sir."

"Very good, Gordon."

Charles Weyland approached the skipper. "How soon to landfall?"

Leighton glanced at the Breitling on his wrist. "At this speed I should say within two hours."

Weyland nodded, his jaw tense.

"Let's get our people ready, Max. I want to disembark as soon as we arrive."

Two hours later, the *Piper Maru* weighed anchor in the shadow of a dark mountain. Within minutes, a solid sheet of ice had already frozen around her stationary hull. Roughnecks swarmed across the decks, and the crane was busy once again, lifting tracked vehicles and drilling machines off the deck and lowering them onto the pack ice.

On the bridge, Captain Leighton directed Charles Weyland's attention to the three mountains in the distance, a snowcapped gray-brown blot on an otherwise moonlit, snow-white terrain.

"The closest one is Olav Peak—the whalers used to call it the Razorback. Not much of a mountain compared to Vinson Massif or Erebus, but whalers used Razorback as a navigational beacon in the days when such trade was still profitable."

Weyland gazed through the lens of an AV/PVS-7 lightweight, high-performance passive image intensifier system. These military-issue night-vision goggles turned the Antarctic twilight into day.

"You'll find your whaling station in the mountain's shadow," Leighton continued. "I'm sorry I can't take you closer, but the draft is just too shallow."

Weyland scanned the distance until he spied the cluster of buildings a few miles away from the foot of the mountain. The whaling station was at least ten miles away—too far to make out much detail.

"You've done enough, Captain," said Charles Weyland. "Just don't go home without us."

CHAPTER 9

Five Hundred Miles Above Bouvetoya Island

The Predators were awake now, and active.

Naked, their pale, mottled flesh still gleamed from their immersion in the pool of primordial ooze. Five powerful beings swaggered onto the starship's bridge, their eyes gleaming with innate intelligence.

Computer monitors flickered all around them as red, green and violet ripples of energy pulsed throughout the chamber. The cybernetic brain's voice—a constant, sibilant hiss like the sound of an angry rattlesnake—greeted its masters with an endless barrage of data. The bridge itself was dominated by a wide window that offered an awesome view of the planet Earth.

Silhouetted against a backdrop of the blue-green planet shimmering below, one of the figures ran a talon over a crystalline control panel. With a whizzing pop, an airtight section of the wall opened to reveal suits of gleaming body armor, five demonic face masks, a plethora of weapons, and an array of short-barreled, shoulder-mounted cannons.

Wordlessly, the creatures girded themselves for the coming battle.

Moving with mechanical efficiency, the Predators draped flexible mail-clad netting over their pale, hard-muscled arms and broad, barrel-like chests. Segmented battle armor was snapped into place, sheathing thick, corded arms and powerful legs. Reinforced boots, loin-plates and chest protectors followed. Then a bulky mechanism was attached to each creature's forearm, just below the elbow joint. A similar device was strapped to their right wrists.

One of the creatures tested the mechanism. With a simple jerk of its sinewy arm, a long, curved, razor-sharp telescopic blade deployed with a soft snick. The formidable hunter examined the honed edge of the blade, then grunted in satisfaction.

Next came a ridged metal backpack attached to shoulder armor, with a built-in mount and power cables for a plasma cannon. Then the flat, heavy face masks were donned. Each mask was different, yet every one obscured its wearer's full face—except the burning eyes and the dangling, metal-tipped dreadlocks.

Finally, a computer was linked to each Predator's left wrist. Upon activation an LED display flickered, and, with a sudden hiss, the armored joints sealed to become airtight. Warm, humid air flooded the interior of the body armor, an atmosphere that mimicked the conditions of the Predators' home world.

With this body armor in place, the hunters collected their weapons—long collapsible spears with serrated tips and curved double-edged blades with ivory grips. Clamps on their gleaming body shields held folded

shuriken that, when thrown, would deploy wicked, retractable blades. Strangely, they left the plasma cannons on their racks, selecting only the less-advanced,
almost primitive weaponry instead.

Only one creature chose a high-tech weapon—a
wrist-mounted net gun—though he counterbalanced
that choice with a more basic, long, curved blade fashioned from a diamond-hard, bony substance.

After they had all completed their preparations for
the hunt, the Predators filed into a small ritual chamber
and knelt in supplication before a mammoth, intri-
cately carved stone effigy of a fierce warrior god, a de-
ity who hurled thunderbolts as weapons like some
mighty, extraterrestrial Odin.

As the Predators prostrated themselves before their
savage god, a static-streaked image appeared on the
bridge's main computer screen. It was the real-time
image of a parade of vehicles lumbering across a vast,
frozen expanse.

CHAPTER 10

Five tracked Hagglunds, followed by the two large mobile drilling platforms, plodded in a long procession across the rugged ice pack. Lex rode in the lead vehicle, a gaudy orange Hagglund branded with the ubiquitous Weyland logo. Little more than a cabin mounted on tank tracks, the Norwegian-built all-weather people mover was the most effective mode of transportation at the South Pole, and its huge windows afforded passengers an excellent view.

Gazing at the pristine beauty of the harsh, moonlit landscape, Lex pressed her cheek against the cold Plexiglas and allowed the polar chill to seep into her. This was Lex's way of acclimating her mind and body to the harsh climatic conditions she was about to face.

"A wasteland," Sven declared. At his side, Verheiden nodded in agreement.

Lex shook her head, disappointed by their powers of observation. All you had to do was open your eyes to see that Antarctica possessed as rich an ecology as any other continent on Earth. This harsh, seemingly hostile environment actually teemed with a variety of flora and fauna—much of it easy to see if one only took the time to look.

Less than five miles from this spot, humpback, minke, and fin whales cavorted in the ocean. A dozen different species of penguin thrived along the coastline, mingling with fur and elephant seals. Albatross, petrel, gulls and skuas wheeled across the sky and snatched krill and fish from the breakers.

The mercenaries—along with men like Charles Weyland, or even that bandit Quinn—all thought of the natural world as something to be explored, tamed or exploited, not cherished or preserved.

"We're about seven miles from the station," Max Stafford announced from behind the wheel, interrupting Lex's thoughts. Next to him, Charles Weyland huddled in his coat.

Sebastian directed Lex's attention to the full moon, which hung so low in the sky that you could practically bump your head against it.

"When I was a kid, growing up in Sicily, you know what they'd call a moon that big?"

Lex shook her head.

"Hunter's Moon."

Twenty minutes later the lead Hagglunds rolled to the pinnacle of a snow rise and halted on the edge of the whaling station. One by one, the other vehicles pulled around it, engines idling. Weyland opened the door, filling the cab with a blast of frigid air. Max shut down

the engine and followed. As the rest disembarked, a
steady snow began to fall.

"There she is," Weyland declared.

To Sebastian De Rosa, the abandoned nineteenth-
century whaling station looked like one of the Wild
West ghost towns he'd visited while digging in the
Southwest. The spare, functional wooden buildings
were made out of the same tarred, rough-hewn timber.
There were hitching posts, a main street fronted by
several large buildings, and smaller shacks in various
states of disrepair.

The difference was that here ice and snow replaced
sand and tumbleweeds. Wood-shingled roofs sagged
under decades of accumulated snow, and drifts as high
as ten feet collected between the buildings and almost
completely buried some of the smaller, heavily damaged structures.

Most eerie was the dark pall that hung over the
place. Bouvetoya Whaling Station was built at the
foot of the mountain, and at this time of year a perma-
nent shadow fell over the desolate ghost town. Sebastian and Miller were tempted to use their flashlights
to illuminate the main street as they moved through
town.

"This place looks like a theme park," said Miller.

"Yes," Thomas replied. "Moby-Dick World."

As the others looked around, Thomas spied Adele
Rousseau. The woman lit a cigarette and took a long
drag.

"Hi," said Thomas.

The mercenary took another puff and said nothing.

"Be honest," Thomas teased. "You're a little disappointed that you didn't get the yellow jacket, aren't you?"

Adele turned and faced him. She was not smiling.

"They give the newbies the yellow jackets so that when you fall down a crevice and die, it's easier for us to spot your corpse."

Thomas swallowed, nodded, and moved on.

"Spread out," Max cried over the howl of the wind. "Locate the structures that are most intact. We'll use this place as a base camp—our tents won't last long if this wind keeps up."

Then Stafford faced the roughnecks. "Mr. Quinn. You'll begin drilling operations as soon as possible."

"I'm on it."

Lex walked past Quinn and continued along the shadowy main street. Miller and Sebastian caught up with her at the deserted harbor. There was a ramshackle wharf and a long dock that stretched far out into the bay, but the bay itself was frozen solid.

A giant black cauldron dominated the harbor from a high cliff. Forged of iron fifteen feet high and thirty feet across, it stood tilted at a crazy angle. The wooden legs under the vat had long since collapsed. Only ice and snow and a single wooden leg prevented the heavy iron pot from rolling over the cliff and tumbling into the harbor below.

Sebastian wondered about the vat. "Witch's cauldron?"

"The Separator," Lex replied. "Throw whale blubber into it, heat it, separate out the fat. Whale oil was big business back then. Almost as big as petroleum is now."

While Miller pushed open a door and wandered inside one of the buildings, Sebastian walked carefully to the edge of the partially shattered wharf, checked the thickness of the ice, and asked, "How did they get ships in here?"

"The station only operated in the summer, when the pack ice melted. It was abandoned in 1904," Lex replied.

"Why?"

She frowned. "Nothing left to hunt, I guess."

She found a harpoon leaning against a dock post and tried to lift it, but the object wouldn't budge. It remained frozen to the ground.

Meanwhile, inside one of the largest buildings, Miller discovered a frozen mess hall. Long wooden tables and rough-hewn benches were sheathed with thick, blue-gray ice. Metal cups and plates, whalebone forks and spoons, even a coffeepot were frozen to the spot where they had been abandoned one hundred years ago.

Miller tried hard to lift one of the cups. With a metallic clink the handle came away in his hand, the cup still stuck to the tabletop. Grinning, he stepped back and raised his camera. "One for *National Geographic*."

When the flash exploded, the sudden light disturbed something in the far corner of the room. For a split second Miller spied a shiny black shape. There was movement, and he heard a weird, scraping sound, like the pincers of some improbably large insect scurrying along the plank floor.

"Hello," Miller called into the shadows.

The movement ceased, but Miller could sense that he was not alone—that something was in here with him.

"Hello!"

Louder this time, Miller's voice reverberated inside the mess hall. He strained his ears but heard nothing. He turned to go when the scrabbling sound returned. This time the noise seemed closer.

Feeling a little anxious, Miller puffed out his chest and thumped it with his fist.

"Come out of there or you'll be wearing your ass for a hat!" Miller shouted in a fair imitation of Verheiden's booming voice.

The noise stopped.

Swallowing hard, Miller's Adam's apple bobbed.

Suddenly one of the tables was knocked aside by something below eye level. Miller stepped backwards—to collide with someone behind him as a hand grabbed his shoulder.

"Jesus!" Miller squealed, throwing his hands up.

"What's the problem?" Lex cried.

"There's something in here!"

Lex looked doubtful. "Like what?"

"Over there—" Miller pointed to the spot where the table fell.

Lex stared into the gloom, her flashlight beam probing the darkest recesses of the mess hall.

"Listen," Miller hissed.

Lex heard it. A scratching sound, like claws on a blackboard. Something was crawling across the ice-covered floor, something small enough to move unseen under tables and between benches.

And it was coming closer. . . .

"Watch out, Lex!" Miller cried.

Suddenly a black shape scrambled out from under a

table accompanied by the now familiar scrabbling sound. Lex shone her light on the creature.

"For God's sake, Lex!" Miller cried, shrinking back.

"It's a penguin!" said Lex, stifling a laugh.

"I can see it's a penguin," he replied sheepishly. "I thought it might be—"

The penguin waddled right up to Miller and cocked its head to stare at the shaken engineer with one beady eye.

"Careful," Lex warned. "They do bite."

CHAPTER 11

Lex and Miller heard shouts as they emerged from the frozen mess hall.

"Over here! You're not going to believe this."

It was Sebastian calling. Hearing him, Quinn and his partner Connors dropped what they were doing. Weyland hurried forward, too, with Max Stafford at his side.

Lex's gaze followed the billionaire as he moved across the snow-covered ice. He was moving with some difficulty, she noted. He seemed breathless and was leaning heavily on his ice pole. Yet when he spoke, his voice had lost none of its forcefulness. "What is this, Dr. De Rosa?"

Sebastian led all of them around the corner of a dilapidated processing factory and pointed. There, in the ice, was a gaping hole ten feet across. The pit was perfectly round, and if there was a bottom, it was lost in the shadows far below.

Perplexed, Weyland looked at Quinn, then at the

mobile drilling platforms that were still being un-packed and assembled.

"How the hell did this get here?"

Quinn crouched on one knee and examined the pit. "It's drilled at a perfect fifty-five-degree angle." He pulled off his bulky glove and ran his hand along the sides of the shaft. The icy walls were perfectly smooth—almost slick to the touch.

Lex peered over Quinn's shoulder. "How far down does it go?"

Sven ignited a flare and tossed it into the pit. They watched it bounce off the smooth walls and fall for many seconds, until the flare's phosphorescent brilliance was swallowed by the dark.

"My God," Weyland said softly.

Max Stafford looked at Dr. De Rosa. "Are we expected?"

Weyland dismissed that notion with a wave of his hand. "It must be another team. I'm not the only one with a satellite over Antarctica. Maybe the Chinese . . . the Russians . . ."

"I'm not so sure," said Lex, staring into the abyss.

"What other explanation could there be?" Weyland insisted.

Lex looked around at the ghost town and the barren glacial ice fields all around it. "Where is their base camp? Their equipment? And where are *they*?"

Max Stafford shrugged. "Maybe *they* are already down there."

Once again Quinn crouched down to examine the mouth of the shaft. "Look at the ice. There are no ridges, no bore marks. The walls are perfectly smooth—this wasn't drilled."

"How was it done?" asked Lex.

Quinn looked up at Lex. "Thermal equipment of some kind."

Weyland nodded. "Like yours."

"More advanced," Quinn replied. "Incredibly powerful. I've never seen anything like it."

Quinn activated his flashlight and turned its beam on a building close to the pit. A large circular hole had been cut into the structure, vaporizing the stout wooden walls and melting the metal machinery inside the building. It was clear from the trajectory that whatever had cut through the ice had also sliced through the structure.

"I told you I'm not the only one with a satellite. It must be another team," said Weyland. He glanced at Quinn. "Whoever it is, they clearly have better equipment than we do."

"Listen," Quinn replied, standing up to the billionaire. "Whoever cut this, sliced through pack ice, the building, the beams and the solid metal machinery. We should find out what cut this before we proceed."

Max Stafford locked eyes with Quinn. "And I thought *you* were the best."

Quinn bristled. He rose, squarely challenging Stafford.

"I *am* the best," he said.

Weyland stepped past Quinn and stared into the pit. "They must be down there."

Lex examined the ice at the mouth of the hole. "No.

Look at the ice. There's no ridges . . . nobody's been down there."

Weyland frowned. "When does the Big Bird satellite pass over again?"

Max Stafford checked his watch. "Eleven minutes ago."

"Get on the horn to New Mexico. Get me that data."

While Max downloaded the satellite reports, Quinn moved one of the Hagglunds forward, directing its spotlights into the pit.

Miller and some of the roughnecks gathered to peer into the hole, but Connors waved them away.

"Don't want nobody fallin' in. Gettin' them out again would be a goddamn waste of time."

Weyland was leaning against the vehicle when Max Stafford appeared, computer printouts and satellite images in hand. He spread the papers across the hood of the Hagglunds as Quinn, Sebastian, Lex, Miller, and Verheiden gathered around.

"There it is, clear as day," said Weyland. His fingers traced the red line all the way across the map, right down to the interconnecting squares.

"And this time yesterday?"

Max unfolded a second printout. Weyland studied it. "Nothing."

Sebastian squinted at the map. "So whoever cut this shaft did it in the last twenty-four hours."

"That's just not possible," said Quinn.

"Well, possible or not, it's here. It's done," said Sebastian.

Sebastian and Quinn locked eyes, and a vein appeared on Quinn's tanned forehead.

"I'm telling you there's no team and no machine in the world that could cut to this depth in twenty-four hours."

Charles Weyland stepped between them. "The only way we're going to know for sure is to get down there and find out."

Then Weyland turned to face the rest of the party. "Well, gentlemen," he said loud enough for everyone to hear. "It seems we may be engaged in a race. If it's a competition, it's one I don't intend to lose—"

Weyland coughed. Suddenly he doubled over, spasms wracking his body. Max held his shoulders as Weyland choked back the urge and regained control of his breathing.

"Okay, let's get to work. I want to know what's down there and I want to know in the next few hours." Weyland's voice was weaker, but his eyes had lost none of their spark.

As Weyland trudged to the door of the Hagglunds, he reached out and squeezed Max Stafford's arm. "There are no prizes for coming in second," Weyland rasped. "Do you understand, Max?"

Max nodded once. "My men are ready, sir."

The area around the pit swarmed with activity. More Hagglunds had been moved up, and their spotlights turned the never-ending dark into day. Teams of roughnecks unloaded coils of rope, and a multiple winch-and-pulley system mounted on a metal tripod had been assembled directly over the mouth of the pit.

Lex was hammering pitons into the ice when Miller arrived, dragging a pallet packed with his chemical analysis gear.

"What are you doing?" he asked.

"Safety lines," Lex replied. "It's a long way down . . . don't want to lose any of you."

As Miller unpacked his gear, he took off his wool cap and scratched his head.

"Put your hat back on."

"Huh?"

"Your hat," Lex said. "Put it back on."

"It itches."

Lex paused, lowering her hammer. "I saw a man lose both his ears from frostbite," she said matter-of-factly. "With the ear canal exposed, you can see a full inch inside your head . . . all the way to the eardrum."

Lex smiled sweetly, tucked the hammer into her tool belt, and strolled away. Miller pulled his hat over his ears.

Dodging roughnecks, Lex crossed the lighted area to the lead Hagglunds. She opened the door to find Charles Weyland inside. He was alone, gulping oxygen from a portable tank. He lowered the clear plastic mask when Lex entered the vehicle.

"You've caught me a little . . . indisposed," he croaked, humbled.

Lex closed the door and sat down by his side.

"How bad is it?"

Weyland looked at her through eyes hollowed by chronic pain. "Bad."

"There's no room for sick men on this expedition."

"My doctors tell me the worst is behind me."

Lex shook her head. "You're not a very good liar, Mr. Weyland. Stay on the ship. We'll update you at the top of every hour."

Crossing the cabin, Weyland concealed the oxygen bottle in a storage bin. When he faced Lex again, some of the fire had returned to his eyes.

"You know," he began, "when you get sick you think about your life and how you're going to be remembered. You know what I realized would happen when I go, which will be very soon? A ten-percent fall in Weyland Industries share prices . . . maybe twelve, though I may be flattering myself . . ."

Weyland slumped into a seat. Concern furrowed his broad forehead.

"The dip in stock prices should last about a week, long enough for the board and the Street to realize they can get along perfectly well without me. And then that will be that. Forty years on this earth and nothing to show for it."

Weyland nodded toward the activity outside.

"This is my chance to leave a legacy. To leave my mark—"

"Even if it kills you?"

The billionaire reached out and squeezed her arm. Lex felt the failing grip of a dying man.

"You won't let that happen," he said.

"You can't go," Lex replied.

"I need this."

Lex sighed. "I've heard this speech before. My dad broke his leg seven hundred feet from the summit of Mount Rainier. He was like you—he wouldn't go back or let us stop . . ."

She paused as the memories returned, and with them the sadness.

"We reached the top and he opened a bottle of champagne. I had my first drink with my dad at four-teen thousand four hundred feet. . . . On the way down he developed a blood clot in his leg that traveled to his lung. He suffered for four hours before dying twenty minutes from the base camp." Lex swiped the dew from her cheek.

Weyland touched her shoulder. "Do you think that's the last thing your dad remembered? The pain? Or drinking champagne with his daughter fourteen thousand feet in the air?"

CHAPTER 12

". . . Warning to all ships at sea . . . weather advisory has been issued . . . States Navy . . . storm . . . dangerous winds . . . force . . ."

The rest of the radio broadcast was hopelessly garbled. In disgust, the executive officer tore off his communicator and tossed it aside. Then he crossed the bridge to check the radar screen. In shades of phosphorescent green, the monitor displayed an ominous mass of rapidly moving storm clouds.

An unexpected blast of frigid wind swirled through the bridge. Captain Leighton appeared, snow clinging to his eyelashes, his shoulders. The skipper's craggy face was bleak as he approached his executive officer.

"It's a huge storm front, Captain," the XO began. "Force twenty katabatic, coming straight off those damn mountains."

Already the wind battered at the windows, and snow came down in a curtain of white.

"How long do we have, Gordon?"

"It's going to hit us in just over an hour. And it's going to be a bitch."

"How's our communications?"

"With the outside world . . . spotty," Gordon replied. "But I can reach the ice pack without too much trouble."

Leighton frowned, then nodded. "Get me Weyland's team. We have to warn them."

Bouvetoya Whaling Station

Quinn popped the door and stuck his head out of the idling Hagglunds.

"Listen up, people. We've got a storm incoming. A big one. If you want to keep it, then you tie it down."

"Christ, boss! You're kidding."

"What's the matter, Reichel?"

"It's the Beakers," he replied. "We've got a bunch of them down in that hole. What if the tripod's blown down?"

Quinn chewed his cigar. "Hell. Then I guess the goddamn Beakers are on their own."

"But Weyland's down there, too. So is that limey Stafford. Connors went with them."

Quinn cursed. "Then you better make good and sure nothing happens to that rig. Get a team together and secure the tripod, pronto. Put an apple tent up around the mouth of the tunnel if you have to, that should hold the tripod in place. And hustle, damn it. . . . If we lose Weyland, we won't get paid!"

* * *

Rappelling down the icy walls of the shaft, Lex was forced to perform double duty. She supervised the descent, which meant swing-running from her safety line to make sure no ropes got snarled, and making sure every one of the two dozen people making the descent was keeping pace.

Still concerned with Weyland's physical condition, Lex also checked on him intermittently. From long experience, she knew that no descent was easy—and this one was being made in virtual darkness, in temperatures colder than the inside of a deep freeze. She wasn't sure Weyland was up to the task, but so far he'd managed to keep pace with the rest of the group.

Using her feet, Lex raced along the sides of the ice tunnel until she reached Weyland's side. She dangled for a moment, steadying herself. Then she leaned close to the billionaire's ear. "How's it going?"

He grinned at her, his face pale in the harsh light of her helmet lamp. Max Stafford deftly rappelled himself to Weyland's side, along with two burly men with shaved heads and Weyland Industries logos on their ice-blue Polartec outerwear. In Stafford's hand, an ICOM IC-4 UHF transceiver crackled.

"It's Quinn. Says there's a storm headed our way."

Weyland turned to Lex. "Will it affect us?"

"We're seven hundred feet under the ice, Mr. Weyland. Quinn could be setting off an atom bomb up there and we'd never notice."

She slapped Weyland on the back, then descended farther down the shaft to check on Miller's progress.

"Tough descent?" she asked.

"A cinch for us heroic types."

"Just keep away from the walls," she told Miller. "Try to stay in the middle of the shaft. You're on a winch—let the machine do the work."

The engineer gave Lex a thumbs-up.

Lex unfastened herself from the winch and attached her harness to one of the safety lines. Then she rappelled down about thirty feet ahead of the expedition, her helmet lamp lighting the way. When the gloom became too intense, she drew her piton gun from its sheath and drove a spike into the ice wall. Then she hung a small battery-powered light there, to help guide the others.

All went uneventfully until they reached a depth of seven hundred feet. Then, as Weyland glanced at his tablet PC, he felt the rope that was lowering him jerk tight. The jolt was so powerful that he was slammed against the ice wall. The wind knocked out of him, Weyland tried to push himself away from the wall when a second jerk of the rope snapped his safety harness and sent him plunging down the shaft.

Max Stafford reached for his boss and missed, tangling himself in his own safety line. Below him, Sebastian saw Weyland dropping toward him. He reached out to catch the man, but his sudden movement—and Weyland's PC bouncing off his shoulder—sent him spinning helplessly on the end of his rope.

"Man down . . . Lex, watch out!" yelled Sebastian.

Lex looked up in time to see Weyland plunging down the opposite side of the tunnel. She kicked off the ice and swung across the void, reaching the other side of the shaft just in time to pin Weyland to the wall with her own body. Before he slipped from her grasp, Lex plunged her axe into the ice and pressed closer. They were locked in an embrace, face-to-face against the cold wall.

"You okay?"

Weyland, trying to catch his breath, nodded weakly.

"Thank you," said Lex.

Weyland blinked in surprise. "You saved *my* life . . . remember?"

"Not for this. For what you said . . . about my father."

The scene was interrupted when the beam from Stafford's helmet lamp sought them out. Max rappelled down to their level and found Lex still hugging the wall like a spider, Weyland shielded in her grip.

The industrialist's complexion looked wan in the harsh light. Weyland gasped, and his wide mouth gaped like a fish. Lex could feel his pulse racing through two sets of winter gear.

"Having second thoughts? It's not too late to go back up."

Weyland shook his head and even managed a smile. "With you taking such good care of me, Ms. Woods? I wouldn't dream of it."

Meanwhile, Max Stafford keyed the ICOM transceiver and shouted into it, "What the hell is going on up there, Quinn?"

Topside, shreds of an insulated apple tent—so named because they are round and bright red to be visible on the snow—had become entangled in the winch. Quinn shoved one of the roughnecks aside and examined the pulley mechanism himself. Then he raised the transceiver to his lips.

"It's the storm, sir," he said, loud enough to be heard over the wind. "A jam in the winch caused by debris."

Quinn waited for a response. It didn't take long.

"Well, see that it doesn't happen again," Stafford said in a clipped, angry tone.

Quinn lowered his eyes and stared at his boots. He spit, then put the transceiver to his ear.

"It won't," he promised. Then he broke the connection, muttering, "English asshole . . ."

Aboard the *Piper Maru*

On the catwalk outside, Captain Leighton scanned the horizon through a pair of heavy-duty Weyland Industries ALM-35 GPS-enhanced night-vision goggles. A savage wind was already battering the icebreaker, and in the distance, the captain could clearly see curtains of snow—tinted green by the NVGs—roaring off Olav Peak toward the whaling station.

Much of Bouvetoya Island was already obscured by the weather, but the Weyland-35 had a built-in geopositioning system that computed distances. A pipper on the heads-up display highlighted the approximate location of the settlement, which appeared to the naked eye as if it was already buried under an avalanche of snow.

"This is going to be bad."

The hatch swung open, and Gordon poked his head out. "Captain Leighton? I think you'd better take a look at this."

Leighton crossed the catwalk and entered the bridge. His executive officer was crouched over the radar screen, waiting for him.

"What is it? The storm?"

"No, sir, something else." The XO had a troubled look on his face.

"Spit it out, son," Leighton demanded. The executive officer tapped the radar screen, just as the blip appeared again.

"I just picked this up," he said. "It's three hundred miles out and bearing one three zero. Whatever it is, it's traveling at Mach 7."

"What?"

"Accelerating to Mach 10, Captain."

Leighton pushed Gordon aside and gazed at the radar screen. "This is impossible. Nothing travels that fast—nothing! It must be a meteorite."

"I don't think so." Then Gordon blinked. "I-I think it just changed course. . . . Yes, it has definitely changed course."

"Give me the new bearing," Leighton commanded.

Gordon sat down at the radar console and punched in data on the keypad. It seemed to take forever for the navigational computer to spit out an answer. When it did, Gordon looked up at Captain Leighton, anxiety clouding his face.

"The object is less than thirty miles away and closing," he said. "And it's headed straight for us."

Captain Leighton bolted for the hatch, his XO on his

heels. Outside, the captain squinted into the twilight sky, trying to pierce the falling snow. Crewmen on deck sensed something was up and followed the skipper's gaze.

"I don't see anything," Leighton shouted over the wind.

"It should be right on top of us—"

"Look!" one of the sailors cried, pointing.

There *was* something in the sky approaching the *Piper Maru*. The phenomenon appeared as a high-speed blur, cutting through the low-hanging clouds and leaving a transparent rippling wake in its path. As the crew watched, awestruck, the optical distortion seemed to increase in speed.

Captain Leighton gripped the rail with both hands. "Hang on!" he cried a split second before the unidentified flying object reached their position.

The crew heard a strange, electronic shriek as the thing approached. When it roared over their heads, the object was accompanied by a powerful sonic boom that shattered windows and shook ice and snow loose from the superstructure. Swept up in the powerful wake, the *Piper Maru* lurched to one side, then bounced back. Collision alarms sounded throughout the ship, and several crew members lost their footing and tumbled over the side.

In the chaos that followed, cries of shock and pain and calls of "Man overboard" echoed across the deck.

"What the hell was that?" shouted a crewman.

Gordon did not reply. Instead, he carefully scanned the sky, trying to pick up any sign of the near-invisible intruder. Finally his sharp eyes spied a swath cut through the low-hanging storm clouds.

"It's headed for the station," he called.

Leighton struggled to his feet and stared into the distance.

"Get Quinn on the horn."

Katabatic winds rolled down the mountain and hit the whaling station with lethal impact. Quinn struggled against the punishing blows of the brutal gusts and the stinging pins of driving snow, barking orders at his men until he was hoarse.

A blast struck a Hagglunds with such tremendous power that it nearly toppled the heavy vehicle onto its side.

Quinn slapped a man's head. "I told you to get that vehicle tied down!"

He threw rope into the roughneck's hands and sent him scurrying. Reichel appeared at Quinn's side and thrust a transceiver into his face.

"Radio for you, sir! I think it's the *Maru*—"

"You think?"

"It's coming through pretty garbled."

Quinn gave his partner a "What now?" look and seized the transceiver.

"This is Quinn," he shouted, pressing the communicator to his ear. He heard a voice and it sounded urgent, but the message was broken and unintelligible.

"Repeat!" Quinn cried. "I can't hear you . . . I can't . . . ah, the hell with it!" Quinn thrust the radio back at Reichel. "Get this kit inside."

"Should I try and raise the *Maru* again?"

"Don't waste your time. Just get everybody under cover. We'll hunker down and wait this monster out. Should die down in about a week."

Quinn scanned the snow-blasted area. His men had secured the vehicles and the equipment. The mobile drilling platforms were secure, too, and the tripod over the mouth of the tunnel had a tent thrown over it and was lashed tight.

The expedition's bright red tents were mostly in tatters, so Quinn directed his men to the only shelter available—the stout wooden structures that had protected generations of whalers a century ago.

"To the buildings. Everybody inside!" he bellowed, clapping his gloved hands. "Come on, people! Move it, move it . . ."

The crew scurried to find shelter in the century-old buildings while Quinn took one last look at the mouth of the pit. For a moment, he wondered how Weyland and Stafford were doing down there.

Then, as Quinn turned his back on the storm to follow his roughnecks into the mess hall, an impossibly large object passed overhead, silently cutting a swath through clouds and pelting snow. . . .

CHAPTER 13

Over Bouvetoya Island

Impervious to the winds that battered it, the near-invisible spacecraft hovered several hundred feet above the whaling station. Saint Elmo's fire danced along the hull as the cloaking device disengaged.

With a series of dull thumps, five gleaming metal missiles fired from the belly of the Predator craft. Like gigantic bullets, they slammed into the ground, each punching a deep crater into the solid pack ice. A field of energy rippled, then as quickly as the vessel had appeared, it transformed into an optical blur again. Its task complete, the starship silently wheeled into the sky and sped away.

At the bottom of one of the newly formed craters, one of the shimmering steel projectiles began to hum. Although the katabatic winds raged around the missile, it was still possible to hear the loud hiss of escaping gases.

A hairline crack appeared on the smooth surface of the missile where there had been no joint before. More smoky phosphorescent green gas vented into Earth's atmosphere as the crack widened.

Finally, the projectile opened. Inside, something stirred—something alive.

Suddenly, the air was pierced by the savage howl of a predatory beast. Its cry drowned out even the clamor of the wind and the rush of the driving snow. . . .

CHAPTER 14

Two Thousand Feet Below Bouvetoya Island

In contrast to the hurricane force winds on the surface, all was silent as the explorers reached the bottom of the shaft. All sounds—voices, even footsteps—seemed muffled, subdued by their echo rather than amplified. Lex had always found this to be a curious phenomenon, unique to the Earth's deepest caverns.

Weyland sat on his backpack, his head hung low, resting.

Meanwhile Connors and a big fellow called Dane—with the help of several Weyland technicians in their ubiquitous ice-blue parkas—unpacked banks of portable halogen lamps and began setting them up.

Stepping away from the others, Lex crouched low and ran her hand along the floor. Like the walls and ceiling, it was made of ice. Ancient ice, glacial in origin—probably frozen a million years ago. Which meant they were inside an ice cave and not under the Earth's crust.

Two thousand feet down and we haven't even touched solid ground yet.

Lex rose and drew a flare from her belt. A moment later a cool, flickering blue glow illuminated a scene of ethereal beauty. They were not in a cave, but in a grotto. The vast chamber was lined with stalactites and stalagmites, like crystal fangs in a sparkling glass jaw. In this light, everything shimmered and pulsed. The ancient ice was translucent, and like the heart of a diamond it seemed to radiate with an inner brilliance.

Sebastian gasped. "It's . . . beautiful."

"Quite the way you have with words," Lex said, approaching him.

Ahead, the grotto opened into a much larger space roofed by a vast ceiling vaulting into the darkness.

"No telling how large this cavern is," Sebastian said.

Lex touched his arm. "By the way, thanks for the heads-up back there."

Sebastian grinned. "Well, seeing as Antarctica is the most hostile environment on God's Earth, I just figured we should be looking out for each other."

Lex laughed. "Nice to know someone was paying attention to my lecture."

Maxwell Stafford stared apprehensively into the darkness beyond the grotto. "Let's get those lights up."

"Any second now, boss," Connors replied.

"How do those cables look?"

Dane grinned. "Nobody's talking to us from up there, but the generator's still humming." He touched the wires together, and a spark leaped between them. "These cables are hot."

"Good," said Max. "Let's start hooking them up."

Charles Weyland rose and crossed the grotto. The descent had taken its toll on the man's weakened constitution—his shoulders slumped, and he seemed more haggard and drawn than Max had ever seen him, even during the worst of the chemotherapy.

"I don't understand," Weyland said, breathless. "No equipment. No sign of another team—"

"Well, this tunnel didn't dig itself."

"We have power!" cried Connors.

Max nodded. "Let's light her up."

All at once, multiple banks of halogen floodlights blinked to life. For a few seconds the sudden brilliance and the twinkling reflections off the ice blinded them all. Squinting against the glare, it was Lex who slowly lowered the hand shielding her eyes.

"Oh my God."

Sebastian, who had turned his back on the intense light, spun around at Lex's gasp—and was instantly transfixed.

"It's awesome," Miller cried. *"Awesome . . ."*

A massive pyramid towered over them, its top brushing the roof of the cavern. The structure had smooth sides and a narrow stairway comprised of hundreds of steps running up one side. It was obvious to Sebastian that this structure was the largest pyramid ever discovered, dwarfing the Great Pyramid of Giza by half.

Sebastian lurched forward, eyes devouring every inch. The pyramid's surface seemed intact and unblemished, though the icicles that hung from the stone blocks partially obscured the details beneath. The smoothly carved steps—each one shimmering with ice—led to a flattened pinnacle at the top. Along those

stairs pictographs were visible, even from this distance—and Sebastian immediately deduced that the
characters were neither Egyptian nor pre-Colombian
yet seemed vaguely reminiscent of both.

"This is . . ." Thomas's voice died.

"Impossible?"

"*Amazing,* Sebastian," Thomas said softly. "Simply
amazing."

Lex rested a hand on Weyland's shoulder. "Congrat-
ulations. Looks like you'll be leaving your mark after
all."

Weyland nodded, and despite his suffering, he managed to offer Lex a broad smile.

"Look! Farther in the ice," Sebastian called. "A
whole temple complex! Connected with a ceremonial
road. The overall design looks like an amalgam of
Aztec, Egyptian and Cambodian . . . but those hieroglyphics . . . I think they reflect *all* three languages."

Thomas lifted his eyebrow. "Is that possible?"

"If it's here." Then Sebastian pointed. "It looks like
an entrance down there, at the base of the pyramid."

Weyland stepped forward to face the explorers.
"Thank you all for this," he said in a voice that sounded
surprisingly vigorous. "Let's make history."

While Max gave orders for Connors and Dane to secure the base camp, the others gathered equipment—
flashlights, lanterns and flares, mostly, but also
cameras, chronometers and compasses, Miller's chemical and spectrum analysis kits, extra oxygen tanks for
Weyland, a first-aid kit, plenty of canteens and even a
few provisions.

After departing the grotto, the group crossed the

broad, broken ice plain stretching right up to the base of the pyramid. Along the way, their footsteps echoed hollowly, a dull and insignificant sound, swallowed up by the enormity of the ice cavern.

On the trek it became clear to Lex that Weyland was getting weaker. Max carried extra oxygen tanks, which Weyland hit on intermittently. Most of the time, the industrialist relied on his ice pole to walk, but as they crossed especially treacherous patches, he was compelled to lean on Stafford for support.

A short, ceremonial stairway—with thirteen steps, Sebastian noted—led to the pyramid's yawning entrance. The door was somewhat narrow but very high. Through it, the pyramid opened into a long hallway lined with many more hieroglyphics than were etched on the exterior of the structure.

Thomas and Sebastian traced the ancient writing with their flashlights and pointed out various characters, pictographs, or cartouches, speculating on possible translations.

"I recognize the Egyptian, but not the other two," said Thomas, pointing to three sets of inscriptions carved into the floor in front of the door.

"The second line is Aztec, pre-conquest era," Sebastian explained. "Third is Cambodian. Looks like a mixture of Bantu and Sanskrit."

Sebastian looked up to find Lex watching him. "Impressed?"

A smile tugged at the corners of her full lips. "Maybe."

"Then you were right," Weyland said. "The pyramid does contain all three cultures."

"That's what it looks like," Sebastian said. "This goes against every history book that's ever been written."

Thomas got down on one knee and traced his fingers along the carved pictographs.

" 'You may . . . choose . . . to enter'?" He paused in his translation and rubbed his neck. "Or maybe it's 'Those who choose may enter . . . ' "

"It's like an ancient welcome mat," said Miller.

Sebastian stepped forward and gazed at the inscription. "Who is the incompetent who taught you to translate?"

Thomas grinned. "Funny, he looks just like *you*."

"It's not 'choose,' partner . . . it's 'chosen,' " Sebastian declared. " 'Only the chosen ones may enter.' "

While they theorized, Verheiden pushed Thomas aside and moved forward, into the pyramid. The first step he took through the door landed his booted foot on an ornate stone tile, activating a hidden trigger. No one noticed as the team moved across the threshold into the entranceway.

CHAPTER 15

Inside the darkest heart of the great pyramid, where none of the Weyland explorers had yet ventured, infernal machines awoke with a throaty rumble. Within a vast stone chamber dominated by a central pool of swirling, ice-cold vapor, clanging reverberations erupted from deep beneath the surface mist.

Barbed, razor-sharp chains dangled down from narrow slits in the high vaulted ceiling and extended deep into the pool's billowing, spectral haze. The chains stirred and clanked, then were suddenly pulled taut as invisible pulleys hauled a massive object out of the simmering pool.

First to emerge was a long, curved bone crest patterned with wavy, rippling contours resembling coral. The bony crest was etched with fine cracks, like ancient ivory. Its hard, horned borders were pierced by spiked hooks welded to the chains. An eyeless, elongated head jutted out from just beneath the crest.

With each rotation of the invisible pulleys, more of the creature was revealed. The elaborately shaped head rested on a long, segmented neck swathed in an osseous shell and corded with machinelike tubes. The creature's knobby backbone was roughly the length of a blue whale, and it was traced by sharp, curved spikes. The torso was protected by a thick protuberance, which tapered down to an impossibly thin, almost skeletal waist and pelvis.

Long black pipes splayed out from both sides of the creature's back, and thin, wiry-tendoned, insectlike arms were fronted by hands that looked eerily human. The overall contours were graceful, feral, and lean. Though impossibly huge—larger, even, than the legendary Tyrannosaurus rex—the imposing creature appeared to possess strength, speed, and agility.

Apparently, it was also quite dangerous. In addition to the cruel-looking restraints piercing its hooded crest, the monster's arm joints and wrists were bound by barbed chain, as were its rib bones, collar bones, and shoulder plates—all in an effort to immobilize the creature.

And there was more.

Visible through the mist was an immense machine with a grotesque, almost organic appearance. Hoses filled with frozen liquid, twisted wires and tubes that resembled chicken gizzards emerged from this machine and penetrated the creature's body in a hundred different places, like some savage, medieval torture device. Many of the thickest tubes clustered around the monster's lower abdomen, where, directly below the tapered pelvis, a bulging, segmented, near translucent tail merged completely with the machine in a bizarre, biotechnological symbiosis.

As more of the creature was raised above the shifting vapor, additional shackles were revealed—restraints were bound to every extremity. As the chains drew tighter, the alien's arms were forcibly outstretched until the elongated head lifted into a strangely regal pose and the creature's bony crest radiated outward like an obscene halo.

With a final clank, the chains locked. Splayed in midair over the pool like a great dragon caught in flight, the Alien Queen floated, motionless. Icicles of frozen drool hung from her toothy jaws, and a sheen of frost covered her black hide, making it difficult to discern where inhuman flesh ended and biomechanical device began.

With a sudden, sharp crack the ice around the creature's muzzle shattered. Spears of ice fell away, then huge chunks followed as the crack widened into a rift, dropping more and more ice into the swirling vapors below.

With a bestial hiss, the Queen's great jaws opened wide to reveal a secondary mouth inside the first. Gnashing its teeth, the Alien's fangs chewed empty air. Almost immediately, the Queen launched into a paroxysm of rage, struggling against the unbreakable chains that held it captive. Limbs were thrashing, teeth were grinding, and chains were clanking as the creature tossed her head from side to side in a futile effort to escape.

The struggles continued for long minutes, sending ice and hot spittle splashing in every direction. But soon the creature surrendered, sagging limply on her own chains. The Alien Queen discovered that despite her immense size and preternatural strength, inside of this chamber she was nothing more than a prisoner and a slave, serving a cruel, as of yet unnamed master.

Inside of the biomechanical contrivance, energies were generated and pumps began to churn. Electrical and chemical impulses were transmitted through the myriad tubes and wires buried deep in the Alien Queen's body, to activate specific portions of the monster's anatomy.

The Queen's lower abdomen began to quiver. Red ooze churned and bubbled beneath the surface of the tail's clear skin. The armored flesh above the pelvis convulsed, and gouts of clotted bile gushed onto a long metal slide that connected the mechanism to a long conveyor belt.

The first birth was painful.

The Queen thrashed, rattling her chains. Then, with tremendous effort, she lifted her head, strained against the hooks that grasped her crown, and emitted a high-pitched screech as she opened the fleshy flap on the underside of her tail and released a leathery sack. Coated with ooze, the egg literally slid down the incline, coming to a rest in a shallow stone cavity.

The block of stone carrying the egg slid along a recessed track cut into a ledge that ran along the wall until it reached another machine. Here robotic arms looking more like an abstract sculpture than functioning machinery emerged from a crevice in the wall.

A powerful laser light bathed the egg to reveal its contents—a motionless malformation. With a metallic hum, the machine rejected the egg, and it continued its journey along the ledge until it approached a stone door that slid open with a grating sound.

Beyond that door a furnace roared, its burning light filling the chamber with a hellish, unnatural glow. The stone carried the egg to the threshold of the furnace, then dumped it in.

When the Alien Queen saw her egg being destroyed, she again exploded into action—straining against the chains in an effort to rescue her doomed progeny. Minutes later, another egg rolled down the conveyor, to be rejected and immolated too, as was a third egg.

But when the fourth egg was scanned, the form floating inside reacted by thrashing its whiplike tail about. Another pair of robotic arms emerged from a trapdoor in the wall, seized the fertile egg and carried it off.

The Alien Queen strained once more against the chains and let out her anger and frustration by howling loud enough for her cries to reverberate throughout the massive pyramid.

CHAPTER 16

Lex paused in the pyramid's entranceway, listening. She could swear she'd heard something—a disturbing howl like the shriek of a wild beast. She looked around at her companions, but no one else seemed to have noticed.

After a moment, Lex shrugged, deciding it was her imagination.

"It's perfectly preserved," Thomas marveled. "These carvings are as pristine as they were the day they were etched into the stone."

"I've never seen anything like it," Sebastian murmured. "The hieroglyphics look to be some kind of hybrid language containing both Aztec and Egyptian characteristics. Perhaps an Ur-language—a lost and forgotten tongue that was the mother to all human languages."

Miller had his spectral analysis kit out and was already working. He blinked at the digital readout that appeared on his tablet PC.

"This reading says these stones are at least ten thousand years old."

Sebastian shook his head. "That's impossible. Check it again."

"I already did."

"Amazing," said Weyland.

"If you like that, you're going to love *this*," Lex called, waving her flashlight to get their attention. She was standing on the threshold of a pitch-black corridor that led even deeper into the massive pyramid.

Weyland hobbled forward, his pole clicking on the tiled floor. Sebastian and Thomas raced up to Lex, their expressions eager. But before they could enter the tunnel, she waved them back. The rest watched as Lex placed a small strobe light on the floor behind her and another on top of a carved stone shelf.

"They'll burn for six hours. We'll be able to find our way back."

Then she led them forward, into a short passage ornamented with carved stone lintels and lined with elaborate pictographs. At the end of the passage, there was another door—more impressive than even the entranceway. The doorjambs were engraved with thousands of hieroglyphic characters and framed by stout bas-relief columns.

"This is obviously the central ritual chamber," Sebastian whispered, his tone reverential. "The reason this structure was built."

Probing the darkness, their flashlights illuminated a mammoth circular stone chamber with a high ceiling that arched into the shadows. The walls were covered with terra-cotta columns etched with the same hieroglyphics, the floor dominated by seven raised stone

slabs, each the size of a large man and each occupied
by a mummified corpse. The slabs were arranged head
to head in a circular shape like the petals of a flower. In
the center of the circle was a carved stone grille. Beneath that grille, all was dark.

Weyland touched a cold stone slab. "These are . . . ?"

"Sacrificial slabs," said Sebastian.

"Just like the Aztecs and the ancient Egyptians.
Whoever built this pyramid believed in ritual sacrifice," Thomas explained.

Lex directed her flashlight beam toward the far wall,
at a mound of human skulls six feet high. "You can say
that again."

"My God," Max Stafford whispered softly.

Miller leaned over a cadaver. "It's almost perfectly
preserved."

Like the others, this corpse had been freeze-dried by
the harsh environment. Flesh and tendons still clung to
the bones. The dead man wore a ritual headpiece and a
jeweled necklace, its stones and precious metal gleaming dully under the dust of millennia. Though there
were no injuries beyond a hole below the rib cage, the
face on each mummy was contorted, jaws gaping as if
frozen in agony.

"This is where they offered the chosen ones to the
gods," said Thomas.

Miller gingerly touched the remains. The flesh was
leathery, the bones calcified to roughly the texture of
stone.

Meanwhile, Sebastian played his flashlight across
one of the slabs. Darkened spots stained the surface—

mute testament to the ritual slaughter this chamber had witnessed.

"Those that were chosen would lie here," he told the others. "They weren't bound or tied in any way. They went to their deaths willingly . . . men and women. It was considered an honor."

"Lucky them," said Lex. She ran her fingers around a circular, bowl-like indentation at the base of the slab. "What's this bowl for?"

Sebastian shrugged. "Opinions vary. Some archaeologists think it's where the heart was placed after it was torn from the body . . . the living body."

Weyland shone his flashlight through the stone grate in the center of the floor. "Look at this!"

Max struck a flare and dropped it through the grate. Crouching over the hole, he watched while it fell. Everyone heard it strike something.

"How far down does it go?" Weyland asked.

"Can't really see," said Stafford. He was on his knees, face pressed against the grate. "Maybe a hundred feet. Looks like another room."

Weyland upped the intensity of his flashlight and played it along the walls. The beam illuminated more stacks of human bones. Many of the skeletons were still intact.

Weyland caught his breath. "There must be hundreds of them."

"At least," Max replied.

As Weyland moved away from the main group, Adele Rousseau remained at his side, one hand on the pistol in her belt. Like the others, she gazed in horrified fascination at the mountain of bleached bones.

Rousseau examined the rib cage on one of the intact skeletons. Like the mummies on the slab, there was a hole punched through the ribs.

"What happened here?" she asked, tucking a finger into the cavity.

Thomas moved to her side. "It was common in ritual sacrifice to take the heart of the victim."

But the woman shook her head. "That's not where your heart is. Besides, it looks like the bones were bent straight out. Something broke *out* of this body."

Thomas found something in the stack of human remains. He stood up and displayed his grisly discovery.

"Incredible," said Miller. "The entire skull and spinal column removed in one piece."

With Miller's help, Thomas turned the skeleton in his hand so they all could see the severed rib bones.

"The cleanness of the cut . . . remarkable," Miller said, scratching his head through his wool cap. "Straight through the bone. No abrasions. You'd be hard-pressed to do this with modern knives, maybe even lasers—"

Miller's speculations were interrupted by a long, echoing howl, like an animal in torment. The sound continued for another moment before fading.

"Did you hear that?" asked Lex, sure now that what she'd heard earlier had not been her imagination.

"Air?" said Miller. "Moving through the tunnels."

"I don't know," Sebastian said, looking around. "Maybe . . ."

Searching for the origin of the sound, Sebastian spied a low corridor hidden between two ornate wall columns. Shining his light into the gloom, he still couldn't make out any details beyond the entrance. Stepping around a skeleton, he cautiously edged his way toward what he thought was the source of the sound.

"Do you see anything?" Miller whispered.

Sebastian *did* see something—or so he thought. He was forced to crouch low because the ceiling at the rear of the antechamber sloped downward dramatically. Futilely, he tried to shine the flashlight rays into the darkest reaches of the tiny, claustrophobic chamber.

Suddenly something dropped on Sebastian's back. He stumbled backwards and fell on his spine. With a dry clatter, the thing—heavy and pale white, with multiple crablike legs—landed on the tiles next to his head. He felt a cold, clammy tail lash against his face.

With a yell, Sebastian rolled away from the object just as Lex caught it in her flashlight.

"What is that thing!" Sebastian cried, his calm demeanor shattered.

The creature was approximately the size of a bowling ball and looked like a crab without front claws, though it did have a long, snakelike tail. It was milky white and nearly two feet long stretched out on its back. Miller stooped low, prodding the creature with his flashlight.

"Be careful," Stafford warned.

"Whatever it is, it's been dead a while," said Miller. "The bones have calcified."

Lex looked at Sebastian, still not quite recovered from his scare. "You must have dislodged it from a crack in the ceiling."

"No idea how long it's been there, but the temperature has kept it preserved," said Sebastian. "Looks like a kind of scorpion."

"No. This climate's too hostile for a scorpion," said Lex.

"Ever seen anything like it?"

Lex shook her head.

"Maybe it's a species that's never been discovered."

"Maybe," Lex replied, but her tone was doubtful.

From the belly of the creature dangled a hard, petrified tentacle that looked to Lex, more than anything else, like a shriveled umbilical cord.

CHAPTER 17

Bouvetoya Whaling Station

Quinn was making his rounds, checking on the comfort and safety of his crew. His men were scattered throughout a rambling, drafty structure that had housed whalers a century before. A few of the roughnecks were clustered around a blaze sputtering in the stone hearth, and as Quinn went by, he tossed more splintered pieces of antiquated furniture into the fire.

Outside, the storm still raged off the mountain, bringing with it an impenetrable curtain of snow. So violent were the katabatic winds that gusts of frigid air penetrated through the joints of the century-and-a-half-year-old structure, and mounds of drifting snow accumulated around doors and under windows.

There was little for the roughnecks to do other than keep warm and ignore the continual howl of the wind's angry blasts. Since they hadn't had much sleep in the past twenty hours, most chose to bundle up tight in their sleeping bags and try to catch some shut-eye.

Which was why Quinn was surprised to come upon five of Weyland's "security detail" busily unpacking long wooden crates and suiting up for battle. Quinn noted that the big one, called Sven, had a tattoo on his bicep—the eagle and fouled anchor emblem of the Navy SEALs.

"What the hell is going on here?" Quinn demanded.

"Just doing our job," said Sven. "I suggest you stick to yours, Quinn."

Next to him, the bull-necked man named Klaus locked eyes with Quinn as he tested the bolt action on a Heckler & Koch MP-5 machine gun. On his hip Klaus wore a Desert Eagle pistol in a Velcro holster, and he had a survival knife strapped to his boot.

Two others were swapping weapons and ammunition as they drew them out of the packing crates. They spoke Russian to one another and ignored the newcomer.

Quinn stepped forward. "Nobody told me we were going to war."

One of the Russians—tagged Boris—looked up and said something to his friend, Mikkel. Both chuckled. Then Boris slapped a magazine into his machine gun and looked up at Quinn. He wore a cruel half-smile that didn't reach much beyond his thin lips. His eyes were watery blue and as cold as the ice outside.

"Perhaps you should've asked, comrade," said Boris, with no trace of a Russian accent.

Quinn took in the machine guns, the pistols, the Kevlar vests.

"You fellows ought to know that it's against The Antarctic Treaty of 1961 for any nation to bring this kind of military shit up here. Nobody cares about a few handguns—even rifles—but this heat you're packing is a violation of international law."

"Well, Weyland Industries is no nation," said Sven as he strapped his tight, well-muscled physique into a bulletproof vest. "And I don't remember signing any treaty."

Inside the Pyramid

Before they moved deeper into the pyramid, Lex faced her party.

"The ambient temperature in here is a lot warmer than ground level," she said. "You can take off your jackets."

Happy to shed their bulky gear, Sebastian and his partner Thomas, along with Miller, Weyland, Max Stafford, Connors, and Adele Rousseau, dumped their stuff in a huge pile.

Lex shed her coat until she was clad only in a bright red, cold-weather pantsuit. Donning her backpack, Lex activated a strobe light and dropped it on the stone floor nearby. Its constant flashing would act as a beacon to lead them back to their gear.

She looked up to find Sebastian watching her.

"Why don't you leave crumbs of bread for us to follow, like in the fairy tale," he teased.

Lex smiled. "The birds would eat them and we'd be lost forever."

"I don't think you'll find many birds down here, and I doubt bats are fond of bread."

As the others repacked and rearranged their belongings, Lex moved a few feet into the next corridor, Sebastian at her side.

"Leaving the bones behind?"

"Thomas will take care of that end of things," Sebastian replied. "He's the type of archaeologist who's half coroner. Anyway, Weyland ordered him to remain in the sacrificial chamber and catalog everything."

"Weyland's good at giving orders."

"Thomas won't mind. That blond Amazon, Adele, is staying behind with him. They could get acquainted."

"And in such a romantic place."

They walked along in silence for a moment, their flashlights stabbing the darkness in front of them.

"What about you?" Lex asked. "What kind of archaeologist are you, Dr. De Rosa?"

Sebastian fingered the Pepsi cap hanging from his neck. "I love old things. There's a special kind of beauty to an object made a long time ago—something timeless, immortal."

"Speaking of beautiful . . . look at the way they catch the light." Lex gestured to the ceiling of the wide hallway, where the stone was encrusted with a forest of shimmering, blue-tinged stalactites.

As she moved the flashlight beam across the frozen surface, the icicles seemed to change color, from cool blue to azure to purple. Weyland hobbled down the corridor and stood at Lex's side, leaning on his ice pole and looking up.

"Must be some kind of mineral impurities in the water," Sebastian deduced.

"That's what I thought at first," said Miller. "But it's not."

"Not an impurity?"

"Not *water*."

Sebastian was surprised. Miller held up his spectrometer. "I ran a quick test on another patch of this stuff, back there."

He consulted the liquid plasma screen. "We've got your tricresyl phosphate, zinc alkyl, dithiophosphate, diethylene gluycol, polypropylene ether . . . and some trace elements."

"Which makes it what exactly?" Lex asked.

It was Sebastian who answered. "Hydraulic fluid," he said. "Or near enough."

Everyone stared at the archaeologist, surprised.

"I own a '57 Chevy. It's my hobby." He shrugged and gave Lex a little smile. "Like I said, pretty much anything old."

Weyland turned to Miller. "So what do you make of it?"

"I don't know. But I can't imagine that the ancients used hydraulic fluid."

"Coincidence?"

Miller opened his mouth to reply, but Sebastian spoke first. "I doubt it, Mr. Weyland. If five thousand years of human history have taught us anything, it's that coincidence is for the birds."

Bouvetoya Whaling Station

Once his men were settled, Quinn took a break and slept for three hours. When the alarm in his watch went off—too soon—Quinn climbed out of his sleeping bag and went outside to check the pit.

He was relieved to find that the rigid, cherry-red "apple" tent over the hole was still intact, and the pul-

ley seemed in working order, with no trace of ice on
the gears. Quinn checked the readout on the depth me-
ter. The pulley had spooled out over 2,011 feet worth
of steel cable, which meant that the underground team
had reached the bottom of the tunnel hours ago, some
time after the storm had begun.

He sat down, yanked off his gloves and cranked the
radiophone, which was hardwired to the team underground. But they didn't bother to answer.

Quinn wasn't surprised. Charles Weyland had become obsessed with security since they'd discovered
the hole in the ice. He'd ordered a complete communications blackout with the outside world, not that they
were hearing much with this storm, anyway. Then that
ex-Navy SEAL and his four buddies from who-knows-
where had dropped their disguise as "security" and
started throwing guns around like a special forces pla-
toon arming for a mission.

He concluded that this whole job was beginning to
stink worse than roadkill on a hot Texas highway.

After determining that everything inside the apple
tent was secure, Quinn stepped outside. The wind hit
him like a baseball bat, with snow pelting his parka so
hard that the individual flakes stung like shrapnel. He
tied his hood and pulled his hat down to cover his face.
Quinn estimated the katabatic gusts in excess of sev-
enty miles per hour, which was very, very bad.

As he walked through town, Quinn could barely
make out the black shape of the mess hall against the
white curtain of snow.

"Hold it right there. Identify yourself," a voice demanded, the cry muffled by the falling snow.

"It's Quinn. Quinn, goddamn it!"

He lowered his hood and stepped forward, to find himself staring down the barrel of the largest handgun in the world. Quinn angrily tore off his hat so the man could recognize him.

Klaus holstered the Desert Eagle.

"What the hell are you doing?" Quinn barked. "I don't like guns shoved in my face."

"Orders," said Klaus with a defiant shrug. He pulled Quinn into the relative shelter of the doorway and leaned close so he could be heard. "Weyland wants this area secured."

"Secured? From *what*?"

"Claim jumpers," the man replied. "The Russians, the Chinese . . . another corporation. There could be anybody out there."

Quinn looked out at the storm. "Trust me. There's nobody out there."

As he turned to leave, Klaus stopped him. "Where are you going?"

"Well, seeing as you boys have got the mess hall covered, I'm going to check on the Hagglunds. Now let me go. I have a job to do."

Klaus released Quinn's arm and stepped back into the shadows. He watched as the roughneck struggled through the snow until it swallowed him up. Then Klaus opened the stout wooden door to the mess hall.

Sven looked up when he felt the cold blast of air enter with Klaus. His eyes narrowed. "You're supposed to be on guard."

"Just wanted some hot tea," Klaus replied.

Sven looked at Boris the Russian sitting in the corner, singing to himself in his native language as he boiled water on a camp stove.

"It ain't ready yet."

Klaus cursed and shut the door behind him as he went back outside.

"When are you going to get that heater started, Mikkel?"

Mikkel looked over his shoulder at the Swede, then punched the stubborn machine. "It's coming, it's coming . . ."

Back outside, Klaus spied another figure moving through the whiteness. He drew the Eagle and aimed.

"Hold it!"

The shape continued to approach, shimmering in the storm.

"Quinn?"

Still, it came closer.

"Identify yourself!"

The figure paused, and Klaus squinted against the snow for a better look. He blinked, and his fingers tensed on the trigger.

There were two shapes now—dark holes in the storm.

"I said, identify yourself!"

A third appeared, next to the others. Together they silently advanced on him.

If they were friendly, then Klaus figured they would have answered him by now. So he leveled the crosshairs, targeting the featureless shape in the middle, and squeezed the trigger. . . .

CHAPTER 18

Bouvetoya Whaling Station

The mercenaries reacted as soon as they heard the shot. Before the echo even faded, an MP-5 replaced the screwdriver in Mikkel's hand. At the samovar, the incessant Russian singing ceased as Boris traded his tin cup for a machine gun.

With the second shot, Sven was on his feet. He threw the iron bolt on the stout wooden door and backed away in case someone shot through it.

"Mikkel," he hissed, shouldering a Heckler & Koch. "Get on the radio. Now."

After an eternity of silence, the door blew open with a deafening crash. Fierce wind and billowing snow saturated the room. Sven aimed his weapon at the doorway, but all he could see was a blur of shimmering white powder.

He turned. "Boris! Secure that door."

The Russians moved to the threshold and peered into the storm. Through the torrential downfall, Sven saw Boris glance his way and shrug. *Nothing.*

Mikkel, meanwhile, was speaking into the ICOM transceiver.

"Base camp to *Piper Maru* . . . We have a situation. Repeat. Base camp to *Piper Maru* . . ."

When he received no reply, the Russian cursed and rekeyed the mike.

Snow and wind continued to surge into the mess hall. Finally, Boris struggled against the storm to push the door closed.

Mikkel felt Sven's grip on his shoulder. "Come on, man . . . I need you to raise the ship."

"I'm trying, but the storm—"

Sven felt Mikkel shudder under his grip—then the man was forcibly ripped from his hand.

He whirled to see the Russian hoisted in the air by an invisible force, the transceiver falling from his limp fingers. Still alive, still aware, Mikkel's face mirrored agony and bewilderment. He knew he was going to die, but he did not understand what was killing him. His eyes locked with Sven's. His mouth gaped, but only to emit a wet gurgle. Then, dead at last, Mikkel hung from a now-visible spear like a piece of meat dangling on the end of a fork.

At the door, Boris reeled as invisible blades lopped off his right arm, then the left. Finally his throat exploded in a red mist before his sundered limbs plopped to the floor. The fist clutching the MP-5 convulsed once, sending a burst into the far wall.

What Sven first saw as a blur was now framed by cordite smoke—the silhouette of an impossibly large, humanoid creature. The ex-Navy SEAL took a step backwards and aimed the MP-5. But before he could pull the trigger, a blow sent him spinning to the floor.

Nose smashed and gushing blood, Sven fumbled for the gun that had been knocked from his hand. Instead he burned his fingers on the pot of boiling water still simmering on the camp stove. With both hands he hurled it, dousing the specter with scalding water.

The aluminum pot bounced harmlessly away, but the water elicited an angry roar as electric charges silhouetted the humanoid shape. Then, in a shower of rapid blue sparks, the Predator's cloaking device shorted out for an instant—long enough for Sven to see his own terrified reflection in the mirrored eyes of the creature's armored face plate.

The shots were loud enough to be heard over the storm. Quinn, returning from inspecting the Hagglunds, threw open the door.

"What's all the damn noise about—"

Quinn's mouth stopped. Bloody bodies and hacked-off limbs greeted him, as did something massive, formless and invisible. Wielding twin blades tinged with human blood, the phantom was in the process of ripping great chunks of flesh from a howling man cowering in the corner. As snow billowed into the mess hall, Quinn dimly perceived a blur of motion. The silhouette was altering its shape again.

Suddenly the razor-edged tip of a spear materialized right in front of Quinn's face. He slammed the door and ducked as the weapon passed through the thick wood and gouged a chunk of muscle from his left arm.

He choked back a cry. Then he turned and ran.

Stumbling through white-out conditions, Quinn heard the mess hall door ripped off its hinges. He traipsed around the corner of the building, pushing through deep drifts. His breath came in hot gasps while splatters of his warm blood left a crimson trail in the snow.

Fearing pursuit, Quinn peered over his shoulder— and blundered into something dangling from the over-hanging roof above. He fell backwards, staring up at what was left of Klaus—identifiable only by the name tag on his Polartec overcoat. The dead man was strung up by his ankles, and where his head used to be there were now only long, red-black icicles flowing from a ragged stump.

Through the white haze, beyond Klaus, Quinn saw more shapes—he didn't need to see their faces to rec-ognize their clothing. It was the rest of his team. Rei-chel, Klapp, Tinker and the others, strung up by their feet, swaying in the wind.

Gagging, Quinn looked away and spied something gleaming in the snow—Klaus's Desert Eagle handgun.

No sooner did Quinn's fingers close on the handle than he sensed something at his back. Instinctively, Quinn flopped over in the snow and squeezed off a shot. The revolver bucked in his hand, and over the rag-ing tempest he heard a satisfying roar of pain and rage. Eerily, Quinn saw the bullet punch a green hole into the invisible shape trudging out of the storm. At his feet, steaming, phosphorescent-green gore stained the ice.

Quinn lurched to his feet and tried to run. He didn't even take two steps before something swatted him back down to the ground. Pitching headlong, Quinn grabbed for something to stop his fall. His fingers closed on a ribbon of tattered red canvas—what remained of the apple tent that had been erected over the pit. Since he'd been here last, something had shredded the tent to pieces.

Hearing the ice crunch behind him, Quinn rolled onto his back and aimed the handgun, which was just as quickly slapped out of his grip by a spectral hand. Quinn tried to crawl away when an invisible foot slammed down on his lower leg, snapping the bone in two with a crack so loud it could be heard over the roar of the wind.

The invisible foot lashed out again, the fresh blow cracking Quinn's ribs and sending him spinning into the pit and down the two-thousand-foot shaft.

The cloaked Predator hopped onto the tripod mounted above the pit and peered into the abyss. With powerful legs braced against the storm, its ghostly outline flickered and changed with the intensity of the wind and pelting snow. The creature could hear Quinn's muffled screams as he bounced off the icy walls, despite the howling storm.

A steady stream of green ooze still bubbled up from the now-visible cavity in the creature's chest. But if the Predator felt pain, it did not show it. Throwing its massive head back and its thick-muscled arms wide, the hunter from the depths of space bellowed out an unearthly battle cry that reverberated throughout the whaling station.

A few moments later, four shimmering wraiths melted out of the snowstorm to join their leader at the mouth of the abyss. As fingers of energy crawled across their formless shapes, the creatures uncloaked.

Ignoring the hole in its armored chest plate—a hole that still oozed gore—the leader activated his wrist computer. With a high-pitched hum, a holographic image appeared among them, glowing faintly, and the Predators huddled close to examine the map of the pyramid complex far below.

In the center of that three-dimensional grid, inside the heart of the large, central pyramid, an electronic pulse throbbed. Grunting with satisfaction, the Predators cloaked again and vanished from sight.

Inside the pit, Quinn opened his eyes, surprised to be alive. His relief ended when he realized he was still plunging down the icy shaft, gaining speed with each passing second.

Desperately, he felt for any kind of purchase. His fingers slid along the ice, then nicked the wires running from the generator to the lights at the bases. Quinn quickly yanked them back, for he was falling too fast to stop himself that way. He would have to find a way to slow his fall a bit more before he grabbed the cable again.

Reaching for his belt, Quinn drew his ice axe and swung it. As the tip bit into the frozen wall, white shards sprayed Quinn's face, blinding him. He still did not slow down.

The *Piper Maru*

Captain Leighton heard a sudden crack above him, like the sound of a tremendous bough breaking off an oak tree. Instinctively tucking in his head, Leighton raised a dented bullhorn.

"Take cover on deck!"

His voice boomed, loud enough to be heard over wind that whistled through the masts. Crewmen scattered as hundreds of pounds of gray-white ice dashed itself to pieces on the steel deck—ice that had accumulated on the ship's superstructure, only to break free when it had become too heavy to stick.

Men dropped behind lifeboats and down stairwells as great chunks of frozen snow bounced across the deck. One piece the size of a football took out the bow light. Another shattered the glass covering a porthole.

"Clear it all away, double-time!" Leighton commanded. "More snow is on the way."

On catwalks along the superstructure, crewmen chipped away at crystal-encased safety rails and knocked down massive icicles from stairways, cranes and cables. Suddenly a frigid blast cut across the deck, catching a seaman and nearly carrying him over the side.

"Mind your safety tether," a deck officer bellowed. Without the benefit of a bullhorn, his cry was snatched away by the tempest.

Swathed in a fur-lined parka, with ice crusting his eyelashes and oil staining his faded white parka, the ship's radar specialist appeared at Captain Leighton's side.

"I've checked the upper decks," he yelled. "The radar antennae are fouled and can't be cleared until the storm is over. My instruments seem to be working, but I wouldn't try to power up the radar anytime soon—the dome is frozen solid and you might damage the dish mechanism."

"So what's the good news?"

The man offered Leighton a half-smile. "The Giants won in extra innings."

Leighton called to his deck officer. "Another fifteen minutes of work, then clear the decks of all personnel. It's too dangerous for the crew to be out here."

With that, Captain Leighton headed for the bridge, where his executive officer and a crewman from the radio hut were waiting for him.

"Sir, communications has just received a message fragment from Quinn's team. I think they're in some kind of trouble."

Leighton's shoulders sagged under the weight of yet more disturbing news. "How's the storm progressing?"

"We're caught in the windfly, and the wind speeds are still picking up," Gordon said as he gazed through the frosted windows. "We're going to have a hard time weathering this storm ourselves, Captain. Whatever's happening on the ice, Weyland and his team are on their own for five or six hours—at least."

CHAPTER 19

Inside the Pyramid

Flashlight beams stabbed the darkness as Sebastian and Lex cautiously entered the new chamber. From the cavernous way their footsteps echoed, they deduced the room was vast.

"We're at the heart of the pyramid," Sebastian declared.

Lex spied a soft glow ahead of them. As she moved closer, she realized it was a flare. Looking up to the ceiling, she saw a stone grate and realized that the chamber they were in was directly beneath the sacrificial chamber.

Passing the sputtering flare, Lex moved forward, Sebastian at her side. Weyland, Max and Miller came next, with Verheiden and Connors bringing up the rear. Weyland played his light along the tiled floor, then up at the high, ornate stone walls and the vaulted ceiling. Sebastian paused to study the inscription on a clay urn as Lex continued to move toward the center of the chamber.

"My God," she cried.

Immediately, everyone trained their flashlights in her direction—to illuminate a large, bullet-shaped crate sitting on a slightly raised platform made of tiled stone. The object was constructed of dully gleaming metal coated by a thin film of glimmering ice. Fifteen feet long, four feet wide, it looked like a coffin. No hinges or joints were readily discernable, but the shape was unmistakable.

"Some kind of sarcophagus," Sebastian speculated. "Egyptian in design. These were built to protect the dead for their journey to the afterworld."

Weyland touched the cold surface. His fingers came away glittering with ice crystals. "Can you open it?" he asked.

Sebastian examined the sarcophagus. On what he first thought was a smooth surface, he noticed shallow etchings on the lid—a series of circular symbols, all virtually identical.

Sebastian looked around, to find a larger version of the same design pattern on the wall.

"Look," he cried. "The symbols on the wall correspond to the face on the lid of the sarcophagus."

"So it's a burial decoration to honor the dead— maybe an inscription," Miller suggested.

But Sebastian shook his head. "It's a combination."

"Like on a safe?" said Connors.

"How are we going to get this open?" Weyland demanded.

"I have an idea," Sebastian replied. He wiped the ice away from the sarcophagus lid. Then, for what seemed like quite a long time, Sebastian compared the pattern on the wall to the one etched into the coffin. As his mind raced, he spoke his thoughts out loud.

"These ancient people would have based the combination on something they could see. It wouldn't be a number. But what could they have seen? The planets?" Sebastian shook his head. "Only nine planets . . . the stars, perhaps. But how would they use stars as a combination? Wouldn't the sky always change—"

"There's only one clear constellation visible this far south that lasts year round," Miller interrupted. "That would be Orion."

"Orion!" Sebastian cried.

Then he reached out his hand and touched one of the circles on the wall. To everyone's surprise it began to glow with a dull white light. Sebastian pressed another circle, then another, until a map of the constellation of Orion glowed faintly on the wall.

Everyone parted to make room for Sebastian as he crossed the chamber to the sarcophagus. Touching the circles etched on the metal lid, they began to glow like their cousins on the wall. Then the lid began to open.

Miller moved in to get a better look. "How is that possible?"

Sebastian grabbed Miller's coat and pulled him aside. He pushed the others away as well. "Stand back. We have no idea what is in there."

From a safe distance, they watched as the lid opened completely and slid to a smooth stop.

Weyland arched an eyebrow. "Well, Professor De Rosa. You're the expert. What do you suggest now?"

From a safe vantage point, Sebastian tried to probe the black interior of the sarcophagus, but there was no way to see without peering over the edge.

"Everybody else, stay back," Sebastian commanded as he cautiously moved forward. At the coffin, he paused. Then, leading with his flashlight, he cautiously peeked inside.

"I . . . I don't believe this."

"What?"

"Take a look for yourself, Mr. Weyland."

The sarcophagus contained three futuristic-looking artifacts, probably weapons.

Sebastian locked eyes with Charles Weyland. "The master culture," he whispered ominously.

In the Grotto

Sprawled on the icy floor, a coating of frost already shrouding his motionless body, Quinn twinkled like a spun jewel in the harsh glare of the halogen lamps. Light stands and wooden crates were scattered about—otherwise the grotto was deserted.

A chilly gust of air spilled out of the mouth of the tunnel. As soon as it passed across his face, Quinn's eyes opened. He tried to move, but his limbs were numb. He was virtually frozen in place. While unconscious, spittle had run from his slack jaws, and blood had flowed from the gash in his shoulder. The liquids had frozen and now he was glued to the icy floor like a bug stuck to the bottom of a roach motel.

Too cold and too weak to shiver, Quinn opened his mouth to moan for help, but the cry died in his throat when he spied an ominously familiar optical distortion rippling near the mouth of the shaft. The monster that had attacked him on the surface had followed him here—and he'd brought a friend. The two of them had probably come to finish the job they'd started.

Quinn trembled as the shimmering wraiths glided toward him. Moving as one, their invisible feet left their mark in the hoarfrost. He squeezed his eyes shut and held his breath. A heavy boot crunched the ice next to his head as Quinn waited for the fatal blow.

To his amazement, it never came. Long moments passed before Quinn opened his eyes again, but when he did it seemed as if the ghostly killers had gone, their tracks forming a trail that led to the ice-encrusted pyramid on the horizon.

Using fingers nearly paralyzed by frostbite, Quinn tore himself loose from the ice floor. Frozen saliva shredded the skin off his cheek, and the scab that covered his shoulder wound was also ripped away.

He didn't care much about the pain he felt—not his broken leg, his shattered ribs, or even the frostbite that had claimed his fingers and toes. Quinn simply could not believe his luck: He was alive, and that was all that mattered.

But as he rolled over onto his back, his eyes went wide. A third Predator stood over him, wrist blades unsheathed. Before the roughneck could even scream, the twin blades scythed down, carving deep into his brain.

In the Sarcophagus Chamber

To Weyland, the found objects looked like guns, but impossibly large ones, making them all the more impressive. The keen eye of the industrialist noted a recoiling barrel configuration swivel-mounted on a rather broad shoulder plate. Two other weapons were in the coffin as well, similar in construction but smaller, and minus the shoulder armor.

Miller leaned close and studied the devices. "Any idea what those are?"

"Nope," said Sebastian. "You?"

Miller shrugged, then shook his head.

Max Stafford scoffed. "Good thing we brought in the experts."

"Hey," Miller cried defensively. "We just found the equivalent of a DVD player in Moses's living room. Why don't you give us a second to figure it out."

Lex noticed Weyland was having difficulty breathing. He signaled Max, who brought him a portable oxygen tank. With shaky hands Weyland held the mask to his face and took great gulps of air.

"Is he okay?"

Lex faced Sebastian. "It's just asthma. He's fine," she said, covering for Weyland.

"Let me see if I can get a base reading off the metal," Miller said, producing his spectral analysis kit and tablet PC. While they waited for the results of Miller's test, a debate raged among them.

"Who made these things, and why?" Weyland wheezed. Max remained at his side, feeding the billionaire oxygen.

"Well, if you ask me, the ergonomics are all wrong for these things to have been designed for us," said Miller. "Whoever made this stuff probably wasn't human."

Weyland pulled the mask away from his face. "Spare us your science fictional explanations, Dr. Miller."

Suddenly Miller's PC beeped and he studied the readout.

"There are two chemicals here. Tilanium and cadmium 240."

"Never heard of them," said Sebastian.

"They're found in meteorites."

"Meteorites?" Sebastian cried.

Miller smiled in triumph. "Whatever these are, they weren't made here."

"When you say 'here,' you mean . . . ?" Weyland's voice trailed away.

"I mean Earth," said Miller.

Weyland moved the oxygen mask away from his mouth to speak, but he started wheezing immediately.

"How you doing?" Lex asked.

Weyland nodded up at her, but Lex could see he was not doing well at all.

"We've been out long enough for today," Lex announced. "We're going to set up base camp tonight at the whaling station on the surface, and we'll get back at it first thing tomorrow."

Max Stafford rose and blocked Lex.

"You can go back to base camp, Ms. Woods." He placed his large hand on Weyland's frail shoulder. "We're going to stay here."

Lex ignored Max and spoke directly to Weyland.

"You wanted to leave without proper prep and we did," she cried. "You wanted to be the first here, we are. You've claimed the find. It's yours. Now we move as a team, and we're done for today."

Weyland looked up at Lex, then at the others. "You heard her," he said. "Let's move."

"What should we do about those weapons, or whatever they are," said Max.

"Take them," Weyland commanded. "We can run further tests on the surface."

Connors stepped up to the sarcophagus and reached inside. His fingers closed on the smallest of the weapons—a flowing, organic-looking metal barrel with a massive handgrip.

"No! Don't touch them," Sebastian cried.

Too late. When Connors lifted the weapon from its cradle, he triggered a mechanism hidden underneath it. There was an audible click, followed by a loud boom that reverberated throughout the chamber, shaking icicles loose from the ceiling.

Then the walls began to move.

"Sebastian!" Miller cried. "This happens in all pyramids, right?"

"No," Sebastian replied nervously.

Like a giant Rubik's Cube, the pyramid began to re-configure itself. In an ear-splitting sequence of groans, thunderous claps and rumbles, gears grating and stone scraping against stone, walls slid aside to transform dead ends into passageways leading to more undiscovered portions of the pyramid. Other halls, meanwhile, were sealed by tons of solid rock or trapdoors that slammed tight.

Sebastian grabbed Lex, yanking her out of the path of a giant stone slab that descended from the roof. Other slabs closed off the passage leading to the sarcophagus chamber, crushing the string of glow sticks Lex had used to mark their path and sealing off their only escape route.

The movement in the ancient structure after so many millennia shook icicles, terra-cotta fixtures, and even stone blocks loose. Objects dropped all around them, bursting apart like mortar shells.

In the sacrificial chamber, Thomas and Adele Rousseau, along with several assistants, were instantly trapped when the entrances were shut by mammoth etched stone barriers that rose from the floor or dropped from the ceiling.

In the sarcophagus chamber, Lex gaped at the moving walls, the shapes surreally shifting, her perspective morphing, as if she'd been dropped into an Escher print.

"What the hell is going on?" Connors screamed.

But his cry died out in the cacophony of grinding gears and sliding rock. Within seconds there was no escape.

CHAPTER 20

Inside the Sacrificial Chamber

Adele Rousseau had been standing in the doorway when she'd first felt the floor shudder. She locked eyes with Thomas, who'd been standing over the mummies, helping four of Weyland's archaeologists catalog the vast array of objects inside the chamber.

Tremors followed, powerful enough to shake ancient dust loose from the masonry. Adele looked up to see a thick stone door descending on her. Just before the heavy portal slammed shut, Thomas yanked the woman out of the way.

In Thomas's grip, Adele watched as another stone door came out of the ceiling, restricting access to the only other exit from the sacred chamber.

"Get something under there!" she cried.

Two archaeologists slid a heavy aluminum case under the door. It was promptly crushed.

"You okay?" Thomas asked, still holding her. Adele pushed herself away, eyes scanning the room.

"We're trapped."

Thomas looked around. "Not necessarily. Let's try

to trip the door. Maybe it will open as easily as it closed."

"All right, let's go," Adele cried, addressing them all. "We're going to try to open this door."

The archaeologists—along with Thomas—placed their shoulders against the door's ornate terra-cotta surface. Finally Adele joined them.

"One, two, three. . . . Push!"

For long, desperate moments they all strained against the solid stone, to no avail. The door defied the brute strength of six full-grown adults.

"I feel a little like Sisyphus," said Professor Joshi of Brown University.

"Slab's gotta weigh two tons," Adele said mournfully. "We'll never move it." She slapped the stone door in frustration. At her side, Thomas gripped her arm and pointed.

"What is that?" he asked.

While they had been trying to move the stone door, a round, leathery sack had been deposited in the carved depression next to one of the sacrificial slabs. It was unclear where it had come from. The object was ovoid, organic, and it throbbed with an inner life. Four puffy, liplike flaps crisscrossed the apex. The entire egg fit snugly into the bowl—almost as if the indentation had been carved specifically to hold it.

As Thomas and Adele watched, the indentations on the other slabs silently opened in places where no seam had been apparent before.

"It's like some gigantic machine," said Dr. Cannon, an Egyptologist from London. There was awe and fear in his voice.

As they watched, more eggs appeared, to fill each stone depression.

"There . . . another," Cannon croaked.

Now all seven of the sacrificial slabs had an egg sack quivering by its side. The humans instinctively huddled together to form a defensive circle. They sensed that it was already too late—that there *was* no defense.

With a wet, slobbering gurgle, the lips on the first egg peeled back. Adele pulled her weapon from its holster. Out of the corner of her eyes, she glanced at Thomas.

"What did you say this room was called?"

Thomas stared at the pulsating ovum on the slabs. "The *sacrificial* chamber . . ."

Adele fired—too late. The bullet struck the egg a split second after the life form within it leaped at its attacker. The flaccid egg sack exploded like a melon as its contents latched onto Adele Rousseu's face.

Her gun clattered to the floor as she frantically tried to tear the face-hugging creature off of her. But the tail wrapped itself around her neck like a boa constrictor, and the harder she pulled, the tighter the strangling tentacle became.

Adele fell backwards, her screams muffled by the smothering alien parasite pressed over her mouth. Thomas rushed to her side and tugged at the snakelike coils closing in on her throat. Everyone else backed away from the writhing woman and the remaining egg sacks. But in that confined chamber, there was nowhere to retreat to—just as the ancient architects had intended, Thomas realized dimly.

The archaeologists braced themselves as the other six eggs quivered and their fleshy lips parted. More pistol shots rang out, followed by cries of fear and terror, then howls of agony.

In the Chamber of the Sarcophagus

Just as Lex was preparing to move her people down a long corridor, the walls began to move once again. Gunshots and bright flashes, followed by frantic, tormented screams, could be heard through the grate from the chamber above.

"What's going on?" Miller cried.

Lex turned to Max, who already had his communicator in hand. "Get Rousseau and Thomas."

Both Maxwell Stafford and Sebastian got on their communicators, but neither of them was able to raise anyone from the archaeological party upstairs.

Charles Weyland stood before what had been a solid wall but was now a wide passageway, so long that it vanished in the gloom. He held one of the Predator weapons in his pale hands.

"Remarkable," he said, his eyes bright. "Hydraulic fluid, walls that move, tunnels that dig themselves."

Lex faced him. "Is there anything you didn't tell me about this place?"

"Nothing. I have no idea what this is."

"How could the ancients have constructed something like this?" Lex demanded.

"Clearly they had help." It was Sebastian who spoke.

"You mean little green men?"

"I don't know about that," Sebastian replied. "But the one thing I do know for sure—" He pointed to the weapon cradled in Weyland's hands. "Five thousand years ago our ancestors were killing one another with wooden clubs and knives chipped from obsidian. Not these things."

"So little green men may not be so wide off the mark," said Miller from the sidelines. He was rechecking the readings on his spectrometer after a thorough examination of another of the Predator weapons. "I've just completed a basic spectral analysis of the metal. The majority of the compounds here are simply unknown, but the two elements I *can* place we've met before—tilanium and cadmium 240."

Miller closed the cover on his spectrometer.

"Well, whatever it is, we're not prepared for it," Lex said. She stared down the long, dark corridor that had opened up behind Weyland. "We're going to round up the rest of the team and get to the surface. Let's move."

Meanwhile, Max and two security members whose tags identified them as Bass and Stone hauled a large wooden crate to the center of the room and pried it open. Packed inside was an arsenal of heavy weapons, including MP-5s, plenty of ammunition, and a variety of handguns and survival knives. Verheiden began handing them out. Peters took a machine gun and a sidearm. Max accepted an MP-5. Connors took a Desert Eagle.

"What the hell is this, Weyland?" Sebastian cried.

Weyland smiled pragmatically, his skin waxy and pale in the gloom. "We've lost contact with the surface. And this discovery is too important to hand it over to the Chinese or the Russians."

"But this is supposed to be a *scientific* expedition."

Weyland bristled. "This is *my* expedition, Dr. De

Rosa, and I will define it. Until I know what is going on, we will be taking all necessary precautions."

Weyland gestured toward the sarcophagus, and instantly his security team began to unload the ancient weapons rack. They carefully rolled the devices up in protective wrapping and stuffed them into a large backpack.

Lex spied the activity and confronted Stafford. "What are you doing?"

"My job. Yours is over," Max said as he slammed a magazine into his machine gun.

Lex's eyes narrowed. "I told you, when I lead a team, I don't leave my team. My job is over when everyone is back on the boat safely, and that gun doesn't change anything."

Stafford looked to his boss. "Mr. Weyland?"

Weyland looked at Max, then at Lex.

"She brought us here, she's getting us home." He faced Max. "You and your crew back her up."

As everyone assembled on the threshold of the new corridor, Max stepped aside so Lex could pass. "After you," he said.

Lex ignored the slight condescension and consulted her wrist compass. "This bearing should take us back to the entrance. We make it to the surface and we regroup at the whaling station."

"What about Thomas and Rousseau?" asked Sebastian.

Lex glanced at him, then looked away. "We'll find them on the way out."

Minutes after Lex and her group departed the Chamber of the Sarcophagus, a seemingly immovable stone portal rose into the ceiling. Then a shimmering blur appeared at the doorway of the murky chamber, stirring the stagnant air.

Blue lightning crackled and the Predator uncloaked. As the creature stalked toward the open sarcophagus, a low clicking sound reverberated deep within its throat. Standing over the now empty weapons bin, the clicking morphed into an angry rumble.

A breeze stirred as more ghostly figures drifted into the chamber. One by one, they disengaged their cloaking devices and approached the sarcophagus, until all were assembled.

The lead Predator tapped the computer keypad on its wrist with two oddly elongated middle fingers. There was a hum of energy from behind his mask as a ruby-red ray emanating from his glassy eye slits stabbed through the darkness.

Utilizing the thermal sensor built into its battle mask, the Predator scanned the stone floor for any traces of residual energy. With its head twisting to the left, then to the right, the creature's high-tech dreadlocks swung about, scanning every inch of the chamber. Finally, the Predator found the spoor—the residual heat of footprints left behind by the humans as they moved on.

The Predator roared and thrust the tip of its curved spear in the direction of the long corridor, where the trail of ghostly footprints led deeper into the pyramid. Shifting the spear in its hand, the Predator engaged its stealth armor and faded from view. With clicks and grunts, the rest of the Predators followed in a blur, right behind the leader.

CHAPTER 21

Inside the Labyrinth

The long, broad corridor beyond the Chamber of the Sarcophagus stretched off into the darkness. Lex and the others followed the passageway for about three hundred feet until they found themselves crossing a stone bridge constructed of carved blocks as large as houses.

Nothing could be seen on either side of the bridge, just a vast, black emptiness. Frigid blasts rose up from the depths. Lex pointed her flashlight into the darkness, but the beam could not penetrate the abyss. Out of curiosity, she broke a chemical glow stick and dropped it over the side.

For a long time, everyone watched the light fall. When it finally faded in the distance, it was still falling.

"How deep could that be?" Connors asked.

Sebastian managed an ironic smile. "To hell perhaps? If we're not already there."

Miller stared at the huge construction stone under

his feet. "We're standing on a single piece of solid rock that's bigger than a Wal-Mart—and these people built a bridge out of it. How could primitives have possibly moved it here?"

"Clearly—"

"They had help," Stafford interrupted. "You've said that before, Dr. De Rosa. But *who* helped them?"

"An extraterrestrial intelligence from another civilization," said Miller.

"But why?" Max replied. "If some advanced starfaring civilization did come to Earth in ancient times, why hang around? These ancients may have had something like a civilization, but compared to an alien race that could travel across galaxies, they were primitives."

"So are *we*," Sebastian replied.

Weyland hobbled past them, an oxygen bottle slung over his shoulder. The industrialist no longer seemed interested in their speculations. Max Stafford broke off his conversation with Sebastian, then hurried to catch up with his employer.

On the other end of the bridge they found another door—this one framed by panels decorated with even more elaborate hieroglyphics.

"This looks important," said Sebastian.

The darkness beyond the threshold was absolute. Lex drew a powerful storm flare and ignited it. Raising the flickering light high, she led them into a long, broad corridor lined with mammoth jade-hued statues mounted on square stone pedestals. Each effigy was a representation of a vaguely humanoid being between eight and ten feet tall, with impossibly broad shoulders

and hair bound in long dreadlocks. The faces varied—
some were broad, flat and featureless, while others had
narrow, close-set eyes and a mouth surrounded by
mandibles that looked like they belonged on a shellfish.

"The green men aren't so little," Lex observed.

"They have different heads, different faces,"
Stafford added, facing Sebastian. "Do you think they
are supposed to be half-human, half-animal gods, like
the ancient Egyptians worshipped?"

Sebastian shook his head. "The flat faces are actually masks, I think, perhaps ceremonial. These . . .
crab faces . . . may also be masks."

"I hope," said Bass.

Sebastian noted that some of the effigies were depicted in regal poses, but most were more dynamic, engaged in some sort of battle, usually against a strange,
crustaceanlike creature with a long, narrow, eyeless
head and a bony, segmented tail. Despite the unearthly
artistic style and sensibility, it was clear that the heroic
central figure in each sculpture were the humanoids.

"Like St. George," Stafford marveled.

"The English knight who killed the dragon?" asked
Miller, gazing up at a statue.

"St. George was Turkish . . . well, Cappadocian, actually," Sebastian noted. "He was born in Asia Minor,
though he did indeed become the patron saint of En-
gland in the fourteenth century."

"Recognize what's on their shoulders?" Lex asked.

The creatures wore weapons on some kind of shoulder mount—the guns were exact replicas of the devices
Weyland and his men had just looted from the sarcoph-

agus. Squinting through his thick glasses, Miller examined the statues.

"These weapons are carved in roughly life size," he whispered, looking up into the sightless stone eyes of one of the effigies. "Which makes our friends here pretty big dudes."

Sebastian directed them to a large painted mural, which depicted humans bowing in supplication to the giants. Max Stafford appeared at his shoulder.

"We worshipped these things?"

"According to this, we did."

"Surely they were just pagan gods," Weyland said, suddenly impatient with all the speculation. He moved forward, but Miller caught up with him.

"The heat bloom that your satellite detected makes more sense now," said the engineer.

"What do you mean?" asked Weyland.

"A building this sophisticated would require a major energy source. That's what the satellite detected—the power plant for this pyramid firing up . . . preparing."

"Preparing for what?"

Weyland and Miller continued to move on. Sebastian remained behind to examine an etched panel. Soon, everyone but Connors and Stafford had moved down the corridor.

"Try to keep up, Professor De Rosa," cautioned Max.

As they walked, the group moved to the center of the long corridor lined with statues. Sebastian counted over sixty before giving up. More effigies lined the passageway as far as his eyes could see—and the passage seemed to be endless.

Suddenly Lex felt a cold chill. She whirled and extended her flashlight, its column of light probing the shadows.

"See something?" Miller asked nervously.

Lex peered into the darkness. "I thought I saw a blur, or a shadow or something. But if I did, it's gone now. The passage is empty."

"I can't believe the detail in some of these carvings," Sebastian said. "Some of the sculptures are meant to be realistic representations, while others have vague, almost abstract features. I suspect the styles in art changed over the passing centuries."

As they moved forward, Stone and Bass drifted to the back of the group to protect the rear, while Lex and Verheiden took point.

Sebastian, Charles Weyland, Max Stafford, Miller, and Connors gathered together in the center of the group, shielded by the mercenaries and their machine guns.

As soon as the humans began to move, the Predator who was stalking them from behind crossed the passageway and edged closer to its prey.

Meanwhile at the opposite end of the corridor, far ahead of the humans, another Predator morphed to visibility, its face briefly superimposed over the features of a stone statue before vanishing again.

The trap was ready to be sprung, and in the uncertain light of the sputtering flare, it was impossible for the humans to know that they were moving into the Predators' carefully prepared ambush.

The *Piper Maru*

The bridge lights were burning, and despite the fact that the ship was on anchor, a full complement of officers was working on deck. The radar operator made countless futile attempts to pierce the wall of snow, while the ship's meteorologist tried to calculate the duration of the storm based on very sketchy data.

"Is the end in sight?" Captain Leighton asked.

"I'd guess four hours. Six at the outside," the meteorologist replied. "But it's just a guess."

Captain Leighton crossed the bridge and dropped a heavy hand on the radioman's shoulder.

"Anything? Anything at all?"

"Nothing, Captain . . . not since the first message. The one the chief picked up."

Leighton turned to his executive officer. "What exactly did you hear, Gordon?"

"Not much," the XO replied. "The transmission was broken up by the storm. There was a lot of static. Some panicked voices . . . nothing coherent."

"You're sure the call came from the whaling station?"

"They identified themselves as members of Quinn's party. Said something had attacked them . . . or some of them . . . I couldn't quite make out the rest. I tried to respond, but I don't think they heard me. After that, all I got was static."

"An attack? Ridiculous," Leighton declared. "Who could possibly mount an attack down here, and in the middle of a katabatic storm?"

"Maybe it was whoever buzzed our ship," the XO replied.

Leighton stared into the tempest. "We have too many questions and not enough answers. And we're not likely to get any until this storm ends and we can cross the ice to the whaling station to see for ourselves." The captain paused to rub his tired eyes. "By then we may be too late."

CHAPTER 22

In the Labyrinth

Stone was the first to die.

Covering the group's tail, MP-5 in his hand, he never even noticed the wire-thin noose that dropped around his throat until it was pulled tight and his windpipe had closed shut.

With a jerk on the wire his spine snapped. Then, silent and unseen, his twitching corpse was hauled upward, into the shadows.

A moment later, Bass faltered as a breeze brushed his cheek.

He turned at the same moment that a Predator spear appeared from thin air and impaled him with such force that he was pinned to the stone wall behind him. Eyes bulging, the machine gun flew from his hand. Gore spurted from his nose and mouth before he could even shout a warning to the others.

Sensing danger, Max hit the floor, dragging Charles Weyland with him. They landed hard. As Weyland grunted, Max felt the breath go right out of his boss's frail body.

"Stay down!" Connors hissed.

But Max looked up anyway, just as something whizzed over his head. He saw the fleeting image of a disk-shaped object encrusted with gleaming, jewel-like crystals.

Lex saw it, too.

"Down!" she cried, pushing Sebastian aside.

The Predator disk missed his head by mere centimeters—so close it cut a swath through the collar of his jacket.

The disk struck the throat of the statue behind Lex. The vibrating blade hummed, neatly decapitating the stone effigy.

As Lex struck the floor, the statue's head landed beside hers.

Then bright flashes—gunfire—bloomed in the passageway. Rolling into a corner, Lex saw Max Stafford firing at a blur. His bullets gouged holes in the rock around them and ricocheted down the hallway.

Dropping to his knees by Stafford's side, Verheiden opened fire in the opposite direction. Bullets whizzed over Lex's head. She found herself temporarily blinded by the muzzle flashes.

"Here!" she heard Sebastian call. "Over here."

Lex rolled until she was on her belly. Then she rose and began to crawl toward the voice, light motes still bursting behind her eyelids. Suddenly the stone floor trembled under her fingers, and over the booming gunfire, Lex heard a rumble, then the grating sound of stone scraping against stone.

"The pyramid!" she heard Weyland shout. "It's shifting again!"

* * *

Lex crawled across the cold floor toward Sebastian's voice. Her vision was clearing, but not fast enough. A thick panel slid out of the wall next to her head far enough to block her path. Sebastian reached out and grabbed her arm, hauling Lex to safety.

Had she stayed where she was, Lex would have been cut off from the rest of the party.

"Wait—" Miller cried.

Another stone door dropped from the ceiling. Sebastian's and Miller's eyes met a split second before the door slammed down between them.

The gunfire stopped abruptly. Max raised his flashlight and scanned the faces around him—Weyland, pale and drawn; Sebastian, still clutching Lex and playing his own flashlight on a stone wall that mere seconds before had been a long, expansive hallway.

"I think I hear something," Lex whispered. "Someone yelling maybe . . . it's coming from the other side of that far wall. . . ."

She was listening to Connors. He'd been trapped alone when the wall panels had slammed shut around them. Now he was pounding the thick rock that separated him from the rest of the party—first with his fists, then with a booted foot.

"Hello! Can anybody hear me? Is anyone there?"

In another chamber, where Miller and Verheiden were isolated together, Verheiden stumbled to his feet, dazed. He'd seen Bass and Stone die, and it had unnerved him. All his training in the use of exotic weapons, all his prior military experience had not prepared the man for the kind of slaughter he had just witnessed.

Verheiden staggered around the room looking for a way out. Panic was taking hold, and the man was fast losing control. Verheiden paced around the tiny chamber like a trapped animal.

"What are those things? Did you see what they did to Bass and Stone? I hit that son of a bitch. Dead on. He didn't stop. He didn't slow down. He didn't even flinch!"

His voice was echoing off the walls loud enough to drown out Connors's yells from the adjacent chamber.

"Hey, Verheiden."

Miller's yell snapped the man back to reality. "What?"

"I'm no soldier, but I think you should calm down. We're not dead yet."

"Thanks, *Professor*," Verheiden said, unimpressed.

"Actually, it's *Doctor*. And you're welcome."

Verheiden rubbed his face with his callous hands. "We're never going to get out of this place."

"Don't say that."

Verheiden looked down at Miller, sitting on the floor. "Whatever you believe in, you should start praying to it . . . *Doctor*."

"Hey," called Miller. "You have children?"

A smile curled Verheiden's mouth. "A son."

"I have two," Miller said brightly. "You know what that means? We don't have the luxury of quitting. We're going to make it out of here. You hear me? We are going to survive this if I have to drag you the whole way."

Verheiden lifted his eyebrows in surprise. Since when did a Beaker have more guts than him?

Max yanked the strangely designed spear out of the wall and eased Bass's bloody corpse to the floor. He tore the backpack from the dead man's shoulders and tossed it aside.

Immediately, Weyland snatched the bag and ripped it open, to examine the weapon inside. "No damage," he said thankfully.

Max looked up. "One of our men is dead."

Weyland touched Stafford's arm.

"I'm sorry," he said in a tone of genuine regret.

"I need to know what this man died for."

Weyland blinked, surprised. "He died trying to make history."

"Whose?" Max demanded. "Yours?"

Lex turned her back on the two and squatted beside Sebastian. She strained to hear Connors's voice again, but he had gone quiet—which was probably a bad thing, she decided.

Lex noticed Sebastian staring into the distance and fingering the Pepsi cap that still hung around his neck on a frayed leather strap. She lifted her hand and touched his. "Careful. That's a valuable archaeological find."

Sebastian managed a wan smile. "Nervous habit."

"Can't think why you're nervous."

Lex followed Sebastian's eyes, and they both stared at the cold stone slab that trapped them.

"Imagine," said Lex. "In a thousand years, *I* could be a valuable archaeological find."

Suddenly the alarm on Sebastian's digital watch went off—a harsh, unexpected sound in that tiny stone cell. He stood up and helped Lex to her feet.

"Don't go writing yourself into the history books just yet," he told her as he silenced the alarm.

"What's that about?" She pointed to his watch.

Sebastian smiled. "Just a theory. Listen . . ."

In the distance there was an explosive sound, like rolling thunder. Then the familiar grating of stone against stone—far away, but coming closer.

Sebastian placed his ear against the wall. He listened for a long time as the sound continued.

"I hear it!" Lex said softly. "But what is it?"

"I think the mechanism of the pyramid is automated," Sebastian explained, his ear still pressed against the stone. "I believe it reconfigures every ten minutes—the Aztec calendar was metric, you see? Based on multiples of ten."

Suddenly Sebastian stepped away from the wall he'd been leaning against. Three seconds later, the stone door slid aside to reveal a brand-new passageway.

Lex was impressed. "Give the man a Nobel Prize."

"I'd settle for a way out."

Max jumped to his feet, weapon in hand. Now that they were free, he was impatient to move.

Weyland rose slowly and seemed to have trouble getting to his feet. Despite his increasing infirmity, the industrialist would not relinquish the backpack containing the mysterious weapons.

"Everyone ready?" Lex asked.

Max stared into the dark abyss. "Ready? I'm ready," he replied. "But just where the hell are we going?"

"It's a maze," Sebastian declared loud enough to break the tension. "A labyrinth. We're meant to wander through it. I'm sure this was built to trap its victims, and we're bound to run into trouble. But *all* mazes have a way out—that's the point. So let's move before the walls come down and trap us again."

With a final glance at Bass's corpse, Stafford shouldered his MP-5 and took point. Lex and Sebastian watched him go. Weyland hobbled forward, leaning on his ice pole, the heavy oxygen tank weighing on his back.

From up ahead, they heard Max Stafford's voice.

"The labyrinth awaits."

CHAPTER 23

In the Labyrinth

Verheiden scrambled when the wall he was leaning against slid into the ceiling, opening a small, cramped crawlspace that had not been there before.

"What now?" the mercenary moaned.

Crouching down, Miller peered into the darkness. "We never went this way before."

"Yeah, so what's that mean . . . *Doctor*?"

Miller did not reply. Instead he raised his flashlight and traced the walls of the tunnel with it. The corridor went on for about twenty-five feet, then split abruptly in two. When Miller saw the fork in the road, he actually grinned.

"It would seem that we're rats in a maze."

Verheiden saw Miller's expression and scoffed.

"Sorry," the engineer said sheepishly. "But I really like puzzles."

With Miller in the lead, they crawled inside.

They traveled for a few minutes. Then Miller heard a voice ahead of him in the confines of the narrow duct.

"Hello?" Connors cried. "Can you hear me?"

"Who is that?" Miller called. It was difficult to make out where the voice was coming from. Sound bounced all over the place inside the shaft.

"It's Connors," called the voice. "Where are you?" The sound echoed hollowly, and from far away.

Suddenly, the man began to scream, his chilling voice reverberating throughout the pitch-black duct.

"Connors!" bellowed Verheiden. He hurried forward, trying to catch up to Miller. But suddenly the floor opened under the mercenary and Verheiden plunged through a trapdoor.

With some difficulty, Miller managed to turn his body around in the tight shaft. He pounded on the floor Verheiden had fallen through, but he couldn't even find a joint.

"Verheiden?" Miller called. "Can you hear me?"

The reply was faint and distant. "Miller . . . get me out of here."

Miller looked around, trying to find a way into the trap. "Hold on!" he yelled. "I'll figure a way to get to you. . . ."

Verheiden had fallen into a small, restrictive tunnel too low to stand up in and too tight for his lanky, six-foot-plus frame to find much comfort.

Above his head he could hear Miller trying to find a way into his prison. He pushed on the ceiling a number of times, but if the door was still there, he couldn't find it now. There were walls on three sides of him. The fourth side, however, wasn't a wall: It was a cramped corridor stretching beyond his vision. But

Verheiden had no intention of going down it alone. He intended to wait right there until Miller found a way to get him out.

Settling in for the long wait, Verheiden leaned against one of the walls, accidentally placing his hand into a pool of slime. Searching blindly for a surface on which to wipe his hand clean of the slime, he encountered a pile of dead skin, like the hide of a snake. More slime dotted the floor, and the mercenary couldn't help but recoil.

Suddenly, he heard a scraping sound echoing down the corridor. He took a few steps forward and shone his flashlight into the dark. Fearing a force moving toward him, he stumbled backwards, toward the wall.

Unfortunately, something more harrowing was waiting there to greet him.

From the chamber above Verheiden, Miller could hear screams and the sound of ripping flesh. He feared the man was dead.

Lex, Sebastian, and Weyland made their way through the forbidding underground maze, Max Stafford, his machine gun ready, leading them forward.

"Keep up, people. Keep it tight."

When they reached a fork in the corridor, they halted. Lex consulted her digital compass, then gazed into the darkness, deciding which way to proceed.

Max caught her arm. "Do you even know where you're going?"

"If we stay on this bearing we should keep going up. If we can do that, we'll make it to an entrance . . . eventually."

Lex noticed that Weyland seemed to bend under the weight of his backpack. She touched his shoulder.

"Leave it," she said. "It can only slow us down."

Weyland shrugged her off. "Too much has been lost to walk away with nothing."

Lex blocked him, eyes imploring.

"No," spat Weyland. "Unknown alloys, alien technology—the value of this find is immense."

"The device belongs to those creatures. Perhaps we should just give it back."

Weyland shook his head, eyes defiant.

Lex tried again. "Whatever is going on here, we have no part in it."

"This is *my* find," Weyland cried. "And I'm not leaving it."

They locked eyes, but it was Lex who finally relented.

"Then give it to me," she insisted.

She took the pack from his shoulders and placed it on her own. Then she curled her arm around Weyland and helped him walk.

"I'll tell Max you need a rest," she whispered.

Weyland shook his head. "Let's get out of here first."

They walked for a time, then Max halted the group. His eyes squinted into the shadows ahead. Finally, he raised his flashlight—just as a Predator emerged from the darkness.

"Move!" Sebastian cried.

Everyone scattered—everyone but Max Stafford, who dropped to one knee directly in the path of the creature and opened up with his machine gun. In the narrow, confined space the noise was deafening, the bursts blinding. This time Lex averted her eyes to preserve her night vision, and Sebastian—despite the exploding chaos—managed to spot the Predator's thick-muscled arm as it materialized out of thin air.

In the half-second that the arm was visible, Sebastian observed a device shaped like an abstract sculpture of a turtle shell strapped to the monster's wrist.

Max Stafford, blinded by his own muzzle blast, never saw the creature's arm or the unusual device on his wrist. All Max saw was a metallic net hurtling at his face.

The steel mesh struck him before he had a chance to react. It met his body with such force that he was catapulted backwards. The machine gun flew from his hands as Stafford struggled against the steel cocoon that enveloped him. But the more he fought, the tighter the net became. He tumbled to the ground and thrashed there, helpless as a caught fish.

Like razors, the steel threads bit into his clothing—then his flesh.

Stafford's cries of naked torment cut Weyland like a knife. With a moan of agony that mirrored Stafford's, he dropped to his knees at Max's side and clawed at the metal web.

"We'll get you out of there!"

The piercing threads lacerated Weyland's hands until they were slippery with blood. Yet he would not give up. The cocoon tightened, and Max's howls intensified as the mesh chewed deeper into muscle and bone.

"Back off!" Sebastian cried.

He grabbed Weyland's shoulders and dragged the

man away from the sight. Then Sebastian drew his survival knife and cut the net—or tried to. But the thread literally severed the knife, and its broken titanium steel blade rattled to the floor.

"Stay back!" Weyland croaked, leaning against a wall. "That damned trap gets tighter every time you touch it."

Blood pooled on the flagstones as red, raw agony sapped Stafford's consciousness. Fighting to stay alert and alive, he forced his eyes open, to see a blur appear behind Sebastian's right shoulder—a *second* Predator.

His lips writhed soundlessly before words finally came.

"Look out—"

But the hoarse whisper came too late.

As the other Predator uncloaked between Sebastian and Weyland, it kicked its powerful leg. The clawed foot hit Weyland like a jackhammer, dashing him to the ground.

Visible now, the second Predator grabbed Sebastian by the throat and lifted him off the floor. Sebastian kicked once, slamming his boot into the creature's belly, but the blow had no effect.

Arm extended, its helpless prey struggling in its grip, the creature threw its head back and unleashed a guttural roar. Sebastian pounded the monster's fist with his own until, annoyed, the Predator slammed him against the stone wall.

Sebastian's head lolled, and his arms dangled like empty sleeves.

Still clutching the stunned human, the Predator raised a long, barbed spear. With his other hand he braced himself to administer the fatal blow to the man still ensnared in the net.

Lex, back against the wall, cast about for a way to rescue her comrades. In the wavering light she saw Stafford's MP-5 and lunged for it.

But the Predator was faster. A shimmering shape crossed the corridor and slammed an armored boot down on the machine gun, crushing it.

Then the Predator swatted Lex aside with the back of its hand.

She struck the wall and slid to the hard floor. Immediately, she tried to rise, but the Predator administered a kick that sent her spinning back against the stone. Blood spurted from her nose and the room spun. Swallowing the pain and her own blood, she quickly rolled aside, narrowly avoiding a second savage kick.

The Predator roared and chased her.

Meanwhile, held fast in the ever-tightening web, Stafford shared a look with Charles Weyland, who leaned against the wall only a few feet away from his faithful assistant. Weyland was winded, helpless, with blood seeping from his hands and wrists.

"I'm sorry . . ." he sobbed.

Stafford's eyes—red-rimmed and pain-ravaged—were resigned as the Predator drove the spear through the net, through Max Stafford's heart, and into the hard stone floor beneath him. A red tide flowed outward, and Stafford twitched once. Then it was over.

Through tears of pain, Lex watched Max die.

"Oh, God," she cried.

Her eyes darted, seeking a way out. Then Lex spied

Sebastian still hanging limply in the second Predator's grip. She called his name.

Sebastian's eyes fluttered, so she knew he was still alive, if barely. Seeing him there and Max slaughtered on the floor filled Lex with a cold, helpless fury. With a defiant shriek, she reeled to her feet, searching for something, *anything* to use against the monsters. She wanted nothing more than to lash out, to hurt them, butcher them—the way they'd murdered the members of her party.

Then cruel fingers encircled her head and forced it back to expose her tender throat. The reptilian stink of the invisible Predator curled her nostrils, and Lex heard a metallic snick as twin curved blades slid out of their sheath and touched her throat.

The creature's arm and face were visible now, though the rest was still cloaked in a shivering blur. It was as if some hunter's ethic compelled this race of warriors to reveal themselves to their prey at the point of climax.

Her head was wrenched from side to side, yet Lex saw the monster staring at her through slits in its expressionless mask. Snarling, the warrior drew its arm back for the killing stroke.

Powerless in its grip, she refused to struggle any longer, or to look away. Death held no terror for Alexa Woods. She would face it squarely, eyes open.

The woman's fearlessness disconcerted the Predator. The creature actually hesitated for a moment— long enough for a black shape to drop from the ceiling and for its razor-sharp tail to plunge through the Predator's reptilian flesh.

Suddenly the hand that held Lex convulsed. Then the fingers parted, releasing her. She stepped back as bright fingers of raw energy crackled across the Predator's torso. The monster twitched and flung its arms wide.

Flattening herself against the wall, Lex heard the crunch of snapping bone and a wet gurgle. Then a black, barbed spike burst through the Predator's chest in a torrent of phosphorescent gore.

Lex whimpered as the hot, steaming liquid spattered across her cheek, but still she could not turn away.

Unbelievably, the Predator was now helpless in the grip of a destructive force more savage than itself. Limbs flailing, wailing madly, the hunter was hauled upward, disappearing in the shadows.

Lex heard bestial sounds, and the ripping of meat and bone. Sparks rained from above, followed by a deluge of gore. In the intermittent flashes Lex observed a black, insectlike shape curling in the arches, its long, clawed arms tearing at the beleaguered Predator.

With a final crunch of bone, the Predator died, its corpse dangling limply on the barbed tip of its killer's tail. Gouts of flesh and streams of reptilian blood plopped onto the flagstones, steaming in the frigid air.

The second Predator spied the black obscenity as it dropped to the ground and crouched on two spindly legs. Tossing Sebastian aside, the Predator assumed a fighting stance, an undulating rumble gurgling in its throat.

The Alien whipped its bony tail around, dislodging the dead warrior and hurling its battered carcass into a dank corner. Legs spread wide, clawed arms raised, the

Alien kicked Max Stafford's bundled corpse aside as if it were clearing the arena. Slime oozing from its lipless mouth, the Alien bobbed its shiny, elongated head and thrashed its tail from side to side as it issued a sibilant challenge. Finally, its toothy mouth opened and the black beast spit at the Predator in angry defiance.

Only dimly, Sebastian had felt the crushing grip relent, and he'd slid down the wall. He would have remained there, too, except for the strong hands that encircled his waist and hauled him to safety.

Sebastian looked up to see Lex standing over him, her face stained with an eerie green phosphorescence, like some strange, futuristic war paint. Then he heard hissing and an angry roar. Rolling onto his side, Sebastian watched two demons out of hell squaring off for a duel.

CHAPTER 24

In the Labyrinth

The tittering obscenity and the reptilian humanoid slammed together with a shuddering impact that sent both creatures reeling. Howls and thrashes accompanied their charge.

The Predator lashed out, striking a backhanded blow against the Alien's gnashing jaw. The Alien staggered. Then, in a scorpionlike motion, the black monster attacked with a flash of its spiked tail. Springing back, the Predator used its wrist blades to counter the strike—and in a quick twist, it severed the Alien's tail.

Yowling, the Alien whirled, spraying deadly venom from its bloody stump. Whatever the steaming droplets touched burned, sizzled and pitted.

The Predator pulled back its arm to thrust again but discovered that its wrist blades had been reduced to smoldering, molten stubs by the Alien's acidic blood. Snarling, the Predator leaped at the Alien and brought it down.

As they grappled, sparks—struck from solid stone

or from the Predator's shredded armor—created distorted shadows that writhed on the walls, floor and ceiling.

"We have to move!" Lex cried, tugging Sebastian's coat.

He nodded and stumbled to his knees, grabbing a flashlight that had rolled to his side. Sebastian looked up to see Lex haul Weyland to his feet. The man sobbed and held his useless hands palms up, their fingers encased in congealing black blood.

Sebastian grabbed Weyland's arm, and together they carried him toward the far end of the corridor, into the darkness. Behind them, the two unearthly creatures grappled on the stained flagstones as the savage battle raged on.

Bodies intertwined as one, the thrashing creatures rolled end over end, kicking and clawing, their wails of rage and pain echoing throughout the tunnel. Gaining the upper hand, the Alien hovered over the humanoid, and its black maw opened. A second set of jaws burst forth from the first—stopping mere inches from the Predator's battle-damaged face mask.

With an echoing roar, the Predator heaved the black, yammering creature aside and sprang to its feet. Whirling to face the Alien, the warrior raised his wrist and aimed the net gun—

The Alien, its gangly black arms flung wide, launched itself into the air in a powerful bounding leap—

And the Predator fired—

A metal net enveloped the creature in midleap, forcing the kicking, mewing Alien to the floor. The Alien's exoskeleton clattered on the flagstones as the net pulled tight, crushing it.

The Predator, unsteady and bleeding from its wounds, grunted with satisfaction as the mesh closed on its enemy, piercing through the Alien's chitinous hide.

Blood and gore spurt from a hundred places, spraying the flagstones and the walls and burning holes wherever it splashed. Unfortunately for the Predator, the acid also burned the net, and in a few brief seconds the mesh melted enough for the Alien to break free.

Spitting angrily, the Alien clambered to its feet and faced the battered Predator. Its black, misshapen body smoked and sizzled where the razor net had cut it. The Alien was determined not to be dominated. Its segmented tail-stump flailed from side to side, beating the stone walls.

The humanoid was clearly overmatched, for the Alien was far more powerful and formidable than the Predator had thought possible. Now there was little to do but face death with honor—and die fighting.

The Predator threw back its arms, extended its chest, and roared in the face of doom.

With a final spitting hiss, the Alien was on him, driving the humanoid to the ground and crushing him under its weight. The Predator struggled against the onslaught, but there was no defense. Clawed hands grasped the Predator's dreadlocks, holding its head fast.

Then the Alien's inner mouth punched through the broken faceplate to smash the Predator's flesh and bony skull beneath. A fountain of gore erupted from the shattered head, spraying the walls and flagstones with clotting brain matter and a steaming green fluid that glowed with a sickly radiance.

On the Staircase

Abruptly, Lex and Sebastian—with Weyland draped limply between them—staggered out of the labyrinth and into a vast chamber lined with stout, rough-hewn stone pillars. The room was a maze of pitch-black shadows, but a dim illumination radiated from an unseen source, though it was still difficult to penetrate the darkness for more than a few yards.

Lex was starting to think like the survivors she'd lived amongst—the Sherpas of the Himalayas and the subsistence hunters of Alaska. She knew that anything could be hiding in this forest of carved stone cenotaphs. For the first time in her life, she wished she had a weapon.

They found a wide stone staircase lined with ornate square pillars. After climbing several steps, Lex and Sebastian slowed and released Weyland. He leaned against the wall, avoiding their eyes.

"What was that thing?" Sebastian croaked, rubbing his bruised throat.

"I don't know, and I don't *want* to know."

Lex drew a compass from her utility belt and, with the sleeve of her coat, wiped the Day-Glo green blood from her face. She read the compass, then glanced around the column-lined stairway.

"What now?" Sebastian asked.

"We keep moving and stay on this heading."

Weyland clutched his chest and moaned. A cough wracked his frail body. He dropped to his knees and began to hyperventilate. Lex hurried to the man's side.

"Take it easy," she said, grabbing his shoulder.

Weyland's face began to turn blue. His mouth gaped like a suffocating fish.

Without breaking eye contact, Lex took Weyland's head in her hands and held it. It was clear that he had taken too much air into his lungs and that they were beginning to freeze.

"You have to control your breathing," she coaxed. "Take slow, steady breaths . . ."

She took shallow breaths herself, to teach Weyland by example, and soon his own breath became less forced, less labored.

"Slow, steady . . . that's it," Lex said as the tension drained from Weyland's face and he visibly relaxed. Finally, Lex led Weyland to a step and sat him down.

"I'm okay . . . I'm okay," Weyland croaked, trying to wave her away and rise again.

Suddenly a looming shadow appeared at the bottom of the stairs.

"Come on, we have to get out of here," Lex cried, hauling Weyland to his feet. Hobbled, the billionaire tried to use an ice axe as a cane, but his arms were as tired as his legs—too exhausted to support him now. Slowly, Weyland slumped against the wall, teetering on unsteady limbs.

"No," he gasped. "I can't . . . it's hard enough to stand . . ."

Every word Weyland spoke seemed to sap more of

his waning strength. Lex could see that the strain of the chase and the constant exposure to the frigid air had ravaged what little remained of the man's disease-ridden lungs.

"Weyland—"

But the man cut her off.

"Save it," he said with some of his old authority. "This is all my fault."

His intentions were clear. Weyland was going to sacrifice himself in order to give her and Sebastian more of a head start.

"I'm not letting you die down here," said Lex.

Weyland grinned. "You didn't, Lex. Go. I'll buy you whatever time I can."

The Predator was coming, moving very deliberately up the stairs. Weyland spied it and grabbed the ice axe, brandishing it like a weapon.

"Go! Go now," he cried.

Lex reached for Weyland, but Sebastian grabbed her arm and dragged her up the stairs. Weyland and Lex shared a final look, then the man turned to face the presence growing nearer.

Not bothering to cloak itself, the Predator walked right up to Weyland. The human rose to his full height, staring impassively at the otherworldly creature. For a long moment, Weyland faced the Predator squarely, eye to eye, then lifted the axe and charged.

The Predator reached out, snatched the axe out of Weyland's hand and tossed it aside as Weyland's futile swing carried him past the Predator and set him stumbling down a step into an elaborately etched wall panel.

The creature turned and stared down at Weyland. As

blank eyes on the Predator's faceplate glowed with crimson fire, the human felt a strange warmth inside his chest. Reaching out, the Predator clutched Weyland's shoulders, held him fast and examined him from head to toe.

Then, snorting contemptuously, the creature pushed Weyland aside and turned his back on him.

Weyland understood what *that* meant. Somehow the Predator could sense his frailty and did not regard him as a threat—in fact, Weyland was sure that, to this monster, he was nothing more than a sick, helpless animal!

Choking on a rush of helpless rage, Weyland clenched his teeth and searched for a way to strike back. He had no weapon, but his fingers closed on the oxygen tank slung over his back.

Ripping the cylinder off his shoulder, Weyland set the tank down and propped it against his foot. Kneeling, he opened the valve until it was gushing full blast. As pure oxygen filled the chamber, he yanked an emergency flare from his utility belt and held it up.

"Don't you turn your back on me!" he cried.

At the sound of the human's voice, the Predator spun—and Weyland ignited the flare.

The combustible oxygen instantly exploded in a bright yellow fireball that engulfed the Predator. Clutching the tank and directing the oxygen flow, Weyland doused the thrashing, flailing creature with blistering fire.

When Weyland heard the Predator's pain-wracked cries echoing off the walls, he laughed like a madman. "That's right, you son of a bitch! Burn . . ."

The black silhouette in the center of the conflagration screeched again. Then, still wreathed in flames, the Predator lurched forward as it unsheathed twin wrist blades. With one quick thrust the Predator plunged the long, wicked knives into Charles Weyland's soft, unprotected belly.

Weyland died with scarcely a sigh, blood starting from his nose and mouth. Snarling, the Predator hauled the limp, bloodstained body into the inferno to be consumed. But with Weyland's corpse came the oxygen tank, still clutched in his dead hands. Licked by the flames, the pressurized contents of the cylinder detonated like a bomb. A billowing orange blast and a bright yellow fireball surged along the stairway, scorching everything in its fiery path.

In the Labyrinth

Lex and Sebastian stumbled blindly through the semidarkness, once again lost in the maze of stone corridors. The pyramid rumbled as it shifted shape yet again, shaking the dust of millennia loose to choke and blind them. Over the noise and the pounding of their boots on the stone floor, they heard Weyland's cries, then the explosion.

"Weyland!"

"You can't help him," Sebastian said, dragging her along.

Lex struggled against him.

"Lex, we have to go . . . hurry!"

From behind came a blast of hot air—and something else. They both saw a flickering light at the far end of the corridor. Then a fiery figure hurled out of the darkness toward them—the Predator, its form sheathed in roaring flames that did not seem to harm the creature in the least.

Sebastian grabbed her arm and they both ran. They hadn't gotten more than a few yards before Lex heard the sound of massive feet pounding through the darkness, gaining on them.

Sebastian rounded a corner and spied a stone barrier rising up from the floor directly in front of them. If it closed before they got through it, they would be trapped in the corridor with the Predator.

By the time they reached the threshold, the barrier was halfway up. Sebastian lifted Lex and practically threw her over the stone wall. Then he leaped up and caught the edge, hauling himself across the top of the door and down the other side.

Just as the opening was about to seal, one of the Predator's throwing disks sailed through and ricocheted off the far wall in a shower of sparks.

On the opposite side of the door, the Predator turned away from the stone barrier to see a black monstrosity uncoiling from a pillar, its segmented black exoskeleton blending in perfect camouflage with the architecture.

Rearing up, the Alien prepared to strike.

But the Predator was faster. Its throwing disk streaked through the air and bit deep into the Alien's shoulder, severing its arm. Then the metallic disk arced gracefully around and vanished into the shadows.

The Alien flailed its ravaged limb, spraying acid blood on the surrounding pillars.

The Predator slammed into the Alien, its booted foot snapping its foe's bony chest plates. The monster howled as it was hurled to the floor, the Predator weighing it down. They battled, hand to hand, as the Alien's lifeblood gushed from its hemorrhaging stump.

Finally, the Predator pinned the squirming Alien to the stone floor with one clawed hand. A throwing disk whizzed over their heads, and the Predator lifted its free hand to snatch it out of the air.

With one quick, violent motion he brought the disk down on the Alien, severing its tittering head from its thrashing body. Bubbling acid gushed from the wound, sizzling on the cold flagstones beneath it. The dead Alien twitched once, then stilled.

In the Hieroglyphics Chamber

Sebastian and Lex raced through another doorway and discovered a new chamber.

The cavernous room was lined with millions of hieroglyphic characters and dozens of elaborately painted panels covered in pictographs and artistic representations depicting, Sebastian assumed, events of historical significance to the long-lost civilization that had built this pyramid.

Sebastian approached a thick stone wall etched with a swirling, abstract design. A dozen or more small peepholes had been cut into the wall—each affording a glimpse into the chamber of pillars from which they had just barely escaped. Sebastian peered through one of the holes.

"Look!" he whispered.

Lex joined Sebastian and glanced through the opening.

From high above they could observe the grisly brutality of the scene. The Predator loomed over the bloody carcass of the Alien it had just decapitated. As the humans watched, the hunter threw back its arms and looked heavenward, as if in prayer. Drawing a knife from a hidden sheath strapped to its waist, the Predator sliced off one of the fingers from the Alien's double-thumbed hand.

Next the Predator reached up and fumbled with the pressure valves at the base of its mask. With a hiss of escaping gasses, the vacuum seal was broken. A moment later the creature lowered its faceplate to reveal two feral eyes, a noseless face covered with pasty-gray flesh, and crablike mandibles that flexed and clawed at the stagnant air.

Clutching the faceplate in one hand, the Predator used the severed finger as a writing implement, etching a design into the faceplate's hard, cold metal with the Alien's acid blood. A sizzling hiss could be heard as he carved a stylized thunderbolt design onto the mask's smooth forehead.

"What is he doing?" Lex whispered.

The Predator held up the mask, displaying it in the feeble light. Grunting in satisfaction, it flipped the mask over to reveal a mirrored surface lining the interior of the eye slits. Using that reflective surface, the Predator lifted the bloody finger and branded the same pattern on its own forehead. The acid smoked and sizzled, and the Predator roared with pain. But the alien hunter did not stop until the thunderbolt design was complete.

"He's blooding himself," Sebastian replied after a long silence. "Tribal warriors of ancient cultures do it. Mark themselves with the blood of their kill. It's like a rite of passage—a sign that they've become a man." Then he grinned. "This is all starting to make sense."

He turned away from the peephole and scanned the hieroglyphs around him, tracing the patterns with his eyes and caressing the carvings with his fingers.

"Yes!" he cried, eyes bright with the rapture of discovery. "This *is* starting to make sense. . . ."

CHAPTER 25

In the Hieroglyphics Chamber

"I want to show you something."

Sebastian led Lex to a panel between two stylized cenotaphs that rose fifteen feet from the flagstone floor. He pointed to a particular section of hieroglyphs carved into the stone wall.

"This outlines some kind of manhood ritual . . ." he began. Sebastian pointed to a pictograph that strongly resembled the now-you-see-it-now-you-don't creatures that first attacked them. "These creatures. These *hunters*. They've been sent here to prove that they are worthy to become adults—"

"You're saying they're what? Teenagers?"

Sebastian shrugged. "Who knows how long these creatures live? Perhaps for thousands of years. However old they are, this is their rite of passage."

His hands traced a pictograph—a stylized star field with what appeared to be a predatory raptor winging its way across the void.

"That's why they didn't carry those guns with them to begin with—"

"Part of the ritual," guessed Lex.

"Right. They had to earn them, like a knight earning his spurs."

Sebastian slapped his palm on the hard stone. "The whole story is here. The glyphs themselves are difficult to comprehend—not quite Aztec, not quite Egyptian—but they're perfectly preserved. And with a little bit of informed speculation I can fill in the blank spots. . . ."

He traced his hand along a stylized pictograph. Despite the bizarre, primitive iconography, Lex easily recognized the image. It was the Earth, as seen from outer space. And over the planet hovered a circular disk of fire, undoubtedly meant to represent a spacecraft dropping toward the planet from deep space.

"As I said before," Sebastian began, "the Aztecs used multiples of ten. These symbols right here roughly approximate the Aztec symbol for ten, so a little mathematics is in order. . . ."

Sebastian paused, calculating.

"Five thousand years ago they found a backwater planet . . . our planet Earth. They taught the primitive humans how to build and were worshipped as gods . . ."

His finger moved down the pictograph, to a familiar triangular shape, with a fiery disk hanging above it. Wavy lines surrounding the disk were clearly meant to depict a mysterious power source radiated by the spacecraft.

Knowledge, perhaps?

"In their honor, thousands of primitives labored for decades—perhaps centuries—to construct this pyramid and others like it."

Sebastian paused over a shape etched in the wall, a

twisted loop that turned in on itself like a snake swallowing its own tail.

"Like the great Ouroboros Worm of Gnostic mythology, in the broadest sense this kind of image is symbolic of the passing of long eons of time and the continuity of life. But in the symbolism of the ancients who built this place, it is meant to represent two things—a repetitive cycle, or a tradition. Something which occurs over and over again. But it also represents an actual creature, a being referred to here as "the Great Serpent." Through this text and probably others, the ancients were taught that their gods would return every hundred years, and that when they did, they would expect a sacrifice. It appears that humans were used as hosts for the Great Serpents."

"Serpents?" Lex asked.

Sebastian nodded. "The ones that don't look like us."

Sebastian went on to explicate a mural depicting a parade of sacrificial victims being anointed by feathered high priests who were then laid out on slabs. Below this image was a pictograph representing eggs, and ritual instructions showing how each egg should be placed in the depression on the slab.

"This . . . egg is what was placed in the carved bowl, not the victim's heart," Lex observed.

"Apparently. And somehow these eggs fertilized the chosen ones who gave birth to the Great Serpents. Then the gods would battle them."

Sebastian showed her a large-scale mural depicting the Great Serpent and the gods clashing in mortal combat.

"This image?" Lex asked, pointing to another mural

depicting a single stylized Predator standing atop a pyramid, a crown of stars encircling its head.

"Like gladiators in a coliseum those two alien races would battle," Sebastian explained. "Only the strongest survived. And the survivors would be the ones deemed worthy to return to the stars, to return *home*."

"What if they lost?"

Sebastian showed Lex three images in sequence, a grim, doomsday triptych. The first was an image of a great pyramid, three stylized Predators standing on the pinnacle, a horde of Great Serpents slithering up the sides. The next image showed the Predators, arms raised, with wavy lines radiating from their wrists.

The third image was hauntingly familiar. It showed an explosion—a green tinted blast with a mushroom cloud hovering over it, an explosion that destroyed everyone and everything in its path.

"If the gods were defeated, then a terrible disaster would overtake the land, and their civilization would vanish overnight . . . total genocide . . . an entire civilization wiped out at once."

Lex went numb. A mystery that had haunted her family for decades was finally solved.

"Then these creatures have been here before," Lex said. It was not a question.

"Undeniably," Sebastian replied. "Thousands of years ago, and many times since—perhaps recently."

Lex faced Sebastian. "In 1979, right here on Bouvetoya Island, there was a mysterious nuclear detonation. No nation ever took the credit—or the responsibility— for the explosion, and Air Force scientists couldn't figure out where the radioactive isotopes were mined, despite the fact that all uranium mined on earth can be traced by its unique molecular signature."

"How do you know this?"

Lex crossed her arms. "My father was an Air Force researcher. Although he spent twenty years studying the event, he failed to trace the uranium isotopes used in the blast to any known source on Earth."

Sebastian scratched his chin. "So they *have* been here before."

"These . . . Predators," said Lex. "They brought those creatures here to *hunt*?"

"Yes," he replied.

"So we didn't discover them?"

Sebastian shook his head. "I think the heat bloom was designed to lure us down here. This whole pyramid is a trap. Without us, there could be no hunt."

In the Labyrinth

Two rippling, translucent shapes appeared among the statuary. In a crackling burst of unleashed energies, the Predators winked into existence. Immediately, one warrior dropped into a fighting stance and scanned the area, spear at the ready.

The second Predator searched the corpses of Bass and Stone, looking for their missing weapons. Then it spied the acid-burned metal net. Ignoring Max Stafford's corpse, the creature inspected the damage to the mesh caused by the Aliens' caustic blood.

Unseen in the shadows, a horde of glistening black shapes slithered silently along the vaulted ceiling.

Hunting in a pack now, the Aliens scrambled among the walls, lurked in the darkness above, or curled around pillars.

Suddenly, choked to silence by the agile tail that looped around its throat, one of the Predators was hauled, kicking, up to the shadowy ceiling. A shower of luminescent blood and the clatter of broken armor striking the flagstones warned the second that death was stalking it, too.

The Predator whirled in time to see its comrade drop to the stone floor in great bleeding chunks of flesh. First a leg, then an arm, then the gory torso.

The Predator roared and drew twin throwing disks—one in each hand.

Suddenly, out of a black corner, an Alien face hugger launched itself at the Predator's mask. In one smooth motion the warrior ducked and hurled a disk. The blade sliced the grasping, pink-white hugger cleanly in half. The creature exploded in a spray of acid blood that spattered the Predator's mask and chest plate.

The Predator dropped the second disk and frantically struggled to remove the mask before the acid blood ate through to the soft flesh beneath. With a hiss, the vacuum seal was breached and the smoking mask clanged to the cold stone floor.

The Predator feverishly tore at its chest armor, which was already pitted and molten from the corrosive blood. The smell of burning flesh filled the corridor, and the Predator howled as acid burned deep into the muscle on its ribs, neck and chest.

Finally, the armor was thrown aside to reveal

patches of chemically scorched skin still smoldering on the Predator's torso and crablike face.

Naked and unmasked, the creature roared defiantly as it faced its attackers—two full-sized Alien warriors scrabbling across the floor to flank him. The Predator thrust its barbed spear, nipping the shoulder of the nearest Alien. The monster shrieked and retreated, even as its cousin knocked the spear aside to bear down on its opponent.

A third Alien dropped from the ceiling, its exoskeleton splashed with glowing green gore. The monster's bony tail curled around the Predator's leg, then yanked. The Predator shrieked in raw agony as the muscle was ripped from its leg bone. Hobbled, the hulking warrior tumbled to the floor as clawed hands tore at its now-vulnerable flesh.

Pinned down by the Alien's weight, its movements restricted by the whiplike tail that enveloped its ravaged leg, the Predator thrashed and struggled, waiting for death to claim it. But even though the black obscenities crawled across the Predator's heaving chest and spilled hot drool onto its naked face, they failed to deliver the anticipated fatal blow. Instead, the Aliens held the fallen Predator still and hissed expectantly . . .

Weakening, the Predator saw something stir in the blackness above its head. Craning its neck for a better look, its close-set eyes widened. The warrior had spied a huge alpha-Alien creeping out of the shadows, its teeth gnashing vigorously. Larger than its brothers, and more aggressive, it was clear to the helpless Predator that this being had taken command of the pack.

As it emerged from the gloom, the monster's battered exoskeleton was revealed. From head to toe the Alien's body was crisscrossed with wounds—including the burning brand made by the Predator's high-tech metal mesh net.

The other Aliens backed away in deference as the monstrosity shambled forward. Bending low over the fallen Predator, the creature lowered its elongated snout as if sniffing its victim. Then two ebony hands encircled the Predator's skull in an obscene caress before clutching the creature's head and holding it fast to the floor.

The Predator thrashed about and its mandibles snapped empty air, but it was still helpless in the powerful grasp of the battered monstrosity.

As the warrior's futile struggle continued, it felt cold, clawed feet crawling up its naked torso. Looking down, it spied another face hugger moving inexorably toward its head. Growling, eyes wide and darting from side to side, the Predator felt fear for the first time in its life.

Working quickly and efficiently, the face hugger slowly settled over its prey's snapping mouth, muffling its whimpering cries. . . .

Miller's eyes opened abruptly. For a moment he didn't know where he was. A feeling of ominous dread was his first clue.

He was standing—or at least he was upright. But when he tried to move, he found himself locked in place. A hard, black substance cocooned nearly his entire body. Only his right arm was free. The sleeve was ragged and heavily stained with blood.

Miller turned his head to the right, saw the two men hanging next to him, and his memory returned.

"Verheiden! Can you hear me?" he cried.

Verheiden, his face smothered by a face hugger, twitched and pulled against the hard shell that imprisoned him—the same substance that cocooned Miller. As Verheiden struggled, the parasite's ropy tentacle tightened around his neck. After a moment, Verheiden stopped fighting, and his body slackened.

Next to Verheiden, Miller saw Connors, or what was left of him. The dead man's chest had exploded outward, and he hung limply from the wall like some sick work of shock art. Although no face hugger clung to his features, which were frozen in an agonized expression, the Alien culprit that had robbed Connors of his last breath lay dead at his feet, legs pointed up toward the sky.

Miller heard a wet, dripping sound. Straining, he looked down. The egg of a soon-to-be-born face hugger was on the ground before him. Its petal-like lips were oozing as they began to open.

Miller pushed and squirmed against the cocoon. Then he saw Verheiden's gun, still in its shoulder holster.

With one eye on the twitching egg, Miller stretched his arm. He could just barely touch the butt of the weapon.

The egg quivered and its lips parted. Long white legs emerged, probing the air.

Summoning all of his strength, Miller threw his body forward until his fingers closed on the handle. As the hugger leaped, Miller pulled the gun out of its holster and fired off a shot.

The hugger blew apart in midair.

Yet when it struck the floor—even with half its legs blown away—the stubborn creature still struggled to rise. Miller fired off two more rounds; each smashed the thing like a hammer.

"Score one for the Beakers," he said.

Though sweet, Miller's triumph was short-lived. Just beyond the dead face hugger, the stone floor was littered with dozens of quivering eggs, each one pulsing with unearthly life.

CHAPTER 26

In the Hieroglyphics Chamber

Lex watched through the peephole as the Predator who had just bloodied himself now gutted and dressed its kill in the adjacent chamber. The thunderbolt he had seared onto his own forehead had not only earned him his warrior status but it had also earned him the name "Scar" to the sole humans who had witnessed the events—Lex and Sebastian.

Using its ceremonial knife, Scar stripped the black, rubbery flesh away from the Alien's jaw and severed the tissue holding the monster's inner mouth in place. Then the Predator doused its trophy with a liquid solution that neutralized the Alien's acidic blood. When the task was completed, Scar lay the grisly relic aside and suited up for battle.

For a moment, the creature vanished from sight. Lex pressed her face closer to the peephole, straining to see it. Suddenly, the Predator reappeared—staring through the very peephole she was using. The monster's shark-like eyes were only inches from her own.

Lex gasped and jumped backwards. After a second or two, she regained her courage and peeked again.

The creature was ready to return to the hunt. It had reattached its metal faceplate, covering its still-seeping, self-inflicted brand of honor. Despite the gloom in the adjacent chamber, Lex could clearly see the same thunderbolt design etched into the creature's metal mask.

Armor donned, the Predator hefted its spear, draped the trophy around its neck, and moved to the stone slab that separated the chamber of the pillars from the room the humans now occupied.

"He's out there. Waiting for the door to open," Lex whispered as she quickly slid on her backpack. At that moment, Sebastian realized they had another pack with them. The one Weyland had carried—the one that contained the Predators' weapons.

"I think when we took the guns, we upset the order of how things work down here. We tipped the scales."

Lex retrieved the pack. "He needs his guns back."

Sebastian glanced at his watch, then shook his head. Time was running out. "When that door opens we're dead."

"Not if we set things right."

Sebastian was astonished. "You can't be serious."

"This pyramid. It's like a prison. We took the guards' guns and now the prisoners are running free. To restore order, the guards need their guns."

Sebastian shivered. "Don't ever use that metaphor again."

"When the door opens, we're going to give that thing his gun back."

"Are you crazy?" Sebastian cried. "You want a

metaphor? During a big game hunt, the animals being hunted don't *arm* the hunters."

"They're not hunting us. We're in the middle of a war. It's time to pick a side."

"We're on a side. *Our* side."

"We have to consider the possibility that we might not make it out of here," said Lex. "But we have to make sure that those serpents don't reach the surface, because if they do, everything, everywhere could die."

Sebastian was quiet for a moment. Then he nodded. "The enemy of my enemy is my friend."

Lex nodded too. "Look. We give him his guns, and if he leaves us alone we can get out of here. All we have to do is hold it together and make it to the surface."

Sebastian's watch alarm rang out. Next came the sound of rolling thunder and scraping rock as the pyramid began to reconfigure itself.

"Let's go find our friend," Lex commanded.

Sebastian took her arm as they both faced the door. The rumbling continued, but the portal did not budge.

"What happens if this door doesn't open?"

Lex frowned. "Try to think positively."

Just then, the stone slab behind them lifted into the ceiling. Sebastian looked over his shoulder. A door on their left had opened too. Beyond it they saw a shambling shape moving through the darkness toward them. It was not humanoid.

"Come on," Sebastian urged. "We have to get out of here."

The two ran into the empty corridor, once again lost in the maze of stone. As the pyramid continued to rumble, the walls shed layers upon layers of blinding dust.

Sebastian, who was in the lead, rounded a corner and spied the deep chasm that had opened up in front of them. The pit seemed to be close to a dozen feet across.

Even running at top speed the leap seemed impossible, but they had no choice.

"Get ready to jump!" Sebastian cried.

Without hesitation he hurled himself forward, arms outstretched.

As he arced through the empty air, Sebastian realized how impossible a jump it was—yet he almost made it. Almost.

The breath exploded from his lungs as he slammed into the far ledge. The impact shattered ribs, but he fought back the stabbing pain and clung to the edge nevertheless. His fingernails dug into the joints between the flagstones as he fought to gain a purchase.

Lex struck the wall a moment later, but much lower than Sebastian—so low that her fingers were not able to reach the ledge. Gloves scraping along the rock, Lex slid down the wall, poised to fall at any moment.

With one hand, Sebastian reached out and caught Lex. It was a harsh jerk that stopped her fall. More pain exploded in his chest, but Sebastian refused to let go. Groaning, his fingers dug into Lex's sleeve and clamped tight. Lex twisted and dangled precariously over the dark abyss.

Hanging there, neither human noticed Scar approach from the opposite side of the chasm. It squatted on its haunches, observing their struggles. Activating its thermal vision, the Predator focused on the woman's back. Inside of the backpack the plasma gun Lex carried was clearly visible.

Gasping from his Herculean efforts, Sebastian managed to throw one leg over the ledge. He then endeavored to pull both himself and Lex to safety. As sweat poured down his face and burned his eyes, he heard a scrabbling sound—like a hard-shelled crab crossing a rocky beach. He turned to see an Alien face hugger, its barbed appendages clinging to the sheer side of the ledge, closer to Lex than to him.

Sebastian shouted out a warning.

Another face hugger scuttled out from an opening in the rock wall, its tail lashing, slapping at Sebastian's arm.

"Hang on!" he cried, trying to keep away from the hugger while dragging Lex to safety at the same time.

Looking down at her, Sebastian noticed movement in the shadows. Behind Lex, yet another face hugger was scaling the wall, its tail reaching out to fondle the tip of her boot.

Sebastian lashed out with his fist to smash the spidery horror tittering near his head. Knocked from its perch, the face hugger emitted a shrill shriek as it plunged helplessly into the abyss.

Only two face-hugging monsters remained. One scrabbled up the wall, its tail slapping Sebastian's cheek as it passed. He nearly slipped from the ledge, but he caught himself just in time. Sebastian's jerky movement came close to dislodging Lex as well.

The face hugger hissed at Sebastian, and suddenly a long, serpentlike appendage reached out of the creature's belly and probed for an opening in Sebastian's face. He raised his arm and slammed his elbow down on it.

Stunned, the face hugger plunged over the edge and into the pit.

Sebastian rolled onto the ledge, arms aching. He looked over to see the hugger scaling the wall parallel to Lex. Before he could warn her, Lex kicked the obscenity with all her might. Legs flailing helplessly, the creature tumbled end over end into the chasm.

"Hang on!" Sebastian cried, still clutching Lex's hand.

As he pulled her toward the edge, Sebastian looked into her upturned face. Her eyes went wide as a shadow loomed over his shoulder.

"What?" he asked, turning.

Sebastian choked. With a look of stunned surprise, his arms flung back and he was ripped away from the ledge. Lex heard struggling, then a crash. She peered over the edge in time to see Sebastian yanked off his feet by a black, bestial figure. With a whipping sound its segmented tail lashed around Sebastian's leg. Whether he was unconscious or dead was unclear, but the man was as limp as a rag doll when the Alien dragged him into a shadowy corridor. A moment later they were both gone.

As Lex clung to the ledge, something rolled past her shoulder—Sebastian's vintage Pepsi cap. It tumbled end over end as it fell into the chasm.

Finally, Lex began to climb, hand over hand, until she reached the lip of the ledge. Pulling herself up onto it she looked around, finding the area around the shattered bridge and the corridor beyond it deserted. There was virtually no sign of Sebastian De Rosa.

Turning her back on the abyss, Lex moved into another corridor. As the beam of her flashlight dimmed, she realized that the battery was dying. Before it faded completely, however, she checked her compass to orient herself—only to discover that it had been shattered in the fall.

Lex cursed.

For the first time since she'd entered the pyramid, Lex felt despair. With no light, no compass, no companionship, and only deadly Aliens and savage, invisible Predators lurking about, she knew it was unlikely she would ever get out of this place alive.

Shadows loomed everywhere. Black doorways yawned forbiddingly. Corridors forked and twisted into more tunnels. Lex was hopelessly, irrevocably lost. Increasing her pace, she rounded a corner and ran into a dead end.

"Damn it."

She turned to retrace her path—and stopped in her tracks when the massive silhouette of a Predator rose to block her.

"The enemy of my enemy is my friend. . . . The enemy of my enemy is my friend." Lex whispered Sebastian's words like a mantra.

The Predator held a short metal tube in its hand, which he raised. Suddenly twin shafts telescoped out of either end to form a deadly spear. The creature puffed out its barrel chest, and when it did, a deep, undulating, clicking sound emerged from its bull-like throat.

Then the Predator swung its spear, gripped it with both hands and plunged it into the stone floor. The meaning was clear—it was time to fight.

Go ahead, make my day, Lex thought with a bravado she didn't feel.

Motionless now, the Predator cocked its head. Its eyes glowed faintly in the oppressive gloom. Lex felt a strange electric warmth tingling her chest, her arms, her spine. She got the distinct impression that the creature had used some device to scan her.

Having determined his mark, the warrior raised the spear again, aimed its barbed tip at Lex's heart, then froze, still poised to strike.

As if hypnotized by the grim tableau of her own doom, Lex stood erect and defiant, waiting for the fatal stab.

Slowly, without taking her eyes off the creature, she pulled off the pack that held the Predator's gun and presented it. When he refused to take it, she set the pack on the floor and slid it toward him.

An endless moment passed. Then the Predator lowered its spear and scooped up the pack—just as the elongated head of an Alien warrior emerged from the shadows behind it.

Lex opened her mouth to cry a warning, but, sensing danger, the Predator whirled to strike before she could even utter a sound.

Swinging furiously, the Alien struck the spear from Scar's fist. A second blow sent the Predator reeling to the ground. Even before the warrior's back hit the cold stone, the snarling Alien was on him. Its tail lashed from side to side, its bony segments struck sparks on the walls and its claws shredded Scar's armor.

The Predator tried vainly to dislodge the monster, but the Alien dug in harder, ripping gouts of flesh out from beneath the armor. Scar howled and jabbed. The Alien pulled back its head, opening its jaws to spray hot spittle on the Predator's mask.

Scar's fingers tore at the Alien's hide until acid blood seeped from a dozen wounds. The Alien then leaned closer to Scar's face. Its jaws opened as wide as a snake swallowing its prey. Its interior mouth moved forward, slathering over Scar's flesh, its teeth gnashing grotesquely.

The Predator showed signs of weakness. Its struggles became less violent, and it seemed to Lex that the creature was as close to accepting its death as she had been just a few second before. Finally, Scar lay still, its sightless eye slits staring impassively at the fate looming above it.

The Alien hissed triumphantly, then tucked its head down to deliver the killing bite to Scar's exposed throat.

Only then did the Predator strike. Using the Alien's weight against it, Scar rolled backwards, throwing the Alien over its head in what looked to Lex like a kind of judo move. To her horror, the Alien had been tossed in her direction. Reaching down, she snatched the Predator's spear from the ground and raised it with both hands.

The Alien bounced off the narrow walls of the tunnel and righted itself. But this time it was facing new prey—Lex.

Scar roared and turned to face its opponent just as a second Alien leaped out of the shadows—the alpha-Alien.

The large Alien, its body burned by a Predator net, threw itself at Scar with all its might. The Predator

pressed its back to the wall and drew a throwing disk.
The device unfolded with an electric hum, revealing
ten-inch blades that projected from its edges.

But Scar never had a chance to use it.

Unleashing an unearthly screech, the alpha-Alien
struck the Predator full on the chest, bringing him
down. Locked in a deadly tango, Scar and the Alien
rolled end over end as the Predator used its own claws
to pound the monster's black, ravaged hide.

Taking its cue from the alpha-Alien, the smaller
creature facing Lex also charged, jaws snapping, teeth
gnashing. The monster leaped in a high arc, intending
to come down with its full weight on the frail human.

But that maneuver proved to be the Alien's undoing.
With calculated calm, Lex stepped back and propped
the Predator spear against the hard stone floor. When
the Alien completed its jump, it landed on the tip of the
sharp spear, impaling itself.

With a dying shriek that shook dust off the walls, the
Alien thrashed and bucked on the end of the shaft. Lex
struggled to hold the spear steady, keeping the monster
twisting on it at bay. Acid blood splashed the walls and
coursed down the shaft, melting the metal. Still the
screaming horror dangling on her spear refused to die.
Risking chemical burns that would easily dissolve the
flesh of her hands to the bone, Lex tilted the spear upward so that the Alien's own struggles, its own weight
would drive the spear deeper into its black body.

Meanwhile, Scar and the alpha-Alien were still
locked in deadly combat. The Predator had rolled out
from under its foe and had recovered its disk. Again
and again, the Predator drove the long, gleaming

blades into the monster's thick hide. The Alien yowled and raked the Predator, even as great rivulets of burning acid flowed from multiple wounds, pitting Scar's shattered armor and scorching his pale gray flesh.

Lex risked a quick glance at the Predator before Alien jaws snapped at her face. The monstrosity she'd impaled refused to die, and as it slid lower on the shaft, it tried to bite her. Lex shook the spear, spraying sizzling drops of acid all over the walls and floor. The Alien screamed again, and so did Lex as the first drop of acid touched the end of her glove.

Recoiling, Lex released the spear and the Alien with it. Both struck the wall, where the monster twitched once, then stilled. Lex gave the Alien a swift kick to the head, then a second—and for good measure a third, just to make sure it was dead. The Alien's jaws gaped open, flecked with foam. Its internal mouth hung limply in its skull. Blood no longer flowed from its wounds.

"The bastard's dead."

Now Lex knew that these things were mortal. She had actually killed one—and it felt *good*.

Suddenly, the floor trembled under her boots as the pyramid shifted again. For a moment, nothing else happened. Then the "dead end" wall rumbled as it slid up to the ceiling, to reveal another chamber beyond.

Lex saw movement and threw herself against the wall. Still grappling, Scar and the Alien rolled past her.

Pinning the Alien to the ground, Scar raised the disk for a decapitating blow. But before the blades reached its throat, the monster slithered out of Scar's grasp, and the blades splintered on the stone floor. Grabbing one of the long, cylindrical horns that projected out of the Alien's spine, the Predator climbed onto its back and slashed at its gleaming skull with the broken knives.

The Alien tried to dislodge him, and both tumbled end over end, through the door into the new chamber.

Lex could see that there was more light in the next room, but she hesitated. If she went the other way, she could slip away from the Predator and maybe get out of there alive.

Then Lex laughed.

Fat chance of that. If Scar didn't get her, the Aliens would.

But there was more reason to stay. Perhaps it was her curiosity, or perhaps it was something more primal—a kind of base admiration—but Lex had just watched the most dedicated hunter in the universe take on nature's most perfect killing machine.

A part of her simply wanted to see who won.

Limping, she approached the door. All along the floor there were patches of sickly green blood and smoldering holes in the stone where the Alien had shed what passed for blood. Lex followed the grisly trail to the doorway.

In the dim light, she saw a long corridor lined with columns. The walls and pillars were elaborately etched with complex hieroglyphics. The battle still raged, with the combatants wrestling in the center of the passageway. It appeared as if the Predator was weakening—and this time Lex sensed it was not a feint. Though he still wielded the shattered throwing disk, his blows were less powerful, and none were mortal. It was only a matter of time before Scar would be dead and Lex would be alone with the thing that had killed him.

But Lex was in for a surprise.

With a howl of defiance, the Predator hurled the Alien aside in a final show of strength. The Alien slammed against a set of pillars and dislodged several huge stones from the ceiling. They came down in a cloud of dust and debris.

Scar staggered back to avoid being crushed—and blundered into Lex.

They shared a startled look, and before Scar raised the disk in his hand, they heard the angry hiss.

Together they turned to see more Aliens—four of them—scrabbling across the floor and along the ceiling. One, who was tossing masonry stones aside, lowered its head and seethed at them. Lex realized the purpose of the troops were to free the alpha-Alien, who had become trapped by the avalanche of debris.

Meanwhile the Predator attached the plasma gun Lex had brought him to its shoulder mount. With a flurry of energy that blinded Lex, Scar drove the Aliens back with blast after blast from that powerful weapon.

When they were fully out of sight, the Predator lowered the smoking disk and dropped it onto the floor. Then he deactivated the weapon on his shoulder and looked at Lex, who stood hypnotized by the sight of the retreating Aliens flowing over rock and along the walls and ceiling.

Without a sound, the Predator turned its back on Lex and stalked away.

"Hey! Hey!" Lex yelled. "I'm coming with you."

She ran up to the creature and grabbed his arm. The Predator turned sharply, nearly knocking her off her feet.

"You hear me, you ugly son of a bitch," Lex cried. "I'm coming with you."

The Predator stared at Lex.

For a long moment, nothing happened. Then Lex simply opened her hands. The Predator stared at the human, arms outstretched. Then, with a grunt, Scar reached into its armor, drew out a knife and placed it into her hand.

CHAPTER 27

In the Labyrinth

No sooner had Scar handed Lex the weapon than the Alien horde swarmed out of the dark in a second attack. Hissing angrily, scrabbling over broken masonry, and running along the walls and ceiling like giant insects, they advanced on Lex and Scar.

Lex backed out of the chamber, into the passageway where she'd killed her first Alien. Its carcass was still there, the melted spear sticking out of its guts.

Lex looked up at the Predator. "A short partnership, but a sweet one."

If Scar heard her, he did not respond. Instead the Predator's long-fingered hands traced the elaborate hieroglyphs running along the side of the doorway.

Lex watched as he tapped several symbols in quick succession, obviously entering a sophisticated code. Each character Scar touched began to glow with an inner light, just like the buttons on an elevator or the features on the star map in the sarcophagus chamber.

Lex glanced up from the ancient keypad to see the Aliens hurling toward them, hopping over one another as they approached. The alpha-Alien, now freed from the rocks that had buried him, was in the lead. Its hide was ripped and pierced and seeping battery acid blood. Out of all of them, he looked the most pissed.

"If you've got a plan, you better damn hurry," Lex said, taking a step back.

The Predator seemed to understand her meaning, if not her words, and redoubled his efforts until practically the entire wall was illuminated.

"Very pretty. But what does it do?"

Then she heard a now-all-too-familiar rumbling within the walls. The Predator took a step back, pulling her along. With a deafening crash, a huge stone slab plunged out of the ceiling and slammed down in front of the Aliens, just as the alpha's raking claws were about to close around Scar's throat.

Lex blinked, amazed to be alive.

There was a loud crash on the other side of the slab as the Aliens slammed into it and beat the stone with their claws. Although they couldn't penetrate the walls themselves, their demonic cries of rage and frustration did.

Lex listened to their shrieks and shuddered. Fearing the dark, she drew her fading flashlight and played the feeble beam around the passageway. Her heart sunk when she realized the corridor was a dead end. Lex was trapped. Her only companion was a savage hunter from the stars, and the only way out appeared to be through an angry Alien horde.

"Great idea you had locking us in here."

Scar grunted.

Unceremoniously, the Predator began stripping off his pitted body armor, some of it still smoking from the Alien's corrosive blood. As each heavy piece clanked to the ground, more of Scar's strange, reptilian anatomy was revealed.

"Whoa, slow down, tiger," said Lex.

Of course she didn't expect Scar to get the joke. Like most of the males she'd known, Scar had a mind of his own, and a temper, too. He was definitely the strong, silent type.

Lex ignited a flare—startling the Predator, who snarled at her angrily.

"It's just light. Light," she said, placing it on the floor.

Scar made that same clicking sound in his throat that Lex had heard these creatures utter before. It reminded her of a frog's chirp. Meanwhile the Predator continued to tear off segments of armor plate.

Lex dropped her backpack and squatted in the corner, as far away from the dead Alien as these narrow confines would permit. In the wavering light, she observed Scar's behavior and tried to deduce the creature's origins.

The Predator's hide was reptilian, but not scaled. At least not scaled the way terrestrial reptiles were. But it was still possible that Scar's epidermis had tiny, near microscopic scales on it. If only she could get close enough to see. Of course, she had no intention of trying. His flesh tone was a pallid gray with a green tinge, though in the flickering light of the bright yellow flare colors could not be easily discerned.

The humanoid's eyes were close together and set forward in its skull. They were the eyes of a hunter. Terrestrial prey—small birds, rodents, deer, oxen— possessed eyes on the sides of their skulls. Earthbound predators—felines, owls, and humans—all had forward-looking eyes that enhanced depth perception and hand-eye coordination.

Scar's eyes were set deep in its massive skull, with a bony forehead to protect them, an evolutionary feature that most reminded Lex of dinosaur anatomy.

The "dreadlocks" that framed either side of Scar's face were puzzling. He never removed them, yet the dangling appendages didn't appear to be natural, either—they had metal tips, for one thing. Perhaps they were some sort of biomechanical aid, a fusion of flesh and technology. Or perhaps they were just what they appeared to be—the Predators' version of hair.

The crablike mandibles around the Predator's mouth were an evolutionary riddle as well. They resembled a feature on an aquatic animal more than the feature of an animal that walked on land. Was Scar an amphibian? If he was, that still wouldn't explain the mandibles. Insects chewed with mandibles, but Scar had teeth for that. Some insects—or was it arachnids?—also used their mandibles as sensory organs, but that didn't make sense to Lex either.

Were they an atavistic trait that had outlived its biological usefulness, like the human appendix? Or perhaps the mandibles were necessary for reproduction or mating rituals—an unsettling thought, but from her knowledge of biology, Lex knew that violence during copulation was not uncommon among Earthbound species.

The Predator's hands certainly resembled reptilian appendages—long, slender fingers, partially webbed, with two central digits that were much longer than the

others. But there were differences, too. Reptiles had
nostrils, though they lacked noses, and many species
of reptiles had olfactory organs in their tongues. Scar
had a flat, hard ridge where a nose should be, with no
breathing slits that she could discern, and she wasn't
sure the Predator even *had* a tongue. Predators also
lacked tails. And despite their formidable skills as warriors, Lex doubted they were capable of regenerating
lost limbs or digits, like a salamander.

Lex noted that Scar wore a kind of mesh underwear
under his plated armor and that the Predator was careful to discard as little of that material as possible,
though Scar did detach a damaged bit of it, discarding
it within Lex's reach. When he was otherwise occupied, Lex casually lifted the mesh and fingered it. It
was made of some kind of flexible metal and was quite
hot to the touch. Even more peculiar was the fact that
the material remained hot long after it was separated
from its power source and, presumably, from Scar's
body heat—if indeed he had any. All this led Lex to
the conclusion that the mesh was some sort of heating
source and was probably as vital a piece of equipment
to Scar as an Aqua-Lung is to a human deep-sea diver.

If the Predator's species had evolved from some
type of extraterrestrial reptile, then they were most
probably ectothermic—meaning their body temperature was regulated by external climactic conditions.

Mammals generated their own body heat, but reptiles depended on external temperatures for thermoreg-
ulation and maintaining a balanced metabolism, which
was why most reptiles thrived in hot climates and es-
chewed places like the polar regions. In fact, weird

things happened to some species of reptile if exposed to a cold environment: They became sluggish and less aggressive, and females sometimes gave birth to live young instead of laying eggs in a nest and hatching them externally.

Reptiles could also die in cold that was too intense or sustained, and Lex noticed several patches of rough, cracked hide on Scar's hands that resembled the chilblains that appeared on humans in icy weather. While Lex was no expert in the fields of extraterrestrial biology or herpetology, it didn't look as if Scar was holding up well in the brutal climate of Antarctica.

Soon Lex began to wonder about her own health.

For one thing, she knew she had the "Martian Effect" to contend with—a phrase coined by a Carnegie Mellon University professor of extraterrestrial biology in homage to H. G. Wells's novel *The War of the Worlds*. Both the Predators and the Aliens could potentially carry dangerous toxins or exotic strains of virus or bacteria to which they were long immune but humans were not. Ancient structures like this pyramid could also hold peril—a long dormant strain of bacteria found in King Tut's tomb decimated the archaeologists who discovered the place and gave rise to the legend of the mummy's curse. And even close contact with earthly reptiles carried some degree of danger—there were species of toads and lizards that secreted toxins capable of paralyzing or killing, and many reptiles carried the salmonella virus on their skin.

Of course, Lex realized that if she lived long enough to actually *catch* salmonella poisoning, she would feel truly blessed.

And creatures like Scar were far from safe to be around even if she had made peace with him. Predators lived for the kill. The ritualistic slaughter of another being, sentient or not, was an intrinsic part of their cultural makeup. By all indications the Predators' civilization was built on cruelty, with the ceremonial hunt as the central tenet of their religion—important enough, in fact, for them to coolly and cynically manipulate a primitive culture, get themselves elected to godhood, and then compel generations of humans to build their pyramids and populate them with "game" hatched out of their own chests.

It was viciousness on a near-genocidal scale, and Lex was suddenly filled with rage toward Scar and his ilk for how they'd manipulated her primitive ancestors, and for what they'd done to Sebastian, to Max Stafford and Charles Weyland—and probably Miller, too.

Lex noticed that Scar had turned his back on her and was busy with a new project. He drew the ceremonial dagger—the one she'd watched him wield as he'd bloodied himself and gathered his first trophy. Now Scar dragged the Alien carcass to a corner of the chamber and yanked out the spear. Scar showed Lex the melted tip of the spear, then cast it aside. Using one arm, he splayed the dead creature out on its belly on the stone floor. With a grunt of effort, he plunged the blade into the small of the Alien's back and pried open the armored shell at the torso until the entire chitin shell split like a cooked lobster.

Black bile, steaming in the frigid air, and slimy green ooze gushed onto the flagstones and immediately began pitting the rock. A vile stench filled the small chamber. Lex retched and covered her nose and mouth with the edge of her scarf. Careful to avoid the gore sizzling on the floor, Scar stepped around the carcass, lifted the Alien's elongated head, and severed the exoskeleton and internal veins and tendons with a sickening crunch. The legs and hips fell away, and more guts spilled out.

Working with speed and precision, Scar stood the head and torso up and sliced the edge of the rubbery, translucent flap that covered the Alien's head. Peeling the thick membrane back, the Predator exposed the Alien's brain, which was—amazingly—still throbbing with life. Finally, the Predator lifted the armored external skull away from the Alien body and placed it aside. The bony shell was completely hollow. The elongated brain remained connected to the torso and still twitched and pulsed.

Both intrigued and repulsed, Lex moved closer, carefully avoiding the acid blood that stained the cell floor. As she watched, Scar removed one arm and began stripping away the muscles from the Alien's shell. While he let the gore slide to the floor, he set the bony armor down next to the hollow skull.

"What are you doing?" Lex repeated.

Once again Scar stood the gory torso up and began to probe the creature's brain with his knife. Even without its skull and its missing left arm, the Alien looked menacing.

Lex watched the brain flop about and wondered, *How do you really know when one of these things is really dead?*

At that instant the Alien's right arm shot out and

raked the air just inches from her face. Lex literally jumped backwards with a yelp.

But the Alien made no further movement, and Scar sat passively behind it, prodding and picking at a lobe of its brain. The Predator looked up at Lex, then plunged the knife into a cluster of nerves. The Alien hand lashed out again. She realized that Scar had frightened her deliberately—and now Lex could swear that the Predator was laughing.

"Ha, ha, very funny."

So Predators do have a sense of humor. Gallows humor, sure, but any kind of humor is better than none at all.

Fun time over, Scar went back to work, stripping away the organs and muscles and keeping only the shell, which he stacked in a pile near the empty Alien skull.

"What are you doing?" Lex asked again. This time she laid her hand on Scar's arm, firmly enough to get his attention.

With an impatient snarl, the Predator threw down the half-mangled arm he'd been working on and held up his knife, as if displaying it. Lex leaned closer and examined the blade. Only then did she realize that it was not forged of metal but carved from some bony substance like ivory, and honed to a sharp edge.

"Okay," Lex said. "It's a special blade. . . . So what?"

Very deliberately, Scar dipped the tip of the sacrificial blade into the Alien's seeping brain pan and covered it with the acid blood. Then he shook the blade over a segment of battered Predator armor. As soon as the drops splashed the surface, the acid went to work, melting the armor.

Then the Predator shook more acid blood off the blade—and onto a segmented piece of the Alien's shell. Nothing happened; the acid just rolled off.

The Predator gave her a look that clearly meant, Get it?

"Of course!" Lex cried. "The Aliens are immune to their own bodily defenses. A porcupine can't stab itself."

And obviously the sacrificial blade the Predator carried was made of the same substance—Alien exoskeleton, carved and shaped and honed to a razor-sharp edge, like the whalebone blades nineteenth-century whalers used to fashion out of the bones of their prey.

Lex nodded vigorously. "I get it, I get it. We'll keep it together and make it to the surface."

Scar reached out and touched her arm, then lifted his hand and touched the mark on his mask.

"Keep it together . . . Make it to the surface . . ." Lex was startled to hear the Predator speak to her using an electronic recording of her own words.

Lex smiled, then he slapped the top of his giant fist with the palm of her tiny hand. "Deal," she said.

Suddenly, an unearthly cry unlike any other they'd heard before literally shook the walls. The cry was more than loud enough to penetrate their chamber, so surely it could be heard all over the pyramid.

Lex and Scar exchanged anxious glances, then Scar snatched a chunk of Alien armor from the pile and slapped it against Lex's chest hard enough to knock the wind out of her. Holding it in place, Scar sized the piece, then tossed it aside in favor of a smaller segment.

Lex understood his plan immediately, and to show

him she got it Lex lifted a heavy piece of armor and placed it on *his* forearm.

The Predator tensed at her touch but allowed Lex to fit the piece of chitin to its arm without protest. As Scar picked through the Alien shells for other usable components, Lex drew her survival knife and started cutting the straps off her ruined backpack.

As they worked side by side for the common purpose of mutual survival, Lex and Scar—human and Predator—began to function like a team.

In the Queen's Chamber

For endless hours, the Alien Queen, powerless to act due to the wicked barbed chains that held her captive, had been compelled to watch helplessly as one after the other of her precious eggs were tipped into the roaring furnace. Only a few of the eggs had been given a chance to yield life, and they had all been spirited away to another part of the pyramid where she could no longer watch over them.

Even now the Queen sensed that some of her offspring were alive and well.

Foam flecked the Queen's long, eyeless muzzle, and her abdomen convulsed as another pulpy egg dropped onto the slide and was automatically carried away by the vast machines that pumped and churned behind the walls.

The female thrashed and bared her teeth in rage when her egg failed robotic inspection and was consigned to the furnace. But before the conveyor reached the fiery chamber, the skin of the egg peeled back, and a pale white face hugger emerged, eager to escape its leathery cocoon. But the machine was pitching the rejected egg into the fire. Extending a robotic arm, it shoved the struggling infant into the conflagration, along with its leathery pouch.

Mewing piteously, the newborn face hugger was instantly consumed.

Witnessing this atrocity, the Queen went berserk. She thrashed and strained at the metal chains, testing their tensile strength to the limit. Even though chunks of masonry and the dust of millennia had been dislodged from the walls and vaulted ceiling by her furious convulsions, the indestructible chains would not give.

Tilting its crested head back as far as the restraints allowed, the Queen opened its slavering mouth and unleashed an awesome, ear-shattering shriek of rage, frustration and utter despair, which reverberated throughout the pyramid.

In the Labyrinth

The alpha-Alien with the net-ravaged hide was pounding its fists against the stone door in a futile effort to reach Scar and Lex when it heard the keening distress call. Pausing, the Alien lifted its misshapen head to listen.

When the Queen's cry came again, the alpha-Alien hissed and bared its teeth, alert for danger. His entourage folded into the shadows, where they swayed like coiled pythons, watching and waiting for its lead.

Tail-stump thrashing, the alpha-Alien turned and hurled itself down the passageway in the direction of the Queen's chamber. The swarm followed, their ebony claws scouring the stone as they scurried into the gloom.

Meanwhile, on the other side of the slab, Scar continued to sheathe Lex in a crudely fashioned battle suit. Using the rib cage of the dead Alien, the Predator created a chest plate, holding it in place with the Velcro straps from Lex's backpack.

Scar had retained his own face mask and the metal powerpack he wore on his broad back. He also kept his shoulder armor with gun mount. These seemed to be the most vital components of his original battle armor, the ones that contained his life-support and internal power systems, and the sensory equipment the Predator relied upon to hunt down its prey. The mesh heat-netting was in place under the Predator's makeshift suit, and Scar also gripped his long, barbed spear in one fist. The other fist was encased in armor, studded with the shattered blades from the Predator's ruined throwing disk.

Lex was smaller, lighter and far less powerful than the Predator, and as necessary as it was to wear this hastily assembled protection, she groaned under the weight of it. Her chest was covered in a segment of Alien plate that had formerly sheathed the creature's thigh. On her extremities Lex had strapped pieces of Alien forearm and shin armor, and she kept them in place with waterproof adhesive tape from her first-aid kit.

Scar had fashioned a large, curved shield out of the Alien's skull for her to carry, and Lex had made a helmet from bits and pieces of chitin held together with rope and Velcro, along with shoulder pads formed from hollowed-out Alien ribs.

In her gloved hand Lex gripped a long, wickedly sharp slashing club made from the piercing barbs of the Alien's segmented tail. She'd also arranged the pitons in her utility belt so that she could pull them out and stab or slash with them in a single easy, quick motion. Next to them, she kept her few remaining flares and her survival knife, unbuttoned and ready for instant use.

Finally, Lex and Scar were ready. They stood side by side, weapons poised, as the Predator's long fingers danced on the ancient keypad. With a grating rumble, the stone slab rose again into the ceiling as the newly attired warriors leaped into the passageway, weapons poised and ready for the savage Alien attack. But to their astonishment, it never came. The corridor was empty, the Aliens gone.

CHAPTER 28

In the Sacrificial Chamber

Feet pounding on the stone floor, the Predator raced through a dark passageway lined with pillars. Lex struggled to keep up. Though a phenomenal athlete in her own right, she was incapable of matching the brutal pace set by Scar. His massive strides more than doubled her own footsteps. Lex was sweating under her winter jumpsuit and heavy Alien armor, and she was also taking in great gulps of frigid air.

Thirty paces ahead, Scar paused at an intersection, as if uncertain which direction to take. Suddenly he bolted to the right.

"No! No! That way," she pointed. "Go left."

The Predator whirled around and spied one of the strobe lights, still flashing where Lex had left it hours before. Lex caught up with him and recognized the area—it was the corridor that led up to the sacrificial chamber where they'd left Thomas, Adele Rousseau, and several archaeologists.

"It's this way up!" she cried, gesturing as she hurried forward.

For a moment it looked as if Scar wasn't going to follow her. Then he took off, running past Lex, leading once more.

"Slow down a little," Lex huffed. "Let me catch up."

To her surprise, he did. After that, Scar paced himself to match her stride, and they ran side by side. It seemed the Predator was beginning to regard her as an equal. Lex didn't know whether she should be flattered or appalled.

Ahead of them a black doorway yawned, two strobes blinking on either side of it.

"The sacrificial chamber," Lex cried.

They slowed and cautiously entered the circular chamber. On the floor, Lex spied a blood-splattered handgun—Adele Rousseau's Desert Eagle. Lex scooped the weapon up and checked the magazine. One bullet left.

From somewhere inside the chamber, Lex heard a faint, ghostly echo. Scar heard it, too. Lex strained to listen, and finally she could make out the sound of a human voice calling her name.

"Lex . . ."

"Sebastian!"

Eyes darting, Lex peered beyond the slabs and the mummies. In an antechamber, she saw a cluster of ghastly statues mounted on the wall—statues she did not remember seeing the last time she was in this room.

The voice called again.

"Lex . . . Help me . . ."

She looped her club to her belt and pulled a spear fashioned from the tip of an Alien's tail off her back.

Then she slowly approached the stone sculptures, her weapon raised and ready. As her eyes strained in the half light, Lex could make out some of the repugnant details of a horrific, terra-cotta mural. It appeared to be the three-dimensional image of a mythical beast with a hard shell for a body and a tiny, humanlike head.

"Lex . . . Please . . ."

Only when the voice called again did the truth become clear. This wasn't a mural. This grotesque tableau was actually alive. The mythical beast was really a human being—Sebastian De Rosa.

The archaeologist was encased in a monstrous Alien cocoon, his arms, legs and feet completely enmeshed in a near-impenetrable shell. On the stone floor lay a deflated egg sack and the translucent shell of a spent face hugger, belly up, its legs stiff with rigor mortis and pointed at the ceiling.

"Oh, God . . . Sebastian . . ."

The man tried to smile, but the effort died on his lips. When he spoke, the words did not come easily. Each breath was labored. He retched, and red foam flecked his pallid cheek.

"Lex . . . I . . ."

"Hold on, I'll get you out of there."

Lex tore at the cocoon with her hands, but it was futile. The surface was as hard as marble. Lex drew a piton and hacked at the enveloping shell, gouging out a few splinters before the steel spike blunted and bent in her hand.

"No!" Sebastian gasped. "It's too late. You have to stop these things."

Sebastian convulsed. The tendons in his neck bulged

as his head jerked from side to side. His mouth gaped open, and blood flowed from his nose.

"Lex . . . They can't reach the surface . . ." he moaned, struggling.

The Predator appeared behind Lex. Gazing impassively at the dying man, he rested his huge hand on Lex's shoulder. She shrugged it off and lunged at the cocoon, beating it with her fists.

"Don't worry, Sebastian. I'm getting you out of there!"

Scar gripped her shoulder again, far less gently now. The Predator dragged her back, away from the cocoon, as she struggled against him.

"Get off me," Lex cried, eyes wet. "I have to help him."

The emotion she'd buried in order to survive overwhelmed her now. She'd watched Max Stafford and Charles Weyland die, and she was not about to give up on Sebastian. Not without a fight.

But still Scar pulled her away.

"Let me go," she screamed.

"Make it to the surface . . ." The Predator's modulated voice replayed Lex's own words to her again.

"I said get off me!"

"Kill me!" Sebastian cried out with the last of his strength. "Do it."

He convulsed again. The pale, naked flesh under his heart began to stretch and bulge. Crimson rents appeared as his skin split open and blood gushed everywhere. Then the man threw his gaze heavenward and cried out in agony.

"I'm sorry," Lex murmured.

She raised the handgun and fired at Sebastian's head. His tormented screams came to an abrupt end.

Lex dropped her head. The Predator stood next to her, watching the dead man, waiting . . .

Suddenly a creature clawed its way out of the dead man's abdomen and launched itself at Scar. With lightning-fast reflexes, the Predator caught it in his hand. He held it firmly in its grip and turned it from side to side, examining it. The tiny creature squirmed to free itself, its jaws snapping at Scar's face.

Casually the Predator snapped its neck between his fingers as if it were a matchstick.

In the Queen's Chamber

The Aliens came from every corner of the pyramid, singly, in pairs, and in clusters large and small. Like a rippling tide of black oil, the swarm flowed down sheer walls and deep shafts, and made their way through drainage tunnels and narrow air spaces between the thick walls. Tittering and hissing, they instinctively responded to the maternal cries of their Queen.

In a great living tsunami the creatures surged into the Queen's chamber, hastening to the edge of the misty, frozen pool. Others crawled down the stone walls or scampered down the long, barbed chains that held their Queen captive.

The largest group of Aliens was led by the alpha-Alien with the net-ravaged hide. They poured in, filling the chamber, hissing and squabbling. Then all movement ceased as the brutes bowed their eyeless heads to their matriarch. For a long time the Aliens remained still, quiet, respectful—a jet-black sea of shining, chitinous hides and slavering jaws, their cylindrical heads bowed and swaying from side to side in supplication.

The Queen rattled her chains and cried out in a sustained, sibilant hiss that inflamed her spawn and spurred them into action.

In a flurry of gnashing teeth and ripping jaws, the creatures attacked their matriarch. Leaping from the edge of the frozen pool, most caught hold of the great harnessing machine that rendered the hive mistress immobile during her reproductive labor—though a few plunged screeching to their death through the rising mist into the vapor pool.

Crawling over one another in a maniacal press to rip their mother's flesh, the monsters moved as a single, sweeping entity, descending the walls and clinging to the chains, while others swooped down from the high ceiling like raptors.

The things caught hold of the Alien Queen in a thousand places and tore at her hide incessantly with tooth and claw. When the tittering mass reached the Queen's head, slobbering jaws gnawed at her great horned crown, cracking the bony crest and tearing the barbed hooks loose from their moorings. Fountains of acid blood flowed in rivulets down the Queen's ravaged frame, splattering her offspring and inflaming them to further savagery.

At last the final hook was torn from her crest in a shower of splintered bone. Although the Queen's head was free and her jaws were more than capable of destroying any of the gnawing, rending creatures within her reach, she still did not fight back. Instead she hung there—manacled arms outstretched, head erect—as if inviting her children to feast on her flesh and drink her blood in a blasphemous orgy of matricide.

The Queen bled from a score of wounds, her boiling blood splattering everywhere. Suddenly there was a shower of sparks as the big machine that held her lower extremities began to melt. Ravaged by the Queen's acid blood, chain metal began to twist, wires snapped and cables buckled.

Triumphantly, the Queen yanked the chain restraining her right arm, casting several of her children into the frozen mist. Fearing for their own lives, the rest of her panicked offspring reversed their course, leaping onto the floor far below, hopping onto the walls, or dangling from the remaining chains like rats escaping a sinking ship.

When both arms were free, the Queen used her claws to shred the semi-molten machine that had enslaved her for so long. Freeing her gangly legs, she still struggled against the great clamp that imprisoned her tail and reproductive organs.

Tension rippled her massive form, jaws locked and teeth clenched as the Queen ripped her trembling tail free. Then, with a snap of cartilage and a flood of bubbling, caustic slime, the Hive Queen tore her own birth canal from her body.

Free at last, the Queen leaped from the shattered platform. Chains dangled from her limbs, clattering as she moved.

Quivering with both rage and triumph, she threw up

her ravaged arms and let loose a shriek that vowed vengeance and retaliatory pain. . . .

In the Sacrificial Chamber

The Alien Queen's bloodcurdling scream echoed through the pyramid.

"What was that?" Lex cried.

She turned to Scar and witnessed a first—a frightened Predator.

"It's *that* bad?"

Scar touched her arm, echoing her recorded words once more like a mantra. "Keep it together. . . . Make it to the surface."

But Lex shook her head. "We can't let these things get out of here."

Acting as if he understood her words, Scar removed a complicated and bulky device from his wrist. On its crystalline face, Alien characters glowed. Scar tapped several keys, and a cluster of symbols appeared. He thrust the device under Lex's nose and tilted his head—his "Get it?" pose.

"I don't understand."

The Predator pointed to the wrist computer. Then he held out a tight fist and turned it upside down. Watching Lex, the Predator slowly unfurled his fist.

"An explosion. That thing is a bomb?"

Then she recalled the mural in the hieroglyphics chamber, which depicted a Predator with its arms raised, then a mushroom cloud.

"It is a bomb!" Lex cried. *Like the one that went off on this island in 1979.*

Lex took the device from Scar's hand. It was heavy, and she could feel it vibrate as mechanisms turned within.

"Well," she said, "I hope it kills every fucking one of them."

Lex tossed the bomb through the stone grate, where it plunged deeper into the heart of the pyramid.

"Keep it together. Make it to the surface," Scar's computer-generated voice repeated.

They started to run.

The path to the entrance appeared to be clear, and Lex could see a dull glow in the distance—halogen lights still burning in the grotto outside the pyramid. But as they reached a wide staircase lined with square columns, another Predator stumbled out of the darkness and lunged at Lex.

Recoiling, she beat the creature with her fist, then kicked out with her booted foot.

Amazingly, the Predator staggered backwards under her weak assault. Lex noticed that the creature seemed injured—its face mask was gone, and its mandibles writhed convulsively. The fanged mouth was flecked with green foam.

Reeling, the stricken Predator stumbled back. Then its knees gave out and it folded to the floor. Head thrown back and twisting from side to side, slime spraying on the statues, walls, and flagstone floor, the Predator howled—and Lex saw its chest cavity begin to bulge.

The helpless creature gagged as the skin stretched

around its heart, then blossomed into a phosphorescent burst of green, gushing gore. Lex stumbled into a column and fell to the ground, watching in horrified fascination as the head of a newborn Alien poked out swathed in pus and ooze, its jaws snapping air, desperate to be free of the Predator's dying flesh.

Only then did Scar step forward and activate the plasma gun on his shoulder. For a split second Lex saw three scarlet dots illuminate the chattering jaws of the nascent obscenity, then Scar fired.

The searing plasma struck the fallen Predator, incinerating its carcass, along with the squirming horror that twitched inside of its gaping chest. Red fire and black smoke filled the chamber, and the awful, permeating stench of burned flesh choked Lex. Turning her back to the conflagration, she watched the flickering shadows play on the walls as both Aliens were completely consumed.

CHAPTER 29

In the labyrinth, hundreds of Aliens raced through the darkness, flowing over walls and rippling along the ground, hissing and tittering, aware that their prey was close—close enough to hear, to smell, and soon to taste.

Behind the ocean of black, blood-mad monsters loomed a massive shape that dwarfed the others—something huge and monstrous and very, very angry. The Alien Queen.

Standing over the smoldering corpse of his fellow Predator, Scar heard the Alien swarm. He paused in midstride to listen, head cocked in an almost human gesture.

After a moment, Lex heard them too. Though she could not see her pursuers, it was obvious that the monsters were gaining on them.

Scar took off, heading for the exit. Lex was on his heels. They emerged from the pyramid in a dead run and took the stairs two at a time. Through a red mist of exhaustion, Lex spied the bright white lights of the underground camp in the distance. It seemed to be deserted.

Sucking in frigid air, she risked a glance over her

shoulder; there was still no sign of the horde that had been chasing them.

In the Ice Grotto

When they finally reached the grotto, they found the expedition's equipment broken and scattered, as if by mad vandals.

It was then that Lex discovered the frozen corpse of the roughneck Quinn at the foot of the ice tunnel. By the look of him, he'd fought hard for his life. While Scar stood guard, Lex quickly searched the camp for others, but everyone was either gone or dead.

At the mouth of the shaft that led to the surface, the roughnecks had set up a winch-and-pulley system to lower supplies underground and haul samples back up. For Lex and the Predator, the device was the only way out of this hell. Looking around, Lex spied a large wooden packing crate. She tore the lid off. Except for a loaded piton gun, there was nothing inside. Lex threw the lid aside and hooked the crate to the pulley cable.

Next she checked the control panel for the winch and discovered that the machine was calibrated with a counterweight of four tons—meaning that a sled with four tons of weight would be hauled up the tunnel at five miles per hour when the switch was thrown. Lex doubted that she and Scar together weighed even half a ton, so with that amount of counterweight their trip to the surface would be quick.

She got Scar's attention and pointed to the sled.

"Get in!"

But as Scar turned to climb aboard, the alpha-Alien lunged at him from the shadows. The severed stump of its tail lashed out and slashed Scar's shoulder. The wound exploded in a shower of glowing green gore.

Lex grabbed the piton gun and turned—just as a second, smaller Alien loomed over her. Startled, she fell backwards, into the empty crate. As the Alien reached for her, Lex rolled over on her back and thrust the muzzle of the piton gun between the creature's snapping jaws.

"Consider yourself exterminated," she cried as she pulled the trigger.

The back of the Alien's head blew away and the creature fell limply to the ice. A few drops of Alien blood sizzled and burned the walls of the wooden crate.

Lex peeked over the edge in time to see Scar decapitate an Alien, only to be attacked by another. Again, it was the alpha-Alien with the grid-ravaged hide, his lightning-fast attack a blur of teeth, claws and a thrashing stump of a tail.

Unrelenting, the Predator slammed the blade of a throwing disk down on the alpha-Alien's head. The wound was deep, but not mortal. Acid gushed from the slash, spraying Scar and pitting his armor. Then the Alien stepped back, raised its claws, and charged again.

Alien and Predator came together with a great crash, and both went down. They rolled end over end, locked in a deadly embrace. Finally Scar kicked out with his mammoth feet, tossing the Alien against a wall of ice.

Lex seized the moment to pull Scar toward the empty crate. At the wall, the alpha-Alien staggered to its feet, segmented tail striking sparks from the ice.

With an angry hiss the Alien took off after Lex and the Predator.

Stubbornly, Scar decided to make a stand. With a roar he turned to face the black monstrosity.

But Lex only wanted to escape. She pushed the Predator backwards with all her might, and her weight carried them both into the empty crate. Reaching over the edge, her fingers closed on the control lever. She pushed it to the line that read Emergency Release.

With a slam, she was thrown backwards, her spine cracking against the edge of the crate. Scar landed at her side at the bottom of the box as it shot up the narrow ice tunnel like an express elevator out of hell.

Up they raced, the sides of the box scraping the ice until it smoked from friction. Lex prayed that the wood would hold together long enough to get them to the top.

As they neared the surface, she noticed flecks of snow around them and looked up. She saw the mouth of the tunnel looming in the distance, cloud-filled sky roiling over the pit, and the tripod platform constructed over the shaft blocking the path of their sled.

Lex managed to cry a warning. "Hold on!"

The box leaped from the tunnel, smashing into the winch rig with a massive impact that shattered it completely and sent the steel tripod supports tumbling down the shaft, clanging as they fell.

Scar was thrown clear. He hugged Lex in a protective hold as they landed in the snow, rolling end over end across the hard, glacial ice.

When the Predator released her at last, Lex tumbled

into a drift, where she lay motionless as wind stirred her tattered clothes and a gentle snow fell around her.

The Predator was up instantly, seemingly oblivious to the wound that still sprayed green gore in rivulets down his chest. He searched around him for danger. A low, cold mist wrapped Bouvetoya Whaling Station in an icy grip, and blankets of snow still fell, though the fury of the katabatic storm had finally blown itself out.

Anxiously, the Predator moved to the shaft and peered down. At first Scar saw nothing, though he heard unearthly, echoing cries rising from underground. Then he saw distorted shadows skimming the smooth walls.

Finally, the Predator spied the Alien Queen, leading her hell-spawn up the shaft to the world of humans. Her claws dug into the ice as her children clambered over her, crawling along every inch of the shaft like ants climbing out of a burning hill. On its mother's broad back rode the alpha-Alien, eyeless head upturned, teeth bared in a savage snarl. When it spotted Scar, it leaped off its mother's back to scale the shaft on its own.

Scar activated his shoulder gun, but the armor sparked and the red aiming lasers went dim. Roaring, he yanked open a panel and fumbled with the controls. After a moment's work, he aimed the plasma gun and fired again. This time a bolt arced into the shaft and an Alien exploded. The Queen hissed angrily as gore rained down on her.

As the weapon on Scar's shoulder began to spark again, the Predator stepped away from the shaft and shed the last of his battered equipment, including his now-useless plasma gun and what little remained of his pitted and broken armor. When he was done, only Scar's mask, a loincloth, boots and chest plate remained from his original gear. Even the mesh netting—rent with a dozen tears and robbed of its energy—was beginning to cool in the relentless Antarctic conditions. The frigid wind bit into the Predator, sapping his body heat and reducing his internal temperature to a dangerously low level.

With one last glance down the shaft, Scar retreated, to wait for the explosion that was mere moments away. . . .

Lex stirred, moaning. She felt the winds burn her naked cheek, and the sting of snow on her face. Then a strong hand grabbed the collar of her jumpsuit and hauled her to her feet as if she were a helpless kitten.

Awareness returned quickly, and Lex blinked up at a familiar face mask.

"Hold on," the Predator said in an electronic voice muffled by the wind.

Hoisting Lex off her feet, Scar ran away from the shaft, toward the abandoned whaling station. Boots crunching in the snow, the Predator carried Lex through the center of the compound. The buildings were all nearly buried by drifting powder. Lex looked backwards, over Scar's bleeding shoulder.

She saw the alpha-Alien emerge from the mouth of the tunnel. The creature hissed when it saw them. Then a bright green flash of light nearly blinded her. She quickly averted her eyes. A hot jet of burning energy surged up the tunnel, scorching all the Aliens in its wake. When the plasma washed over the alpha-Alien, it didn't even have time to scream before it was blown to bits.

As the force of the blast rolled over them, Scar redoubled his pace. But almost immediately, a massive aftershock threw human and Predator to the ground. The force tossed Lex free of the Predator's grip. Staggering to her feet, she saw Scar down on one knee, his shoulder gushing green more intensely now. Then a third shuddering shock wave sent them both reeling to the ice again.

When the blast vaporized everything in the underground cavern, millions of tons of ice were instantly transformed into steam, which melted more ice to create even more steam. Suddenly the ice pack around the mouth of the shaft and the mess hall next to the pit were catapulted into the air. Like a house of cards, the weathered timber splintered and pitched to the ground, fully collapsed.

Then the ground began to cave in on itself as the ice grotto and the pyramid were obliterated. Into the spreading crater, more sections of the whaling station, the abandoned base camp, and the mobile drilling rigs all tumbled, sucked deep into the bowels of the Earth.

Lex watched anxiously as the caving ice continued to spread outward, like ripples in a pond—ripples that swallowed more and more of the landscape as they flowed inexorably toward her and Scar.

Scar grabbed Lex, forcing her to her feet even as the ice pack shattered under them. Pulling her along,

the Predator stubbornly ran on, despite the fact that
there was no hope of outrunning the widening tide of
destruction.

Lex stumbled as the ice shifted under her. Falling
helplessly into the abyss where the collapsing ice
threatened to bury her forever, she yelped as she was
yanked upward so forcibly that her arm was nearly
pulled out of its socket. Before she could react, Scar
threw her like a rag doll onto a patch of unbroken ice.
She spun, then crashed limply into a snowdrift.

Then the Predator made his own desperate leap to
safety as the ice disappeared under his feet.

CHAPTER 30

Bouvetoya Whaling Station

Lex tried to open her eyes, but her lashes were caked with snow. She had to blink several times to clear them.

She was on her back, looking up at the sky and the heavy, black, cast-iron vat still teetering on wobbly legs at the edge of the cliff, despite the earthshaking violence that had rocked the vicinity.

With a moan, she felt something digging into her back. The spear Scar had fashioned from an Alien tail and the shield made from their armor were still strapped there. Lex sat up and looked around. She and Scar were lying on the very edge of a mammoth crater that had swallowed the whaling station; only the huge vat for cooking whale blubber and the wharf and docks over the frozen harbor remained intact. Around the perimeter of the crater a few tiny shacks leaned precipitously, on the verge of collapse.

Lex got to her feet and gazed out at the devastation. Through the fog that curled around her, it was difficult to determine the full extent of the damage. But the crater itself was vast, stretching farther than she could see.

Deep down, near the center of the pit, Lex could make out a few of the timbers from the old buildings and a high-tech drilling machine lying on its back—all that remained of the whaling station and the Weyland expedition base camp. A dozen paces from Lex, a snow-covered building still stood, though it now leaned precariously. An oil lamp, no doubt lit by one of the expedition's murdered members, still burned behind a frosted window with a warm yellow glow.

With an undulating warble welling up from within his throat, Scar rose and shook off the snow, to stand beside Lex. As she smiled up at him, Lex heard a dull plop. Then something hissed and sizzled in the snow near her boots. She looked down to see a great, bleeding chunk of Alien flesh—Lex recognized the grid pattern burned into its hide and felt relief.

More gouts of flesh landed in the snow around them. Still dazed, she watched Scar dig through the snow and carefully lift an object, which he cradled in his misshapened hand.

When Scar opened his fingers, Lex saw the grisly thing he held—a severed Alien digit, somehow thrown clear of the blast, its shattered joint still oozing acid blood. He held the bloody thing in front of her face, and shocked awareness dawned in Lex's eyes.

She nearly recoiled from it, and what Scar wanted to do with it—but in the end Lex decided to accept the honor. She'd earned it, and after all, this final pain would pale in comparison to what she'd already been through.

As the caustic chemical burned her flesh, Lex winced but uttered no sound. The pain seemed endless as the Predator carefully traced the distinctive thunderbolt scar on her forehead.

For a brief moment, human and humanoid stood facing one another in the vast polar expanse, sharing a ritual that was already ancient when mankind was still living in caves and hunting wooly mammoths with fire-hardened spears and stone axes.

But the solemn moment was interrupted when an explosion sounded at their backs and they turned to see the Alien Queen burst out of the crater in a shower of snow and ice.

Snarling, Scar pushed Lex to the ground and hurled the last of his throwing disks at the slavering Hive Queen. The whirling blades slashed the Alien's throat, severing tendons and opening a gaping wound. Acid blood popped and crackled in the frigid wind and drops rained down, to pockmark the snow.

One disk remained lodged in the Queen's flesh. The other passed through her black hide and made a wide arc in the air, returning to Scar like a boomerang. But as the Predator reached to catch it, the Alien Queen lashed out with her tail and batted him into the side of the small building. Wooden beams shattered, and splinters impaled the Predator's flesh. From somewhere inside the tangle of broken wood, smoke and flames erupted from the smashed lamp. Within a minute the entire building was ablaze.

The Predator tore himself loose from the burning debris and staggered to his feet, even as the Queen closed in on him. Before Scar could get out of the way, the Alien dashed the Predator to the ground and crouched over him, claws raised to tear him limb from limb.

But before she could deal a fatal blow, Lex hopped onto the Alien Queen's back and let out a warrior's shriek. Shield in hand, Lex lifted the crude spear over her head and drove the tip into the wound Scar had made. The blow was dealt with all the force Lex could muster, and the Queen howled in surprise. Hissing, her tail thrashing, the Hive Mother howled in agony even as she threw her crested head back, trying to dislodge the human.

Lex redoubled her efforts, driving the spear deeper into the Queen's shiny black hide. Acid blood gushed in a great fountain, drenching Lex and rolling harmlessly off the shield.

Then the Queen rose to her full height, hoisting Lex with her. But still the woman refused to let go of the spear. Instead, she plunged it deeper into the wound. Finally, the Queen whipped her head from side to side with enough force to throw Lex off.

She crashed to the ground, losing her shield. Then Lex rolled away from the Queen, who roared and stamped her massive feet, cracking the ice and trying to crush her flat. Lex leaped to her feet and took off in a dash. Risking a peek over her shoulder, Lex felt a rush of satisfaction when she saw that her spear was still embedded in the Queen's throat.

As the Alien fought to dislodge the spear, she stumbled against the burning building and plunged into the middle of the conflagration. Lex prayed that the monster would burn. Almost immediately the Queen rose from the flames like a phoenix, to attack once more.

But Lex was gone.

The Whalebone Graveyard

Lex hated to leave Scar lying in the snow, but until she finished off the Queen, she could do nothing for the fallen Predator. So when the Queen emerged from the burning building, Lex ran in the opposite direction, toward the frozen shoreline.

Cresting an icy mound, Lex gazed out at a vast landscape of bleached whalebones. The bones littered a beach that was enveloped in a cold mist. Racing toward the whale graveyard, Lex sought shelter, a place where she could hide until she formulated a new plan of attack.

But time had run out. As she stumbled across the whale graveyard, the Queen's black head loomed out of the fog behind her.

Narrowly avoiding the Alien's raking claws, Lex ducked into the nearly intact skeleton of a whale. The bones rose out of the ice to form an ivory cage of protection. The Queen's jaws snapped as she tried to grab the woman, but the sharp whalebone splinters pierced her hide. The Queen let loose with sibilant cries of rage and pain.

Racing among the bones, Lex circled the graveyard and hurried back the way she had come—toward the wharf and the only shelter she could find. Scrambling up the edge of the cliff, Lex dived under the tottering legs of the huge iron separator just as the Hive Mother reached out to snatch her.

"Damn it!" Lex cried, rolling away.

The Queen thrust her head between the separator's support beams. Lex felt hot breath wash over her. It smelled of blood. She grabbed a chunk of ice and threw it at the creature's gaping jaws. Then, narrowly avoiding decapitation, Lex ducked as the Alien whipped a barbed chain at her head.

"Come on then!" Lex cried defiantly as she slipped under the heavy iron pot.

Arms flung wide, chains dangling from her limbs, the Alien Queen bellowed in frustration. Lex dropped to the ground, crawled through the snow, and placed her shoulder against the weak support beam. She pushed against the wooden strut with all of her remaining strength. A tiny rivulet of blood trickled from the thunderbolt scar on her forehead. Lex tasted it, and pushed harder.

The Alien matriarch hissed like a rattlesnake and her toothy mouth gaped wide. Out of that noxious hole the inner jaws shot forward, snapping at Lex. Then Lex heard the wood crack, and she felt the support beam tumble as the iron pot dropped from its pedestal, to slide a few feet down the icy slope. But instead of falling on the Queen's head, it remained in place, held only by a single stout wooden beam sunk deep into the glacial ice.

Collapsed on the snow, Lex panicked. The Queen was advancing, but Lex was out of weapons, ideas and luck.

Just as the Queen's gnashing jaws were about to

close in on Lex's throat, an unholy howl cut through the frigid air.

Scar!

As he raced forward, Lex could see that the Predator was bleeding from a dozen wounds. But in his hand he held her crude spear, and he was ready for a fight. Fearlessly, he leaped, landing on the Alien Queen's broad back. With a powerful thrust, he drove the spear clean through her throat.

The Queen bellowed with rage, and the Predator jumped clear. Spinning in the air, Scar landed in the snow next to Lex, where he crouched in a fighting stance.

While the tormented Queen clawed at the shaft, Lex tried to lift one of the chains linked to the Queen's body and lash it around the iron separator. But the links were too heavy, and her strength, taxed to the limit, finally failed. Dropping the chain, Lex stumbled to her knees.

At that moment, Scar appeared at her side, taking up the task and lifting the chain links, wrapping them around the separator's handle. Lex rose to help, and for a few triumphant moments they labored together, side by side.

Then Scar suddenly stiffened as the spiked tail of the Alien Queen punched a hole clean through his chest. Arms flung outward, the Predator was hoisted off the ground, writhing on the end of the razor-sharp tail.

With a flick of that deadly, albeit maimed, appendage the Queen dashed Scar to the ground and loomed over him, ready to finish him off.

But Lex was faster.

She rose and stumbled forward, slamming her body against the last support beam. The shock of the blow rattled her teeth and bruised a rib, but Lex heard a satisfying crack as the final leg tore free of the ice. Immediately, the huge iron vat slid the rest of the way down the slope and over the edge of the cliff, tumbling toward the harbor far below.

The long chain snapped taut, and with a jerk the Queen was snatched away at the very moment of her kill. Dragged through the snow, she kicked and clawed helplessly as she was pulled toward the ice-bound harbor.

The separator bounced end over end and struck the thick pack ice. Under the weight of the cast-iron vat, the ice cracked—but did not shatter. The roaring Alien was dragged along, but she came to an abrupt halt at the edge of the cliff—right in front of Lex.

Lex watched desperately as a spiderweb of cracks spread outward from the vat, but still the separator did not sink.

Then the Queen struggled to rise, and Lex knew she was doomed.

Suddenly an earsplitting crack echoed up from below, and with a groaning sound the frozen sheet caved in under the three-ton separator. With a splash the vat slipped through the hole and into the bay.

Once again the chain was pulled tight and the Alien Queen was yanked, wailing, toward the widening gap. Tittering and slobbering, the creature clawed at the ice, but to no avail. Limbs thrashing, wailing in protest, with hot gore gushing from the wound in her throat, the monster was sucked into the harbor, where she was swallowed by the cold ocean depths, the heavy separator as her anchor.

As the Alien Queen sank, Lex rose and hurried to Scar's side.

Sobbing, she fell to her knees in the bloody snow, cradling the dying Predator's head in her arms. His body broken, the Predator seemed resigned to his fate.

As Lex held him, Scar reached up a battered claw and gently traced the thunderbolt scar on her forehead with the tip of his finger. Using a distorted version of Lex's own voice, the Predator spoke.

"The enemy of my enemy . . ."

". . . is my friend," said Lex.

Then the Predator shuddered once, and died.

As Lex pressed his face to her breast, a strange wind blew. Something large was passing over their heads. The Predator spacecraft shimmered into visibility, energy crackling across its hull. It hovered over Lex and the fallen warrior, engines humming.

As the shadow of the starship fell over her, Lex looked up. A few feet away, on a low ice shelf overlooking the battleground, a dozen Predators winked into existence before her eyes. Then multiple shadows cast from nowhere played over Lex. With a crackle of strange energies, more Predators became visible.

In a moment they pressed in to surround Lex.

Bowing low, they offered their respects to the lifeless Predator, then they lifted his corpse and carried him toward a long ramp that lowered silently out of the belly of the spaceship.

Lex fumbled at her belt for a weapon but came up

empty—her club was gone, lost in the fight. She crouched in a martial arts fighting stance, fists raised and ready to lash out. Lex was willing to take them all on if she had to. For a long moment there was a tense standoff.

Stepping in front of her, a tall Predator with long, drooping dreadlocks and ornate, jewel-studded armor considered her through blank eye slits. Slowly, the creature lifted its hand and traced the scar on Lex's forehead, then pointed to the same symbol burned into its own mask.

Lex's eyes darted to the others. All of them bore the same distinctive mark.

The Predator elder nodded once, then presented Lex with his heavy spear. As she grasped the object in her hands, the inhuman hunters bowed their heads in a gesture of respect.

Then the elder turned his back on the woman and winked to invisibility. Lex traced his retreating footsteps, along with the prints of the others, as they marched through the snow to the starship.

The ramp silently closed and the craft's main thrusters roared. Saint Elmo's fire danced across its metallic surface and the ship vanished, though Lex could still hear its roar and feel the hum of its engines rumbling in her chest. Finally, in a blast of snow and ice, the spacecraft was gone.

Drenched in blood—human, Alien and Predator—and wreathed by bruises, Lex watched it go. In her own gesture of respect, she touched the tribal scar that branded her forehead. Finally, she lowered the spear and reached into her pocket.

Lex gazed at Sebastian's rusty Pepsi cap for a long moment. Then she turned her eyes skyward once more, where a break in the clouds revealed a brilliant full moon hanging low in the Antarctic sky. Watching the clouds drift across the lunar surface, Lex recalled Sebastian's words, and she spoke them in a voice tinged with awe and sadness.

"Hunter's Moon."

EPILOGUE

His kin had laid him in a place of honor, at the base of the statue of their savage thunder god. His faceplate was off, the scar on his forehead a dark stain on his pallid flesh.

The funeral ceremony was over and the other clan members had filed out to enter their individual cryostasis tubes, where they would hibernate during the long voyage back to their home world.

Alone now, in a chamber heavy with incense, Scar's corpse twitched.

Suddenly the gray flesh below his dead heart bulged and stretched as if some creature was trapped inside his body, fighting to break free. . . .

WHOEVER WINS...
WE LOSE.

AVP

ALIEN VS. PREDATOR™

Diamond Select Toys and Collectibles is out to make collectors the big winners this summer with its forthcoming products based on the most anticipated sci-fi monster match-up in cinematic history, Alien vs. Predator!

• Bookends • Motion Globes • Plush Toys • Wall Sculptures

Look for these items in all fine comic book and specialty stores beginning in August!

www.diamondselecttoys.com

COMIC SHOP LOCATOR SERVICE
888-COMIC-BOOK

AVP

WWW.AVPFANCLUB.COM
OFFICIAL FAN CLUB AND STORE

- **OFFICIAL MERCHANDISE**
- **OFFICIAL FAN CLUB**
- **EXCLUSIVE PROP AUCTIONS**